The First Time
I Saw
Jenny Hall

Also by Eric K. Goodman

High on the Energy Bridge

The First Time
I Saw
Jenny Hall

· A NOVEL ·

Eric K. Goodman

William Morrow and Company, Inc.

New York   1983

Library of Congress Cataloging in Publication Data

Goodman, Eric K.
   The first time I saw Jenny Hall.

   I. Title.
PS3557.O583F5   1983   813'.54   82-22863
ISBN 0-688-01886-6

Printed in the United States of America

First Edition

1 2 3 4 5 6 7 8 9 10

BOOK DESIGN BY MARIA EPES

For those who die still dreaming.

For Willie.

Acknowledgments

I would like to thank everyone who helped in the research and writing of this book. Larry Brezner, Melissa Manchester and Michael Lippman. Mikie Harris and my dear friend Kevin Kane. William Abrahams, in his way. Dr. Richard Kolesnick for his kindness freely given. H. Patrick Sullivan for naming me Writer-in-Residence. The friendly folks at Newfound Sound. The pond at Hulbert Hollow.

Extra special thanks to Mac Benford and The Backwoods Band, particulary to Mac for inviting me into their lives and their van. And to Jim Zimmerman, for his expertise, insight and perfect pitch, who is my partner in the songs written by Potts and performed by Jenny.

Finally, to Susan and my parents, for their love and support.

· PART ONE ·

Time Still in My Hands

Chapter One

•

THE FIRST TIME I saw Jenny Hall she was sitting at the bar in Discovery, smoking a cigarette. Thousands—and if you count a miniature Jenny on the box, millions—have seen her since, but that Thursday night she was just another stranger, a beautiful face I'd probably never know.

A lot has happened since. Some of it I'm proud of. Some of it has taught me about stupidity and evil, especially my own. And sitting at the piano in my new apartment, looking back and wondering, I know I'll never feel the same about the world and being alive in it. That there's a certain innocence of heart, which, once lost, is never recovered.

I remember her cigarette because after I'd been in Discovery's bar awhile, Jenny turned in my direction. The glow from the track lighting lit the upper half of her face, and three stools away, I could see her eyes were this incredible pale blue the sky and girls' eyes are in Kansas or Colorado, but not in Brooklyn, where I grew up. And the smoke—here comes the cigarette again—rising from her left hand drifted past her eyes like clouds crossing that pale sky. Smiling, I thought, Hm. Just Hm.

She smiled back so quickly, I knew she hadn't seen me. A few minutes later Sean Green, the club manager and nominally my boss, dropped an arm over my shoulder. Sean was thirty, maybe thirty-two, and liked touching people. For years Sean, who was good-looking in a preppie way—you could imagine him at sixteen sneaking outside to smoke a butt—had been trying to make it as a singer, but almost everyone, Sean included, knew it was never going to happen. In between introducing Discovery's acts with sleazy one-liners he somehow brought off, Sean sucked the nozzle of a Reddi-Wip can for a nitrous rush that glazed his eyes and deadened his soul against a nowhere job he was good at. If Sean offered you his nozzle that meant you'd reached the inner circle, but that, I guess, could be said about almost anyone.

"Potts," he began, hugging me. "You owe me one."

An arm flung over my shoulder, he led me three places down the bar to Jenny. The fingers of his free hand disappeared under her hair; she looked up, saw it was Sean and smiled.

"Steve Potts, ten-thumbed piano player, meet Jenny Hall."

She turned, again I felt without seeing me, and gave me her hand, which was small and ridged with calluses.

"Jenny auditioned Monday and blew the rubes away."

"Thanks," she said, then added softly, "I guess."

Sean caressed her hair, which was straight, long and off-blond, tinged with red. He slid a finger down the back of her black-and-silver dazzle-thread top, which clung voluptuously to her breasts. Watching, I felt my throat go tight and again I thought, Hm.

Jenny sipped her drink, trying to ignore Sean, except every so often he'd slip her the finger and she'd twitch. Sean pretended not to notice. He had an asshole streak you could drive a truck through, and liked to push the sexual power his emcee job gave him. I thought maybe I should say something. But what if she considered it part of the business? Then Sean moved his hand again and Jenny jumped. Our eyes met, and I saw that her face, which was lightly freckled and from some angles, I thought, incredibly beautiful, a woman's face, and from others a sprite's, a pixie's face, a twelve-year-old boy, I saw she was blushing red. Not with embarrassment, but rage.

"Sean."

Our eyes met as applause erupted in the showroom to our right. And grinning at me, pleased with his performance, Sean eased his hand the length of Jenny's hair, then slithered off.

Jenny sipped her drink, set it on the bar. Under the tight top her breasts rose and fell. I sat down next to her.

"Quite a slimy"—she looked up, smiled—"son-of-a-bitch you work for, isn't he?"

"Sean's a louse, but he knows talent."

Jenny tapped a Marlboro from a half-filled pack, put it in her mouth. "You smoke?"

"Thanks."

She lit mine, then hers off the same match and we sat smoking in Discovery's dark, half-empty bar. Discovery was an improv club but had enough singers in to require a small band. Once a week I subbed for the house piano player. Nothing great, but it was steady money and though I knew better, I still dreamed the next Ronstadt would stride through the door and we'd become a team, someone to put across the songs I was obsessively writing.

I looked up. A comic's patter drifted in from the showroom, some schmo's mouth pressed to the mike for airplane noises, amplified farting, a sure sign the funny man stank.

"You're not nervous, are you?"

Her face ignited in a smile I discovered most men found as sexy as I did. There was something about those pale blues and fluid mouth that started male and sometimes female juices flowing: funky, casually sexed Jenny, though you wouldn't know it the first time you looked at her. Five-two or -three, nice breasts, but slim, little-girl hips and a flat ass.

No, you didn't pick it up the first time, but when you turned back maybe you saw it, maybe felt it, but however, whatever, bub, if you missed the signs, you were a dead one. Or as my grandpa Ziggie, Potzgovitz in the old country, liked to say, a *schtumie,* a noodle-noggin. Missed this incredible rush of life, and not just sex. Jenny made you feel more alive, your life, while she was near you, as vibrant and vivid as hers.

Anyway, she turned. "Me, nervous? Does the Pope piss purple?"

"Depends what he's been drinking."

"Listen, what's your name?"

"Steve Potts."

"I'd tell you my memory's bad, but it's not. Must have been the green slime."

I winked. I have sexy eyes, at least that's what women tell me. Bedroom eyes, brown touched with green, which my father, Arnie, and I inherited from his father, Ziggie, who also passed on the family business: Potts, I Peddle, originally a pushcart, now Potts and Pans, a chain of kitchen-beautiful emporiums with branches in five suburban malls. Five branches, but no new rootstock because Ruth and Arnie's bundle of joy lacked *sachel*. Or as Arnie was fond of saying, "When they were handing out brains, my son, you thought they said trains, and stood on the wrong line."

It's true. I've always had the bad habit, from Arnie's point of view, of taking the wrong things seriously. I believed they meant it when they gave me those culturally enriching piano lessons. How was I supposed to know, eight years old, that Beethoven was a bum and Mozart died young, a pauper?

So I winked the family eyes, began the Potts family joke.

"People usually remember my name. Potts reminds them of pans, and pans [which I pronounced with the hint of a *t* so it sounded like pants], pans remind them of me."

She peered into my eyes; I added, "I bet people remember yours, too."

She pulled on her cigarette, exhaled, and her eyes came back troubled; anyway, less open.

"Why's that?"

"It's a beautiful name, Jenny."

She touched my arm. "What kind of piano player are you, Potts?"

I'd been expecting some sort of silly barstool question, but not that one.

"The best."

She let our eyes meet again.

"Are you sure?"

"No complaints yet, ma'am."

"I guess," she said, "I'm going to find out."

"I hope so."

The back of my throat tightened again. I felt myself smile in a way that meant I was pleased with myself; the smile banging elbows with a smirk because I was pleased, as I finished, "What are you going to sing tonight?"

Jenny sang three songs, "Forever Young," "When Will I Be Loved?" and "Respect," the old Aretha tune. White girls should lay off black material. I've heard so many Westchester princesses sing Bessie Smith that what I used to do, except when paid to play, was leave immediately. There's something so pukey about Bessie's words bubbling out of some white girl's mouth, something so self-inflating—the human ego sick and bare, declaring I've got soul, too, listen, just like Bessie —that it embarrasses me.

So when Jenny announced her third song was "Respect," my heart sank. When she started to sing and it wasn't Jenny Hall trying to sound like Aretha in '69, but simply Jenny Hall, whose voice wasn't as high as Joni Mitchell's or as strong as Baez's, but had a richness like Ronstadt or Billie Holiday's, I knew I'd been wrong.

It was more than her voice. Bobbing like a bantamweight, jeans tucked into boots, belting "*R E S P E C T* / Tell you what it means to me," the mike in her left hand, her right index finger pointed like a lay preacher's at her congregation of out-of-town businessmen, somehow, despite the theatrics, she seemed natural, unpretentious. As if she weren't responsible for, or even aware of, the beautiful music rising through her, the way a forest, say, doesn't notice the wind singing symphonies as it blows through.

Pounding the black and whites, feeling as if someone had hit me in the head, I thought, That's impossible. She must know how good she is. But as we built toward the finish, her voice swelling with the sound, it seemed as if she were unaware, the sprite/sexy woman's face flushed with joy, her ego out of town.

I stopped playing. The audience got up on its collective hind legs and cheered. Looking right, I noticed Sean inside the black curtain that led to the bar, and Sean, whose cooled-out, jade-o persona forbade enthusiasm for anything, Sean was howling with the others.

Then Jenny, who'd been bowing to the drunk and cheering crowd, Jenny turned around. The follow spot fired her hair. Framed by the black and screaming showroom, her face looked like Dietrich's in her cabaret movies, looked like someone, one pale eye shining, as she asked, "You know 'Desperado'?"

I nodded. So did Tim on drums, and Wolf, who was playing bass. "That was great," I called, and maybe Jenny heard me, maybe she didn't. She was putting out the brilliant, self-absorbed vibration of a woman in afterglow. And smiling, still bowing, she strapped on the acoustic guitar she'd shed for "Respect," then nodded. My fingers found their way into a simple intro, and I remembered the only other encore I'd played in a year of working Discovery. Phyliss Randazzo, a fat Italian girl, arrived with her Bay Ridge cousins club because a record producer named Pope was coming in. The family cheered and whistled, pounding tables to force an encore, although Pope, no dummy, departed after the second number.

Then I was listening to Jenny's "Desperado." Not what I'd

do for an encore—you know, slow and sad, makes 'em mad; fast and loud, leaves 'em proud—but for her it seemed right. The lights washed over her, the sound rolled out and her voice held the soft, sad words till they seemed to merge.

Once or twice I craned my neck to watch her. Mostly I played, my fingers finding their own way because I couldn't believe what I was hearing. Talents like Jenny had agents, managers, hangers-on. Yet except when I accompanied someone else, I'd sat with her the hour before she sang. No one. Nothing except her quick smile and pale eyes, which, before she sang a note, I'd felt myself half in love with.

So I played, listening like a member of the audience, which for once wasn't clinking its rude fucking cubes, and decided. I'm going to stay close to her, God am I going to get close. Did I come on too strong in the bar?—as the beautiful words which urged us to be open to love, to allow someone to get close, as the beautiful words sailed on.

The furnished one-bedroom sublet Jenny lived in on Fifty-sixth near Eighth was dark and cramped, but regal compared to my studio on East Seventh. Backed up against her refrigerator, my hand on her butt, her tongue in my mouth, I saw visions, briefly, of Jenny Hall naked, her sheets on fire, Steve Potts stoking it higher.

But when I hit the street and gazed up at the single lit window on the second floor, I was thrilled. Not that she ever asked me to stay. But if I'd only been interested in one night, I would have snuck my hand inside her jeans, and who knows? Instead, walking down Fifty-sixth, then up Eighth toward Columbus Circle, a warm August morning, her number safe in my billfold, I cheered myself for not letting Mister Johnson do all my thinking.

Riding a desolate D train south to West Fourth, I stared at the blackened window across the aisle. Framed by red spray-paint graffiti, *Flatbush Girls Suck, Koch is a Racist,* I saw Steve

Potts, Stuyvesant High School, '69, of the curly-haired, bed-room-eyed Brooklyn Pottses. Mediocre left hand, straight teeth, a red-brown moustache six to eight shades lighter than my hair. Five-seven-and-a-half, and a liar: five-nine to anyone I thought would believe it. A dream-dreamer and songwriter, some good, some bad, some, I knew, real good, though in four years of gigging around and dropping demos at the offices of publishers, producers and stars' managers, I'd begun to think of myself as Potts the Almost, Potts the Near But Yet So Far.

The train hurtled south. I was alone with the rails' singing except for an ancient black man sleeping on an empty seat, hands folded under his neck. Overhead lights tumbled off, then on in series. And now, I thought, Potts the Blessed. Upon whose life true love, anyway incredible luck, has just de-scended. Two weeks in New York, she'd said. A band breakup. A small upstate town near Ithaca.

"What kind?" I'd asked in the cab crossing the Park to her apartment.

"Friendly."

"What kind of *music*?"

"This and that," she answered, eyes wide and laughing, I knew, at me. "Weird, honey. Weird."

I kissed her. She kissed me, then poked me in the ribs. I poked her ribs, and pretty soon we were giggling and hugging like demented fourth-graders. God knows what the cabbie thought, what any New York cabbie thinks of the crazy shit that goes down behind his back. I saw this one though, an old fat man, peer into the rearview right about the time my hand danced across Jenny's breast, which like her ribs felt lovely, delicate, and oh, not so delicate. She looked up, expectant, laughing, and there I was, Jenny waiting while these all-know-ing gray eyes watched in the rearview.

I blushed, sat up thinking that my great-uncle Louie, Zig-gie's brother, a tedious old man who drove a hack forty years, might not have been exaggerating when he used to say, "I've seen it all, Stevie boy. I've seen it all."

I exited at West Fourth, leaving the sleeping black man bound not for glory but Brooklyn. I crossed the gray-brown platform, climbed cement stairs to the street, and headed for Figaro's, an all-night cappuccino bar off Bleecker which served the best Italian cheesecake in the city.

A little background. Tuesdays and Wednesdays I played The Stage, a Bleecker folk club two blocks east of Figaro's. Fifteen bucks a night and I could pass a plate. Again, nothing special, but between the steady gigs, session work and teaching piano and voice to my three high-school rockers, I paid bills and kept myself in grass and an infrequent toot of cocaine without taking money from Arnie and Ruth—who were loving, warm parents, but also, I knew, die-hard capitalists, and never gave without expecting in return.

Rosemarie, the deadshift waitress at Figaro's, waved me in. She had long hair, which she dyed black and teased into a magician's cap. She was married to a bum, who beat her up every few months, then took off. Her eldest son, whom I reminded her of, was also a bum, and Rosemarie bitched to me about him. Tony did this, Tony did that, the fucking snake.

I sat at my usual corner table. Rosemarie arrived with cheesecake and a cappuccino, then left to serve other customers. We had a deal. Rosemarie fed me and I listened to her bitch about Tony. I loved the cheesecake, Rosemarie was lonely, and as far as I could tell, her son, whom I'd seen just once, really was a bum.

A few minutes later Rosemarie sat down.

"How are you?"

"Don't ask. How about you?"

"I think I'm in love."

She examined me for signs of illness. "Her family has money?"

"Rose, she's incredibly talented."

"Talented. You're talented. Can you pay for your cheese-cake?"

"I don't have to."

"Better," Rosemarie said, "if she had money."

"Better she doesn't have any social diseases."

When Rosemarie didn't come back with the filth I'd set her up for, I came down from my Jenny-high and noticed she was upset.

"So how's Tony Two?"

"The little shit's in jail."

"Since when?"

"Since this afternoon when the cops found six TVs and four stereos in the garage so hot you could get burned standing next to them."

"I'm sorry."

"*You're* sorry. In the morning I bail him out. Tonight I'll give him something to think about."

"You're upset?"

She waved her hand as if she were shooing horseflies lost under her cap of hair. "Why should I be upset? Now get going, I'm busy."

I headed east to my apartment, located between First and Second avenues, in an old Ukrainian neighborhood. I felt like a Nietzschean superman—I am up and the world is not, yea, me—as I wandered the empty Village streets, which, no shit, I loved. Partly, it was my own life I loved. Four years earlier, after I'd decided not to become a lawyer or a kitchen-beautiful magnate, discarding briefs and Lucite pepper mills for the hopes and dreams swarming inside me begging to be sung, although no one seemed interested in hearing them, it was the Village I'd come to, making the big move across the East River. The Village and living ghosts. Dylan, Baez and Bobby Hall, who'd come as kids in the 60's to dream their dreams and change the world with their music; radical gods who'd broken in at places I now played.

And if Dylan's marriage to Sara and life in the country had

dissolved last year; and Baez was in semiretirement in some California burb; and if Bobby Hall, the most heroic and certainly the most radical of the three, who'd never compromised his music and always gave, I'd read, his money to the Movement; if he was broke, his voice gone, when was it a month ago if Bobby Hall had tried to hang himself, that was life. It didn't change what they'd accomplished, the beauty of what they'd attempted, and it didn't have to happen to me.

Even if it did, my thoughts racing, my mind's accelerator hugging the floor, even if things went wrong, I wanted to try. Wanted to be here haunting the brilliant ghosts with my ghostly dreams.

It was obvious right then I wasn't getting to bed, and I swung north to Washington Square Park. I smoked Camels until the sun rose, when I started the *Times* crossword: yesterday's, which, like a no-shame New Yorker, I'd fished from a trashcan. Bloody Aurora and Con Ed's vapors were soon turning magenta cartwheels over the East River. The morning air goldened. As I filled in 36 down, "Recess for a statue"— "niche," the windows of the NYU libraries facing the Square reflected a new day. No past, no history, I thought, waxing sentimental after a long night. No meaning.

A little later a kid I'd seen around walked up smoking a joint. I should definitely go home, but I wouldn't mind getting high. No, I decided, I shouldn't.

"You play The Stage, right?"

"Uh-huh."

"Want a hit?"

I'm a pushover. "Sure."

He passed the joint. His face was large, wild-eyed and Slavic; his body seemed too frail to support it. He wore a T-shirt, jeans and a woeful beard. I mean, it was pitiful. Some hairs were two inches long, but most—fine, light-brown fuzz —were short and gapped like teeth on a broken zipper. Suddenly, the kid stuck out his hand.

"I'm Bobby Zimmerman."

We shook hands. I returned the joint.

"Any relation?"

"You mean, am I Bob Dylan?"

"Something like that."

"Lots of people ask. You know"—the kid paused, passed the joint, then nodded as if he'd consulted with himself and decided—"sometimes I think I am. Like maybe I was reborn or something."

I didn't mention Dylan was still alive. Instead, my breath hissing around the resin-stained paper, I took a long hit and thought, This kid's a fucking lunatic.

A few minutes later, Bobby Zimmerman said he had to get going, pumped my hand and walked off. I sat there thinking about the future. Maybe, I decided, he is Bob Dylan. Maybe I'm about to write "Rhapsody in Blue." I stood up, stretched, then headed home through the bright morning streets.

Chapter Two

•

THREE WEEKS LATER, another early Friday A.M., Jenny and I were in bed. It wasn't the first time—that happened the night after we met—but it might as well have been. Bells still chimed; synapses rang not only with what they felt, but anticipating what followed. We were at the hot-lips, hot-stuff new lover stage, and fell asleep in rooms flooded with seminal fluids, sexual swamps. A look, a touch, an errant fingernail. God, Jenny said, when was it, the night before. I do feel alive.

We topped her bed, a king-size in a small room, the curtain drawn, window vented four inches. Predawn drivers growled by gunning their engines. I lay across Jenny, nose and cheek on her right breast, left forearm reaching from her navel to her crotch. Jenny, whose fingers were strong, she'd told me, from four years of living on her own farm, baking bread, splitting wood, milking a cow one summer, the whole country-hippie schmear, massaged my neck. I was half asleep, but every so often, moved by the cosmos, the incredible luxury, by deep wellsprings of lust I'd always known were there, I would moan and lick her warm, bumpy nipple. Simple in concept, simple in construction, but everything, I thought, a man could want.

We'd made love already, a half hour earlier when we returned, excited and turned on from playing Discovery. Jenny had become a fixture and they paid her decent money, whereas most acts performed free for the showcase. But people were coming in asking for her, and Sean the Lecherous was no fool.

Anyway, we'd returned. I ended up kneeling on the rug, Jenny's legs spread hanging over the edge of the bed, my mouth at the gate of heaven, or, if you prefer, at her crotch. She came almost immediately, singing a love song of yipes, yowees, my Gods, and once, at the end, "Oh, Potts," which made me feel like Valentino.

We climbed onto the bed. I rocked and shimmied inside her, losing myself in Jenny's midwestern blues except I now knew she was from California. Reading them and hearing her, I knew she was almost there again, and thought, Oh, God, hold on. Let me hold on.

But the will dissolved. My eyes closed and I felt nothing except the body I was clinging to, the ecstatic swelling of membranes. Deep inside her, and from a great, happy distance, I heard myself whimper and chortle, then Jenny pulled me close.

A half hour had passed. I looked up from her breast.

"You're wonderful to make love to."

"Really?"

Her eyes, less innocent than I'd thought on meeting her, less innocent, too, than I'd thought even a few days ago, looked at me with the pleased, possessive smile of a naked lovely woman holding a man.

"I bet you say that to all the girls."

"Only—"

I felt myself getting hard and moved my left hand, which had been resting harmlessly on her thigh, and teased the lips of her vagina.

"Only," I repeated, "when I've got 'em where I want 'em."

I slipped my middle finger inside her.

I heard her breath catch. Her hand grasped my penis, which, good soldier, stood erect and at attention.

"Who's got who?"

Discretion is the better part of valor. Never more so, I thought, than in certain wars.

"I give up."

"Good, I want to inspect the prisoner."

Jenny led me penis first until, crawling, I arrived beside her. We smiled, me down at her, Jenny up at me, hushed and pleased. Suddenly, a car's engine roared into life on the street. The sound filled the room; I started to lose the erection. Tomorrow, I thought. No, today, Jenny's band was visiting, the car's gears grinding in torment, and who knew, who fucking knew?

The roar ended. Jenny looked up at me, her face flip-flopping from woman to sprite and back again. Her fingers moved, and I was hard as Gibraltar.

"Prisoner Penis and his potts reporting for duty."

She smiled, changed position slightly, and, eyes open, measured the prisoner with her tongue.

"He looks like you," she said.

"How do you mean?"

"A little cocky."

I laughed, she giggled, then it all dissolved as Jenny took me in her mouth.

Early that afternoon we ate breakfast at Jenny's kitchen counter. I'd cooked, so my stool—black, spindle-back wrought iron—was the one in the kitchen, while Jenny's, across the counter from me, was set nominally in the living room. She looked calm and rested. I hadn't shaved and didn't feel calm. She cut into an over-easy, and yolk rushed across her plate like yellow blood.

"This is a beautiful breakfast."

"Runs in the family. You know, have pots, will travel."

We smiled; she began to eat. Watching her, her hair still wet and falling over a blue robe, I felt the day dissolving. A hot wind blew through my head, desert madness.

"Still," Jenny added, her mouth full of egg. "I owe you."

The First Time I Saw Jenny Hall

I watched her. Jenny was a messy eater and tucked a napkin under her chin to protect her clothes. The first time we ate in a restaurant together, I thought she was kidding. I mean, you sit down with a beautiful woman, and it turns out she wears a bib. What was amazing wasn't only that she slopped food— there was already a tear of egg on the napkin tucked into her robe—but that she was honest or unselfconscious enough to admit it.

"Why aren't you eating?"

"Promise you won't move back to Ithaca this weekend."

She grinned, filled her mouth with home fries.

"Don't be silly. Just wait till you hear them play."

"I don't think I want to."

We stared at each other. The Angel of Death circled the room, looking to land. Jenny raised a forkful of egg, and without noticing lost half of it, which slipped off, landing in her potatoes.

"Why not?"

"Danny's your lover, isn't he?"

"That's none of your business."

"Then I'm right."

"You're not only right, you're an ass."

She slammed down her knife and fork. All I could think was, I've ruined everything.

"What do you know me, three weeks?"

"I'm sorry."

"I stopped living with Danny a year ago, but I'm closer to him than anyone."

What about me? What about the brother you mentioned? Your father? (Her mother was dead.) What about *me*?

Instead, I repeated, "I'm sorry," and reached across the counter, entwining our fingers. "I was out of line."

"Were you ever."

We embraced over the breakfast dishes. Her mouth tasted of egg and potatoes.

"You'll like Danny," she whispered, "you'll see. Everyone likes Danny."

I nuzzled Jenny's neck, her wet hair falling against my eyes. I wasn't sure, but it felt like something funny was happening to my right elbow.

"He's the bass, right?"

"Uh-huh. Between the four of us, we have a band."

I sat up. A pat of butter and half a smashed croissant were stuck to my elbow. Jenny, looking luscious and fourteen though I now knew she was twenty-eight, a year and a half older than I was, smiled at me. I removed the croissant.

"If you think I'm playing with your old lover and a drummer named Parakeet—"

"Bird."

"Bird, Jesus Christ."

"Danny's hair." She paused; she was teasing me and I knew it. "Danny's hair is halfway to his ass."

"You know, your relation to Danny sounds sick."

"Soon I'll tell you about my brother."

She was joking, but there was no joy on her face.

"Hey," I said. "Your eggs are getting cold."

She didn't answer.

"I said—"

"I know. Your eggs are getting cold, too."

We ate. My eggs tasted like pot cheese. Jenny said, "If you're looking for someone who's simple and uncomplicated, you're barking up the wrong tree."

"Woof, woof."

"I mean it, Danny still loves me. And he was so much a part of that life." She stopped. "A life I loved. I loved my friends, I loved my house. I—"

"Then why are you here?"

She didn't answer, and I suddenly realized I was falling in love with this girl though I knew she didn't love me, which wasn't at all how I'd run my life until then.

"I left because it wasn't enough."

She started to cry. This time, instead of dunking my arm in her potatoes or the solidifying eggs, I walked around the counter, hugged her and held on, Jenny sobbing against my shoulder in her living room.

That night I was a crazy man. Surrounded by Ukrainians a half-generation from the steppes, I languished in my one-room furnished cave, drinking bourbon and failing to write a love song for Jenny. When she called Saturday afternoon, I was still hung over. We were all, she said, meeting for Sunday brunch.

"Great."

"Danny's been acting funny."

"Oh?"

"I told him about you. That we play together."

My palm started sweating against the phone. I'd wanted her to tell Danny we were lovers, but she refused.

"Since we stopped living together, you're the first person" —she hesitated—"that I've told him about."

"You're sure we're going to like each other?"

"Potts," she said. "Stop thinking about yourself."

That night a song still wouldn't come, and around midnight I walked south on the Bowery toward Sub's, which was a bad sign. Sub's was a punk bar. I wrote pop-rock, my background was folk, and I didn't know or much like new wave. If they were the new wave, I was the old. And being passé at twenty-six, though I laughed about it with friends and told stapled-cheeks and pins-stuck-in-soft-tissue jokes, early obsolescence in a trendy business wasn't funny. Watching sixteen-year-olds bounce like jackhammers, eyes fixed on the stage in slack-jawed devotion, made me dizzy. As if it were 1967 and I still wore a crewcut. Except it was '77, my hair was long, but all the kids in punk bars had cut theirs.

I pushed through the door, paid five dollars, made my way through the darkness. Some British band that knew maybe three chords was pumping megadecibels of lumpy rock into the smoke and gloom. The brick walls ate the highs, amplified the lows, and after three quick bourbons had taken me over the crest of glory, I decided the mix was something a musician in hell for buggering a burro deserved to hear.

Two more drinks and the burro was on top. The next thing I knew it was two-thirty, and I was wondering who ran the ferris wheel concession behind my eyes because it was time to close down, bub.

Whoa. An arm's length down the bar, a tall skinny freak with Dayglo green hair waved a four-inch gravity knife he'd snapped open with a click which sounded like someone hawking up a moist yellow one.

"Fucking-A." His teeth were three inches long and orange. "Fucking-A, straight."

We have moments of genius, of inspiration. Michelangelo experienced many. Newton watched an apple fall and saw God. Watching the knife point dance in the dim light, I was visited by an angel. Do something, she whispered, or this asshole will kill you.

I looked up and down the bar at the other freaks and ghouls. Short spiked hair, leather vests, combat pants with chain belts. *Fucking-A, straight.* I tried to imagine breaking a bottle over Greeny's head.

Imagining, I nearly parted with bladder control, stopped a baby's breath from wet pants. The angel at my ear kept repeating, Do something. Do something or this asshole's going to stick you, but I *couldn't* do anything except sweat and watch the knifepoint glisten and shimmy. All at once, someone banged me hard on the left shoulder and I thought, Oh, God, oh, my God. A big black-bearded bouncer pushed between us.

"Give me the knife."

Over the bouncer's shoulder, I watched Greeny's eyes widen. He was taller, but the bouncer was a walking silo.

"*Now.*"

"Hey—" Greeny started to say. But another bouncer who'd snuck up behind—weaselly-looking, with rat-brown hair—reached up with something hard and clobbered him. Greeny gave a little grunt, a discreet burp, then buckled, dropped the blade and pitched forward. His forehead smacked the bar and he ended up at the big bouncer's feet looking almost lovable, knees curled, thumb in his mouth, baby punk.

The big man picked up the knife, closed it, put it in his pocket, then turned to his skinny partner, who was grinning ear to ear.

"Not so hard next time."

He faced me and grinned. Tiny teeth hid in the cave of his beard like an animal's eyes.

"Hey, there're *scum* bags everywhere."

He spoke with a thick Brooklyn accent. To be friendly, so did I.

"Thanks, man. Saved my ass, ya know?"

He clapped me on the shoulder, muscled me toward the bar.

"Next one's free."

He disappeared with the weasel, dragging Greeny, and I looked around. No one was paying attention to me, and braced on the bar, my hands started to tremble. Heart pounding, I decided to get going before some of Greeny's friends sucked my blood.

I looked around again. The British band was still thumping *Sturm und Drang* nightmares. I took a deep breath and gulped the free bourbon. Then, watching out for green-haired freaks, I headed home through the cool night ripped as confetti, glad to be alive. But what I kept thinking, as I struggled to put one foot in front of the next, was that these things didn't happen to Steve Potts, boy from Brooklyn. It was Jenny's doing, Jenny, and wait till I told her.

A half hour later, head whirling—whiz, whirlywhiz, whiz— I was embracing my mattress to keep from tumbling off, trying to remember what I wanted to tell Jenny. I was in love and the feeling made my head spin. Something was making my head spin, and I passed out feeling safe and full of purpose.

Danny wasn't particularly good-looking. Bird, the drummer, was crazy. Six-two or -three (when you're five-seven-and-a-half, it hardly matters), he had blue eyes, an Irish knife-blade nose and soft reddish hair which stood up like an eagle's crest. He speed-rapped all the way to Puzo's, the West Village café where we were eating brunch, his nose bobbing, attacking the air. Danny he called the Greek. Jenny was Jenny-O. I was Potts the stranger, Potts on the outside, as Bird, talking more than he ate, waved his fork and silver sunlight flashed off the tines.

Danny, who sat opposite Jenny (she was to my right, her chair against the white railing), looked as uneasy as I felt. Though there was no way, I thought, trying to chew my eggs so they wouldn't make any noise, that he could be as hung over. But while I could talk to anyone, especially a blabby maniac like Bird—who suggested that this café, which ground its own sausage, and decorated its outdoor tables with pink carnations, must be run by a gay Italian—Danny was almost silent. Not unfriendly, just quiet. He had an open expressive face—a broad forehead which still seemed to break out, olive skin, straight nose, a long black ponytail and soft eyes—that couldn't help but give away what he was feeling, a traitor in his own camp.

I'm better-looking than Danny. (I know, it doesn't matter. But that's what I was thinking as I watched him across the table.) It was something to hold on to, because Danny exuded an enviable tranquillity, a spacy calm that made me feel hyperactive and comically middle-class.

It occurred to me that this hippie superman, with his embroidered workshirt and long ponytail years after everyone else had cut his, was the kind of man Jenny had loved for years. That worried me. After two months I knew I could love her as I'd never loved anyone else. But I hadn't dropped out, hadn't left the city except for college. Loving me was a big step for Jenny, backward or forward depending on your perspective, but certainly away from her past.

"Danny," I asked, "you guys been playing much?"

"Some."

"Since Jenny left?"

He looked at me, eyebrows tugging his forehead toward his nose. Someday, I thought, he's going to wrinkle like a seat cover.

"Waterfall's still working, but we miss her."

Who's we? I wanted to ask. And in what way exactly do *we* miss her? Jenny had told me that when she left for New York, Danny moved into her farmhouse. Which must feel, I thought, like an awfully hollow homecoming. And watching him, I wondered what had moved Danny, who Jenny told me grew up on Long Island, to an upstate country town? I wondered, too, what he felt facing me in this cutesy café, and if he still had any clothes in Jenny's house when he moved back in.

"Danny also plays in a blues trio," Jenny said.

With the sun shining on her hair and blond freckles, on her small nose and white napkin tucked into a peasant blouse which bared half her shoulders, she looked like an American primitive, Huck Finn with lipstick.

"We miss her," Bird said, "because me and the Greek have to pick up the vocals, which is a mixed bag, you hear what I mean. The most commercial aspect of Waterfall was Jenny-O's boobies shaking when she sang. Now she's gone"—Bird's eyes glowed, and laughing, he emitted a high metallic sound like a bat—"we're your average bunch of misunderstood geniuses."

"I do not shake my boobies. They're tits."

"Boobs," Bird answered. "Bazooms."

"A tit," I said, "by any other name would taste as sweet."

No one spoke, and I thought about Jenny's breasts, of which I was quite fond. About the night, not too long ago, that I'd kissed them, it seemed for hours. And remembering that, the sun shining down on our happy table, on the pink carnation, I grinned. I hadn't actually said Jenny and I were lovers, but I figured Danny had gotten the idea. Looking up at him, I knew I was right. So why, pushing my eggs around the plate and waiting for Bird to say something funny, why did I feel like such a creep?

After coffee we returned to my apartment, Bird driving the old humpbacked red Volvo they'd come to town in. No one said anything, but from the way she grimaced and kneaded my knuckles, I was sure the car was Jenny's. Bird gunned the engine, ignored lights, ground the gears, and at the corner of Hudson and Eleventh, nearly ran down two men in shorts, who leapt out of the way like pins split by a bowling bowl, screaming, "Watch out, you bitch!"

Barely noticing because he was so busy making some ridiculous point, Bird swerved around them, his face and attention shifting briefly from his conversation to the street and back again.

Bird loved to make a point. Making points, making music and taking drugs, there was little else he cared about. So that when Bird, whose full name was John Brian Michael Murphy, managed to combine drugs and making a point about music, his big nose sticking in your face like a finger, he was blissful. Since Bird was often high and always talking, generally about music, he was one of the few truly happy people I've ever known.

We arrived in front of my building, where Bird parked by sound, banging bumpers with the cars fore and aft. The four of us climbed the five flights to the Potts one-room mansion, Bird asking at every landing, "Are we there yet, Potts

Daddy?" then cackling and observing that the scene in the city must really be bad, since in T-burg you could starve without having to walk up and down five flights to do it.

Nothing had been said, but I knew Jenny had mentioned her plan to them, and that the audition was to take place in my apartment. Fine. I was operating from a position of strength —Jenny's bed—and never having heard them play a note, I'd decided they were the real thing. Besides, having gotten so wrecked at Sub's I not only hallucinated green-haired freaks, but somehow conjured one with a knife, I'd been working myself up to accepting whatever Jenny wanted. There was a ripeness about her, a sheen. Two or three times in life, if you're lucky, you meet someone who for some reason, or perhaps for no reason at all, is lit up with possibility like a movie marquee, and that summer, Jenny was one of them.

I mean, she glowed in the dark, and who was I to ask why? Instead, climbing the fifth and final flight to my apartment, the hangover which had subsided to a gray haze during brunch again roaring blood red, I tried to decide if I should play the love song I'd written that morning or stick to older stuff.

Unable to make up my mind, I opened the door and Bird, Jenny and Danny followed me in. Jenny crossed the room and collapsed on my bed, which was set against the far wall on a wooden platform six inches off the floor. Without seeming to consider much, Danny joined her. After looking around, Bird sprawled on the floor at the foot of the bed. That left me the piano bench, which was where I sat.

A word about that apartment: small, a suburban kitchen. The right-hand wall, as you entered, contained my one closet and a built-in two-burner stove. It was followed rapidly by a similarly scaled sink, three cabinets designed for doll's dishes and, in the corner, the door to the john. In the opposite corner, above the bed and gray as a cloud, the apartment's one window let in what little light there was. Close to the foot of the bed was my only cherished possession: the upright Stein-way my parents had given me for college graduation. Much abused but in tune, generally littered with ashes, empty Bud cans and sheet music, it shone, freshly polished.

And me on the bench, back to the keyboard, Jenny and Danny on the bed to my left, Bird stretched out on the floor, a beer he'd found in the fridge perched on his chest like a sleeping cat.

"I guess you're all wondering why I asked you here."

No one laughed. It was a crummy joke.

"Steve," Jenny said, "why don't you play something?"

"You want to sing?"

She shook her head. She was sitting up back against the wall, hands folded on her lap, her jeaned thigh touching Danny's.

"Just you."

As I pivoted on the bench, my eyes swept Danny's. My heart began an excited, skip-beat rhythm. Hell, I thought, why not?

"This is called 'Fall in Love Again.' It's new, written for Jenny to sing."

I started simply, rather slowly, a sweet melody line, then picked up speed and conviction (along with depth in the left hand) as the song evolved. Which was how I'd written it that morning, alone in the apartment, waiting to meet them, sud-denly convinced that instead of writing a love song for Jenny, I'd write one she could sing to me.

Tentatively, I began:

> *"It's taken too long*
> *This time, I know,*
> *I'm gonna find myself and go.*
>
> *"Waved my sorrow in the wind*
> *Like a martyr, it's been*
> *My only friend."*

The First Time I Saw Jenny Hall

I began to play and sing louder, more confidently, too, as someone feeling these emotions would.

> *"Swear I'm gonna fall*
> *In love again, in lu-uve,*
> *Swear I'm gonna fall*
> *In love again, in lu-uve,*
> *Swear I'm gonna fall,*
> *Swear I'm gonna fall*
> *In love again."*

I let the emotions which had welled up well down again, and played an eight-bar break, nothing fancy, that turned the melody to the verse. I sang, my phrasing again tentative because that's what the singer should feel, and because the second *A* part was about Danny.

> *"Been so hung up*
> *On the past*
> *Never thought I'd let it go.*
>
> *"Been so hung up*
> *On long good-byes*
> *I forgot our sweet hello—oh!"*

Then I was singing "Swear I'm gonna fall / in love again," and so forth, pouring my heart out to the blank wall. I was convinced the song was super but afraid to turn and see what anyone thought. Not only was I auditioning, there were these duels. First, between me and Danny. More important, though harder to judge, Jenny and I were dueling.

—Step over this line, I dare ya.

—Oh, yeah?

I had to prove I was worth loving, independent of her wishes, but had to do it without crowding her, or the audition was a wash. In other words, step over the line without stepping over it.

I played. But as Grandpa Ziggie said when finishing a schnapps, "All good things must burn and end." I ran a short arpeggio and turned around. Jenny was whispering to Danny. She noticed me, smiled, but kept whispering.

Bird said, "Not bad, hotshot. You make that up by yourself?"

"Tolstoy visits me. Leo can't sing, but words, he's okay."

Bird wasn't listening. Like me, he was trying to hear what Jenny and Danny were saying.

"Yeah," I said loudly, which made Bird, who was now sitting up cross-legged, turn back, his eyes startled. "I wrote it this morning."

"The bridge is a little schlocky, you know, first-generation. Other than that—"

"It's good," Danny said, his voice round and smooth, a baritone. And I hate to say it because it sounds nasty, his voice was mellow, understated and mellow. "Real good," he added. "Slicker than my stuff, but fine."

I met his gaze. Out of the corner of my eye, I caught a flash of Jenny's hair.

"Thanks."

"I was wondering. What would you think of us playing together?"

"Gigs?"

"I was thinking a demo. You know, work up five or six tunes, see what happens."

"It would be hard," Bird offered, "to gig. We don't live together."

"We're going to cut the demo long-distance?"

"I thought," said Jenny, "we could spend a couple weeks at my house. There's enough room and there's a piano."

"How are we going to pay for it?"

Bird made a pass at his wallet. "I've got ten bucks."

"That'll leave us what, two thousand short for sixteen-track?"

"Let's discuss money later," Jenny said, which I realized was wise, but left me feeling all kinds of things: like maybe she expected me to raise the cash from the Potts and Pans empire.

"Danny," I asked, "you really want to do this?"

"I brought it up."

"You think we can work together?"

Danny frowned, and when he spoke his voice wasn't calm or spacy. But he sounded sincere, which was what I'd tried for, though I hadn't been able to say, "Can you deal with Jenny and me sleeping together while you're in the house?"

"I'm willing to try."

"Then so am I."

"Good," Jenny said, and stood up. Then we were all standing. Bird lit a joint, which we smoked in celebration. Blood brothers, smoke brothers. My hangover receded, and on the white sands of that early afternoon we made our first joined footsteps. At my suggestion, we agreed to call ourselves Jenny Hall and Waterfall. Waterfall, because that had been their name (from the Taughannock Falls in Trumansburg, New York), but with Jenny's name up front because if we were going to succeed commercially in a way the old Waterfall hadn't, it would be Jenny's looks and voice (singing my songs, I hoped) that would do the trick. So it made sense to give her star billing.

The only protests were Jenny's. Influenced by the pot and the intimacy of the small room, a bond grew between us; a special quiet, which was odd given all the reasons I'd been sure Danny and I had for not getting along.

We smoked a second joint sitting together Indian-style on the floor. When it had burned down, Jenny, who was next to me, put her hand on my knee.

"Play 'Time Still,' okay?"

I stood and walked to the piano. "Time Still" was one of the older songs I continued to play. Vaguely country-sounding, it was something I'd written with Ronstadt in mind, hoping to sell it to her. *Sure.* In the three weeks we'd played together, it had become Jenny's favorite. She said it reminded her of Trumansburg and of her brother, who, best as I knew then, she was once close to but no longer saw.

Zipped, my hangover cured, the music floating out in waves, I finished the intro and Jenny started to sing. Each time, I thought, she lit up the room, and not because sunlight was snaking through my one small window and kissing her hair. It was her singing, "Time Still" so transformed I never wanted to sing it again myself.

> *"Time stretches out*
> *Like an unbroken road,*
> *Steals from my hand*
> *Like the mountains erode,*
> *Then they're gone.*
>
> *"I wish I could hold*
> *Time still in my hands*
> *And make it my own*
> *But I can't.*
>
> *"I wish I could hold*
> *Time still in my hands*
> *Like a rock or a stone*
> *But I can't,*
> *Turns to sand."*

Playing the next two verses, I peered at Danny, who was again seated on the bed to my right. Jenny, singing, stood to my left, and Bird, stretched out on the floor, lay behind her. Watching Danny watch her, eyes intent, his lips slightly parted, hands clasped under his chin, elbows on his knees, I took in what Jenny had told me: He still loved her. Best friend or no he was suffering, willing to be in a band with her new lover just to be near her.

Realizing that, whatever resentment I still felt toward him

vanished. Listening to Jenny, my words more than they had been because she was singing them, my heart went out to Danny.

"Time only comes once," Jenny sang, her voice golden as her hair in the baby picture she'd shown me, "then it's gone. / Like the words of this song / you borrow, they never belong to you."

Playing the chorus, Jenny singing, "I wish I could hold / time still in my hands," I glanced at Bird, who rolled his eyes and smiled, as if to say, Hot stuff, man. Then Bird's head inclined or bopped, at least his nose seemed to, toward Danny and his nose traveled from Danny toward me and inclined or bopped again.

A warning? A salute? Maybe I'd imagined the whole thing. Bird seemed to shrug, then I wasn't looking at him because Jenny was singing the second half of the chorus, her voice sad and soaring at the same time, and I heard nothing, nothing mattered, but my words and the music.

Chapter Three

·

THE NEXT SIX WEEKS are a hot happy blur. We soared through September and October on winged Indian-summer days cooler and less humid than August, but warm enough that twice Jenny and I rode the train to Jones Beach. We swam, lazed on a blanket until the wind picked up and the sun set behind a hot-dog stand. Before returning to the city, we ate raw clams and strolled on the boardwalk, arms around each other's waist.

Once or twice we slept apart. Small spats, fatigue, I don't remember. Our routine, though, was to work somewhere together (alone when she played Discovery and I was at The Stage) until one or so, then show at the Hideaway, Max's or CBGB's. We'd do an acoustic number or two, replacing the band when only regulars and scene heavies were still listening, my years of making connections with crews and club managers finally paying off.

Here comes crazy Potts, they used to say when I worked alone.

Crazy as a fox when Jenny and I floated in and blew them away for free. We'd decided that for now only exposure mattered. So all through September and most of October we'd materialize like Kirk and Spock on a strange planet, Jenny shimmering and singing in the light of reflected dreams.

Fleshed, we faded in the night, finishing at Wo Hop's on Mott Street, which was a good place to be seen, frequented by musicians and managers (Jenny loved moo shu pork and hot and sour soup), or at Figaro's. Rosemarie alternated between being quietly and openly hostile to Jenny, whom she referred to as the Princess.

"Hey, Stevie," she'd say, waiting until Jenny was in the head to drop off the cappuccino and cheesecake she knew we shared since she left two forks. "How's the Princess?"

"Fine. How's Tony Two?"

She'd describe the latest bummer—Tony had quit school, he was breaking probation, popping pills, something—and I'd tell her how sorry I was. When Jenny returned, Rosemarie would disappear. But one night in early October, before Rose could leave, Jenny asked, "How's your son?"

From under her black cloud of hair, Rosemarie eyed Jenny. "Fine."

Which meant, and we all felt it, "What's it to you?"

"At his age, I was a real pain. My mom had died."

I glanced from Jenny to Rose. Princesses, nonpersons, didn't discuss dead mothers, and Rosemarie's mouth hung slightly open. Above her narrowed eyes, one penciled eyebrow rose in confusion.

Jenny sensed her advantage.

"Steve's told me about Tony, that he likes music. I thought maybe I could talk to him."

Rosemarie looked lost. Then she seemed to recover and managed a smile. "Thank you."

"What was that about?" I whispered, when Rosemarie moved off. "Tony's a hood. He's crazy."

"So was I. Mom died the fall my brother started college."

I cut into the cheesecake. "How old were you?"

"Twelve."

Chewing, beginning to feel as you do when someone starts in on a secret—fascinated but anxious, because the intimacy will change who you are to each other and it's out of your control—I asked, "You were a hood?"

"I was crazy."

Working from the other side of the wedge, she chipped off a piece, raised it to her mouth. "Uhm," she said, swallowing, "that's good. I roller-skated every day after school and my father, when he finished work, had to haul me home from the park. Of course, he was nuttier than I was. For the first couple months we ate out all the time since neither of us knew how to cook or could stand being in the house, which was large, and without Mom and Bobby, like living inside a bad dream."

"Your brother's named Bobby? Like Bobby Hall the singer?"

"Always has been."

I didn't ask why she was smiling. In two and a half months I'd learned that Jenny, who could be mysterious, even secretive, would tell me herself what she wanted me to know.

"What did your mom die of?"

"Leukemia."

For a moment her eyes projected such sadness, turned inward though they were still very wide and nominally directed at me, that I took her hand as you might with someone who's blind or dying—to let her know you're there.

"I'm sorry."

Jenny's face, which had briefly looked sixty or eighty, was again that of the beautiful woman/sprite.

"The worst part was that before she got sick, or before I knew, we'd been fighting. I guess that's an old story. I'd just entered puberty, my tits were growing and she insisted I wear dresses and a bra, stop fighting with boys, and stop wearing my hair in pigtails. That argument, our last, she won by cutting it short."

She squeezed my hand. When I squeezed hers, Jenny smiled.

"We made up when Mom was in the hospital, but by then she'd given up and it didn't matter. It's hard to explain. She was this dying woman, not Mom anymore."

"I'm sorry."

"I wasn't telling you so you'd be sorry." She laughed. "But don't ask why I am telling you. Maybe you're beginning to feel like a real person, you baby hustler, you."

"You're kinda cute yourself."

"I meant what I said to Rosemarie, though I'm also tired of being treated like the whore of Babylon. Is your mother like that, too?"

"Let's not discuss my mother."

We didn't. Maybe we were scared of how close we were getting. Maybe we didn't have the time. Most nights we didn't arrive home till four-thirty or five. And because we were excited, afloat on a river of dreams, we'd make love, often until the sun rose. Thinking about it now, sitting at my piano in a new, more prosperous apartment, I realize what I couldn't have then: We would never be happier. And remembering, I see us lying face-to-face on Jenny's bed, the ambiguous light of dawn firing the room, and I could cry for the fragility of love and understanding, and for how stupid I was not to realize that a year ago.

I'm getting ahead of myself. Most days we'd wake between twelve and one, eat, then separate for the afternoon. I'd teach whatever lessons I had scheduled, then settle in at the piano. If nothing new came, I'd revise old songs, sharpening rhymes, working on counterpoint, harmony, and in general cutting the schlock level, which, as Bird had pointed out, was a problem for me.

Most days, though, bare-chested, wearing gym shorts and rubber flip-flops Jenny had given me, I worked in a fever of excitement and confidence, sketching words and/or chords in a blue music-lined notebook I kept at the piano beside a pitcher of iced tea. Sometimes I had just a single line, the hook; other days, a chord change I'd picked out, a few lines of melody. But I noted it all, convinced like a convert of his new religion that everything mattered. And I carried that notebook everywhere, even to the crapper.

Around six Jenny would stop by. She didn't generate many ideas but knew instantly what was wrong with mine. Then, me at the piano, Jenny on my bed, guitar in her arms, we'd argue about changes, rhymes, significance, Jenny singing the melody as she heard it, *a cappella* and without words. She'd pause, and wet her lip with the tip of her tongue curled upward like a crooked finger. When she heard the next phrase, her quick smile ignited and she'd begin to sing, smiling because the change she wanted was right, but also because she knew that after a little fussing I'd admit that and use it.

In many ways that was the most important thing we learned during that six-week Indian-summer dream. Not that we might love each other; not that we were real people and her mother had died, while my parents were still trying to run my life. Not even that Jenny was limber enough to grasp her own ankles, both legs straight out, when I was inside her, or that she'd learned where I liked to be touched when I was coming.

No, none of it was as important, or even as exciting, as how well we worked together. Gregarious in our personal lives, neither of us had written songs with anyone before and felt, magically, as if we were completing something in someone else. I mean, everyone's got genitals, but only Jenny and I could make our musical parts fit together so well.

So that's what I remember. Making love at dawn, making another kind of love in the afternoon, iced tea glasses sweating, our bodies sweating, intimate and joined, the world out there somewhere, waiting.

The last Sunday in October I took Jenny to Brooklyn to meet my parents, Grandpa Ziggie, my sister, Karen, her husband, Bob, their girls, Beth, nine and blond, and four-year-old Janey, who was round, dark and giggly.

The First Time I Saw Jenny Hall

Don't worry. I'm not going to describe it. What you need to know is I'd decided to hit Ziggie for the $2,500 demo money. He counted on me in his battles with my parents, with whom he now lived. He had the cash; I was his favorite. But in my family, what figured about money and what actually went down were in anything but a linear relation. If they had been, I could have approached Arnie and Ruth the four years before I met Jenny when I was surviving on knishes and pizza. It's not that they wouldn't have helped: big Arnie and little Ruthie loved their kids. But the anxiety which animated every Potts-and-Pans-made bill complicated matters. I could never ask, "How about two hundred a month? Think of it as med school," because it was too upsetting for all of us.

Or maybe I was too proud.

Anyway, I'd called Ziggie on the Friday. After a pause, a bronchial in-rumbling of wind and wisdom, he said, "You want the moon, too, mister?"

Sitting at Jenny's kitchen counter, I imagined Ziggie, his face long and sleek as a collie's behind another counter, the gray-mottled one in the original store in downtown Brooklyn. Slump-shouldered, I imagined him, gray and lean, his good eye twinkling.

"You can get it wholesale?"

He laughed. "Sunday," he said, "you're coming?"

"Yeah."

"I could die, you wouldn't know for weeks. She's that something?"

"What's this guilt? You sound like Dad."

He didn't answer, and again I saw his expression: heavy eyebrows raised like the Yiddish actor he'd wanted to be. He disliked being compared to his son or daughter-in-law, whom he considered wipeouts, Americans with money and leisure but no class. In Ziggie's opinion, his son, too, had taken the wrong things seriously. Arnie saw only the struggle for money; taking over the business he'd become rich, never understanding what the struggle was for. Ziggie, when he retired, relearned Russian so he could read Dostoevski in the original.

"I'm an old man."

"Who'll probably outlive me."

"If that happens, may God strike me dead."

"If lending me money is so upsetting we have to discuss who's going to die first, maybe it's not a good idea."

"Who said anything," he answered slowly and loudly, never convinced you could hear him otherwise, "about lending?"

"If money changes hands," I said, my palm sweating, "it has to be business. An investment. Music is my business."

"You know, Stevie, you can be a putz like your father."

"And where did he get it?"

The phone line wheezed. Ziggie asked, "You're bringing her Sunday, what's-her-name?"

"I'm bringing her Sunday."

"So we'll talk."

Sunday Jenny and I walked slowly from the D train station through my old Brooklyn neighborhood. I felt like a ghost. The real Sheepshead Bay me was twelve or fourteen, happy, fearless, swinging a stickball bat in the schoolyard of P.S. 98, playing punchball on Twenty-sixth Street and dreaming, though I didn't know it yet, of leaving. Crossing Bedford Avenue holding Jenny's hand—Jenny, who had never set foot in Brooklyn—I expected to see myself and the kids I grew up with still lost in our unconscious, physical lives, though they had died in Nam or moved away, married and become fathers, plumbers, doctors, bums, whatever Brooklyn boys did.

A half block from the green corner house on Twenty-sixth Street, which I'd been proud of growing up because it was bigger than my friends' houses, Jenny squeezed my hand.

"Your mom's not going to like me."

"That's crazy."

Arms bare under the first dress she'd worn since I met her, a blue jumper, Jenny looked like a blond dream walking.

"Mothers don't."

"What are you talking about?"

Jenny flicked her hair out of her eyes.

"Boys' mothers look at me, and I'm not bragging, well, maybe I am." She smiled. "But they look at me and know I'm getting it on with their son. That the sex is good and it matters."

We'd stopped walking. I kissed Jenny on the mouth.

"Why not? We're grown-ups."

"With some girls mothers could tell themselves, well, maybe not. With me, maybe because my mother was dead and that made me an untouchable, they always knew."

"Pretty hot stuff, aintcha?"

"I thought I'd warn you. Is that the house?"

I nodded. We walked to the chain-link fence, opened the gate and started down the cement path which split the lawn and led like an arrow to the scrollwork *P* for Potts on the screen door. Subtle, big Arnie, he isn't.

On Monday I cashed Ziggie's check, bought two grams of cocaine, two dozen hits of speed and called Sean Green, my students and the boss at The Stage to say I'd be away for two weeks. Everyone reacted sanely except Sean.

"You're taking Jenny, aren't you, ya little shit?"

I grinned at Jenny, who sat beside me brushing her hair on the black couch in her living room. Around her middle, a pink towel. Around mine, nothing at all.

"What's it to you?"

"Look," Sean said, and I parted my ear and the receiver, "I don't care if you fuck each other blind."

"Drop dead."

"Listen, Potts. If they find you buns up in the river, covered with shit and rubbers, I wouldn't care. But if Jenny doesn't show four nights a week like her contract says—"

"No can do."

Jenny blew me a kiss. We were high on cocaine, and her breasts peeked over the pink towel like tulips.

"I'll pay her twenty percent more. I'll pay *you* twenty percent more, you rat-turd. Where's your loyalty? I introduced you."

"We're taking two weeks to put this demo together, just accept it."

"Let me put it this way. If you're gone two weeks, don't bother coming back."

"I guess you don't want to see Jenny either."

There was a pause. Then Sean said, "Let me speak to her."

I handed Jenny the phone and lay down, my head in her lap. Jenny held the phone away from her ear, but I didn't listen. Instead, I admired the underside of her jaw and throat, then lifted the pink towel. Her thighs and pubic hair were still damp, and snuggling under the towel, I'd entered a moist, fragrant cave. Sighing, I settled in for winter. But after a minute or two, Jenny tapped my shoulder and handed me the receiver.

"All right, Potts," Sean said, his voice loud and close, "I know what you've been doing."

No, you don't, I thought, and sat up.

"You've convinced that poor girl she needs you. What is she, psychotic?"

"You ought to try," I said, "shoving that Reddi-Wip nozzle up your ass."

"I'll ignore that on account of we're old friends. Be back in two weeks. Jenny will give you the details."

"Huh?"

"And Potts, good luck."

I hung up.

"What's that about?"

"Sean's agreed to showcase the band, hour sets on Friday and Saturday when we get back."

"You're kidding."

"Advertising in the *Voice,* everything."

"What kind of money?"

She laughed. "What was Ziggie's word, *bupkas?* Goat shit?"

I nodded.

"Hundred and fifty a night, split four ways."

"That cheap shit."

Jenny looked at me hard; no, she looked concerned. "I thought we weren't going to worry about money."

"I'm not."

"Then what is it?"

I looked at Jenny and saw I was ruining what should have been a triumph.

"You're right. We'll invite every producer and A & R man in town."

"I can tell," Jenny began, and her eyes glowed. Naked on the couch, I shivered though it must have been seventy-five in the room. "I can tell from the half-assed way you said that something's upsetting you. You're pissed off I arranged it."

"Have you and Sean been negotiating without telling me?"

"There's a lot I don't tell you." Her tongue snuck out, hovered on her upper lip, then disappeared. "Don't you wonder what I do in the afternoons?"

I was now completely chilled.

"You're not turning tricks? Sucking Sean's nozzle?"

"*Steve.*"

She looked straight at me; her facial bones shone naked through her skin. And as she began to reveal herself I saw how she would look at sixty, still beautiful, the fine lines and pale eyes without age, outside of time, which is how someone looks if you love them.

"I've been holding out. You haven't noticed because you don't know me well enough. But after yesterday—"

"What?"

"You don't take money from your family. Ziggie told me you'd never asked before." She paused. "I don't either. It gives them power over you."

"Fine, I'm a hero."

"You don't think it's weird I haven't told you about my family except my mother's dead?"

Was I supposed to answer? Answer what?

"I'm screwing this up," Jenny said, and grabbed my hand, "but what I'm trying to do is share what there is to share." She took a deep breath; her eyes widened. Then, mocking her own intensity, Jenny wrinkled her nose, a little girl flirting with herself in the bathroom mirror. "The whole messy me, you know, and I'm afraid it'll fuck things up."

"It can't matter. I don't say it, but you must know I love you."

"I'm going to hold you to that."

We sat quietly, holding hands.

"I visit my brother in the afternoons at Payne Whitney." When I didn't react, she added, "That's the psychiatric wing of New York Hospital. He tried to kill himself in August, and one of the two reasons I moved was to be near him. The other, the music, you know about."

I didn't understand, although as she spoke I finally made the connection.

"It's no coincidence his name is Bobby Hall, *the* Bobby Hall as you put it, because he is."

I started to say, "You're kidding," but my lips failed me. When I could speak, I said, "You thought your brother being Bobby Hall, who's always been, you'll pardon the expression, one of my heroes, was going to upset me?"

"Not upset you."

And I don't know why, maybe the combination of fear and

pride, but for the past six months the look on her face has filled the darkness before I sleep.

"I'm afraid it will change things, you know? I'm afraid."

I slept badly that night and I knew why: Bobby Hall. When I was in high school and college we were intimate. Bobby, of course, knew nothing about it. My hero, Lord, Bobby Hall, though I understood that musically, and at times lyrically, his songs were second-rate. So what? Dylan I considered a demigod, Blake or Shelley in blue jeans; I'd always known Bobby was human.

I attended all his New York concerts, six or eight before he dropped from sight in '73. Through '69, his voice was high and pure, sweet and angry with the righteous rage of someone who has seen evil, recognizes his own capacity for it and preaches that possibility as his gospel. Showering the morning after each concert, I'd practice singing like Bobby, my voice the second lance of the people's army, until Arnie would pound the bathroom door threatening to break my ass unless I left him some hot water.

On the bare, black stages of the 60's, Bobby Hall looked like an old-time rad, a union man. Performing, he wore workshirts and jeans, a bandanna at his throat and sometimes a Greek seaman's cap stuck on his head, emblem of the working class he fought for but wasn't part of.

His brown hair was never very long. He was often photographed smoking a cigar, which was incredibly unhip, unless you believed, as I did in high school, that he was expressing solidarity with Fidel and Che.

He had full, pale cheeks that made him look like a radical cherub. His eyes were intense, brown and soulful. For years, no matter how much he drank, his body stayed thin, what *Newsweek* once termed "a boy's body, lightly haired, lightly muscled," as if to imply his ideas weren't fully formed either.

Fuck *Newsweek*. Listening from the back of the medium-

sized clubs Bobby insisted on playing, too young to drink, I
believed he was a revolutionary. I believed he meant what he
was saying, and that what he said mattered.

> *It's freedom, don't you see,*
> *Not I, but the wind that blows through me,*
> *Not you, not me, not us,*
> *We'll be turned to dust.*

In '68, with the whole world including me watching, Bobby
led the Chicago protesters through a version of "We Shall
Overcome," the memory of which still sends shivers up and
down my insides. Police sirens howling, clouds of tear gas
funneling past, nightsticks whistling midnight arias, Bobby
Hall stood in the lights, arms uplifted, and the night answered,
"Shall overcome someday-ay-ay-ay-AY!"

"Not someday," he'd shouted, and clenched his fist. "Now.
Not someday, NOW!"

For a time, people believed in now. Sitting on my mother's
slipcovered couch, I believed it. The next night at dinner, a
high school junior, I told my parents I smoked pot and
dropped acid twice a week (a lie); that I had a black girlfriend
who loved oral sex (alas, another lie); and, because it was
important to be honest, I used words like fuck and shit in front
of them for the first time. I finished by telling my father that
because he supported the war, he was a racist pig and crypto-
fascist.

Arnie, you had to hand it to him, threatened to let me have it
across the mouth but good, though we both knew he hadn't hit
me since I was four. We stared at each other, queasy with guilt
and rage, then Arnie opted for his usual double whammy. He
swore he was going to cut off my allowance, then stormed out
of the room, shouting as he climbed the bedroom stairs that
if I masturbated like a normal kid instead of playing the piano
all the time, none of this would have happened.

In the fall of '69, I came in from college with a date and

The First Time I Saw Jenny Hall

listened to Bobby sing at the Brooklyn Academy of Music, a gig which later became known as the silver suit fiasco. The preceding summer he'd been to north Africa, and three goons beat the crap out of him in Fez. Because there was no apparent motive and because they concentrated on his throat, half strangling him and ruining his highest, purest notes, there were those who said that the beating was a C.I.A. setup, payback for Chicago and other crimes against the state.

I didn't believe that. But when I think back on what the craziest, most paranoid people I knew were saying in '69—like how their phones were tapped, half the campus rads were C.I.A. plants, and Nixon was a crazy schizo bastard—I wonder about what happened in Morocco. But I never asked, Bobby never offered to tell me, and he's not likely to now.

Whatever happened, he came out in front of a packed house waiting for the radical songs that had given them courage and made him famous, Bobby came out wearing a silver Presley suit, and under the banner of "sharing" the music that had mattered to him as a kid, played only 50's R & B, primarily Buddy Holly and Bo Diddley.

My date was Cheryl something, a Jewish girl with large breasts and a full moon face. We sat in the first balcony, ripped, joined by the sweat of our palms and my interest in Cheryl's melons. Twenty minutes into the concert, people began to jeer and walk out. I wanted to kill someone. Didn't they know who they were booing? My hero, and how could he be doing this? To me? Who'd worshiped him for years and paid my seven-fifty?

Another ten minutes of R & B, and I'd stopped answering Cheryl, who wanted to know what was wrong with his voice. Why did he keep missing the high notes? What was the radical significance of the silver lamé?

"Cheryl," I said finally in my mature freshman manner. "Shut the fuck up."

The nightmare lasted another twenty minutes. Bobby, who had never been more than an adequate guitarist, embarrassed us both that night. The audience bayed like dogs. Bobby's voice grew more and more hoarse. He kept promising to do the old stuff, then didn't, until it seemed he longed for the first martyring stones, his own blood, when someone, probably his manager, phoned in a bomb threat.

In the middle of a song, without saying why, Bobby announced the concert was over. People began to howl and throw things. I howled, too, although what I wanted to do was weep and throw Cheryl off the balcony. When the second chair seat shattered against the stage, Bobby reappeared. In a voice so hoarse it was hard to believe it was his, he said there'd been a bomb threat, and asked us to proceed quickly and quietly to the exits.

"I'm sorry," he said, "but you got to go."

I saw Bobby perform twice more: once in '71, the last time the spring of '73 in Max's Upstairs. He sang the old songs, but by then they seemed like an act, not part of history. His voice was gone, the words were just words, and we all knew, Bobby, too, that it was over.

I heard nothing about him for three years, then rumors started he had been sighted on the Bowery carrying a matched set of Zabar shopping bags, BOWERY printed on one bag, BUM on the other. Supposedly, he was covering the bags with prophetic scribblings.

I didn't believe it, although one night, late, I saw someone on East Broadway who might have been Bobby. Hunched in a doorway, he seemed to notice someone was watching. Then he stopped noticing or ceased caring, closed his eyes and raised a bottle.

A month later a picture of him ran on page three of the *Daily News*. It was the one taken when he was the pink-cheeked darling of the radical music world, the one which hung in every New York club. The headline screamed: "Ex-Protest Singer Tries To Hang Himself—Saved When Rope Breaks!"

Lying awake beside Jenny, and the next afternoon walking up First Avenue with her, I wasn't thinking about the pain which waits for stars in the American firmament. I was thinking of the Bobby Hall who'd made me want to write songs and right wrongs, and who, for the past three months, had been locked up in a mental hospital.

I was thinking, too, of Jenny, who as we turned east on Sixty-eighth Street took my hand. It was a warm, pristine afternoon, but there was enough autumn in the air that sunlight reflecting off Sloan-Kettering's windows dazzled my eyes, and shadows cut the street like ledger lines. Looking up, I saw Con Ed smokestacks rising on the Queens side of the river like immense carrots, behind what I knew must be the hospital. It was happening, I thought, to me, to us. How could it be?

I tried to regroup. Hall was a common name, more common than Potts. They didn't look like each other. (I glanced at Jenny; maybe a little in the cheeks, the shape of the eyes.) But what did I know from stardom? Stars were stars and my father owned kitchen stores. In high school I didn't dream of being *like* Bob Dylan, I dreamed of being Dylan. In my head I knew better, but my heart whispered that the distance between me (born to sell pots), who had a father named Arnie and a mother who'd always dreamed her son would be a cardiologist, and the kind of life they led, seemed too immense to leap without becoming them.

I had a college friend whose father hosted a TV talk show, and occasionally I'd spend weekends at their house. One Sunday morning I opened the door to what turned out to be the wrong bathroom, and there was Ray's famous father, shaving at the sink. He wore striped boxer shorts similar to Arnie's.

His shoulders—for some reason this amazed me—were covered with black hair.

"Good morning." One cheek lathered, the other already shaved, his famous puss smiled at me in the mirror. "Up early, aren't you?"

"I am, sir," I stammered, attempting to blot Brooklyn from my speech. "Sorry about the intrusion."

I closed that door behind me.

Since the first night at Discovery, I'd known Jenny was keeping something back; known beautiful, talented singers didn't just stroll in off the street. Now that the other guitar, so to speak, had dropped, I was both relieved—I'd been afraid the secret was she didn't and never would love me—and worried that one morning she'd remember she was with Stevie Potts from Brooklyn, and decide it was all a mistake. Or that somehow I'd break the spell, and screw it up. Squeezing Jenny's hand as she led me across York Avenue, I wondered if there was a spell; if one night, late and unremembered, I'd mortgaged my soul.

"So *nu,* Potts? A blonde, nice tits. Great sing—*ger,* famous brud—*der.* Vat's it verth?"

Everything, a voice inside me answered. *Who believes in devils anyway?*

Jenny led me past a wide lawn edged with hedge and flowers, a black wrought-iron fence, low gate, Griffen's Faculty Club, the hospital buildings set back from the street. She led me past a small gatehouse; a uniformed security guard knew her and smiled. Then, turning right, Jenny pointed at the large building which loomed in front of us, and said, "That's Payne Whitney."

If she said so. The first story was constructed of immense granite blocks. Above it, six or eight stories of grayish brick were broken up by granite arch work, arched windows and fancy, on-edge brick pattern work, which created an effect, I thought, feeling us tense as we walked, of strict, gray correctness.

"How's he doing?"

"Better." Jenny turned toward me. "I'm pretty sure he wants to live."

Not knowing what to say, I whispered, "It's a day later and I still love you."

"Potts, you're a baby."

But she was smiling, which was all I'd wanted. A fool for love.

While Jenny signed us in, I inspected the waiting room, which stank of old wood, old money and the fears, I thought, of loved ones waiting on bad news. Opposite the main doors someone had arranged a couch, chairs and four standing steel ashtrays in front of a stone hearth capped by a mahogany mantel which rose to a fourteen-foot ceiling. Reading the inscription carved in three-inch-high gold letters, I began to feel seriously creeped out:

The wisdom and generosity of
PAYNE WHITNEY
established this house for
healing of the sick and troubled
1932

Upstairs, outside the dayroom, Jenny stopped walking and, as if she'd thought about it on the elevator ride up, said quickly, "If he's not nice to you, and he may not be, don't take it personally."

I hugged her. Through our clothes I could feel Jenny's heart beating.

"Don't worry. I'll take it like a tree, like a man"—I winked —"but not personally."

We entered the dayroom, which was done in bright colors designed, I suppose, to cheer up crazy people. Ocher walls, brown carpets, green Ping-Pong tables and couches, and in one corner, a large color TV ringed by lavender love seats. In one of them, older and heavier than in any picture I'd seen, sat Bobby Hall, the hero of my youth. Who'd done more, I thought, suddenly excited, than any other musician to turn America against the war. We approached, and I could hear him singing the songs I'd never believed any one person had written since they lived in the hearts and psyches of everyone I knew, as if he'd known our dreams before we did: "The Man Is Mad," "No More Lying, No More Dying," and of course "White Guns." Feeling like a fool, I wondered what I should say, and flashed on the hairy shoulders of Ray's famous father.

Bobby waved, hand above his head as it had been on his second album, except that in the picture the fingers formed a fist. He stood and Jenny kissed his cheek. Wondering what to do—introduce myself or let Jenny—I didn't wonder long. Bobby turned. Grinning, he said, "You look young to be her old man, you know?"

Uncertain what to say, feeling as if someone had barfed in my lap, I looked from Bobby to the guy standing next to him, who was tall, tanned, handsome, and laughing his ass off at little Stevie Potts.

"Yeah, but I'm well hung."

I held my hand out and Bobby eyed it as if it were a monkey's paw. Then, playing to his small crowd, he turned from his friend to Jenny, and grinning, shook my hand. I squeezed for all I was worth, and Bobby's eyes came to mine.

"All right," he said. "What's your name?"

"Steve Potts," Jenny answered. "Why don't you boys idle down?"

We arranged love seats in a semicircle as far as possible from the TV, on which three patients—two teen-aged boys and an old man—were watching "General Hospital." Bobby's friend, whose head was ringed with tight brown curls, pumped my hand.

"I'm Ethan Marks," he said, and sat.

"Oh," said Jenny. "I didn't introduce you."

She sat, too, Bobby to her right. Which left me and one empty chair, Ethan on my left, Jenny to my right, opposite Bobby. Who cared where I sat? All I wanted to do was be near, look at and listen to Bobby Hall. When someone's crapping on your head it's hard to remember it's not really your head he wants to crap on, but I was so thrilled to be near Bobby Hall, it would take more than insults to upset me.

So I sat and watched Jenny and Bobby, feeling like a kid at his first circus. Ethan also watched, but I soon decided that what he was watching was Jenny's breasts. I caught his eyes, which were almost blond, snake yellow, and he turned away. I couldn't help thinking that Ethan, whose name I'd heard before—"Ethan Marks, antiwar activist"—I couldn't help thinking Ethan was thinking evil thoughts.

A few minutes later I was sure.

"You're a piano player, aren't you?"

"Are my keys showing?"

He grinned. Schlocky music drifted toward us from the TV; from the corner of my eye I watched a nurse plant a moist one on a doctor's waiting lips. Someone entered the room, her husband or his chief of staff because there was a roll of ominous TV drums, as, smiling, Jenny said, "I told Bobby on the phone this morning."

"Billy Joel. He's one of your favorites, huh?"

"Why do you say that?"

Ethan grinned. His grin was elegant; so were his teeth. He was tall, good-looking, a tit-starer.

"He's popular. Same instrument as you. You even look a little like him."

Bobby and Jenny were now the spectators. That's all I wanted. Sit near Bobby, watch him, maybe learn a little. This macho shit I could do without.

"Yeah, I like his stuff."

"What about his politics?"

Even a fool would have known he was being set up.

"Best as I know, he doesn't have any."

Bobby spoke next, pinning me with the brown eyes which had always looked soft and sensitive on his record covers.

"Could that be said about you?"

I sprouted donkey ears. Then Jenny broke in, angrier than I'd ever seen her. Angrier than when I grilled her about Danny and thought she was going to snap off my nose.

"I didn't bring Steve to be insulted, Bobby."

"Then what is it? Does he want my autograph?"

"Fuck off, huh?" She glared at him. "We're cutting a demo with Bird and Danny. I thought, I was hoping"—she glanced at Ethan; something passed between them, and I wondered what I was getting into—"you might want to help. But before you ask"—anger flooding her eyes, her cheeks blood red and Bobby, fire-eyed himself, sitting there taking it—"there won't be any of your goddamn politics on the tape."

"They're your politics, too," Ethan said. "Or used to be."

"Look who's talking," Jenny shot back, and Ethan looked so wounded I wanted to laugh. She was beautiful. She was fantastic, and she went on, "They're also Steve's politics, but that's beside the point."

"That's what you think," said Bobby. "If you, as my sister, believe you can keep politics off your tape by not mentioning them"—he grinned—"you're nuttier than I am. If nothing else, you're making the statement of no statement."

"Fine. For now, like anyone else, I want to sell the music."

Bobby looked at her and I knew what he was thinking. *You're not anyone, you're my sister.*

I could hear Jenny's answer, too. *I know it, do I ever.*

"I'd still like to help," Bobby said. "I've been waiting for you to ask."

"Steve just raised the money."

For the first time Bobby seemed vaguely friendly.

"So you found the bread?"

"I'm also writing most of the songs."

"Triple threat, huh? You taking good care of my sister?"

"I'm doing my best."

That ended it, the rest of the visit shoptalk, music babble. Bobby asked when he could hear the material. Jenny said when we got back to town. I began to relax, and felt—as long as I ignored Ethan—that I'd entered the seventh circle of heaven, which surrounded Bobby Hall even in the nuthouse. He said he was getting out soon. I told him I hoped so, and that when we returned there was nothing I'd like more than his advice on my songs. Yeah, he said, well, sure.

A half hour later, Jenny and I were back on the street. As we crossed First Avenue, I said, "You think he'll like my songs?"

"Why shouldn't he?"

"They're not exactly political."

"They're wonderful, Steve." She squeezed my hand. "I love singing them."

"Thanks."

We walked south. The day was still sunny, the air warm. At the corner of Sixty-sixth, in front of Peppermint Park, which was a chic, East Side imitation of an ice cream parlor, I said, "Bobby won't like them, will he?"

"It doesn't matter what Bobby likes."

"It matters to me."

We crossed Sixty-sixth Street. A phalanx of Japanese tourists passed us walking north, cameras ready like six-shooters.

"It matters to me, too," Jenny said. "But I don't know. Bobby's not easy to get along with, he never was."

"I noticed."

We smiled at each other.

"I thought you were great. Took it like a tree."

"Like a rock. 'And an island,' " I sang, " 'an island never cries.' "

We walked south. There was a warm breeze from the river, and my heart was full of hope.

Chapter Four

•

WE DROVE OUT OF TOWN in a borrowed Potts and Pans Cadillac Jenny dubbed Daddy's Caddy. Silver outside, black plush inside, D.C. bore us across the G.W. Bridge, west on 80, and as the sun was setting, north toward Ithaca. When we saw our first barn and silo, then fields brown with stubbled corn, Jenny smiled and said it reminded her of home. Me, it reminded of "Bonanza."

I hadn't told Jenny, but I'd never been to a farm before. Growing up on a corner lot, I thought we were big landowners. Jenny had twenty-two acres with a pond on top of a hill, five acres of hardwoods facing the pond, and an old barn and fruit trees behind a clapboard house set back from a paved county road.

I grew to love her place, but arriving that night I was worried. Say there was one double bed and Danny insisted on sharing it? What if I said stupid things all the time? What if Danny forgot he was a gentle hippie and slit me ear to ear like a watermelon?

Danny was out when we arrived, but had already moved his things from the master bedroom to the small room off the dining room. Hauling our bags in from D.C. to the kitchen, which was large and white-walled except for the section behind the stove, where strips of barn board met on a bias as if it were a parquet floor, I could hear our footsteps echo in the empty upstairs bedrooms.

We moved everything inside and smoked a joint, sitting at

the kitchen table. Jenny said, "Bobby lent me the down payment four years ago, then refused to be paid back. Even after he needed it."

"He really gave it to the Movement, huh?"

Jenny looked at me oddly, and I promised myself not to ask any more dumb-ass questions.

"He was never practical. He doesn't have health insurance. So our father has to help pay for Payne Whitney, which drives Bobby nuts. Dad's a banker who makes Nixon look like Mister Nice-guy."

I had a short spell of wondering why, if her old man was a banker, I'd had to raise money from Ziggie, but kept it to myself. Jenny stubbed out her cigarette.

"I'm going to walk up to the pond. You want to come?"

"I'm already breathing hard."

"No joke's too low for you, is it?"

"I can crawl under ants' bellies."

Jenny found an Army blanket in one of the house's many closets; as we were heading out the kitchen door, she ran back, returned with a plaid woolen jacket for each of us.

"You'll need it. It's windy on the hill."

I decided not to ask whose jacket it was. That way, I assumed, lay no happiness. But Jenny, who was often so finely tuned it was scary, said, "It's not Danny's. I keep it handy for friends."

We walked past the barn, which was large, red, falling down and half converted, I learned later, to a two-car garage. Jenny's hill rose behind it. She'd brought a flashlight, but except when a low cloud hid the moon there was enough light to see by. We hiked, Jenny leading, through a hillside pasture she said she'd kept cows in.

"You really had cows?"

"You thought I was kidding?"

"Who knew?"

"Actually, steers." She grinned at me over her shoulder, kept climbing. "That's a boy cow with his nuts cut off."

I didn't answer because I assumed what I should be doing was looking out for piles of what Ziggie called good luck. After five minutes of climbing we stopped, out of breath, in front of a barbed-wire fence.

"I used to get up here without puffing."

"The wicked city." I was still wheezing. "A musician's life is hell."

She opened the gate. I followed her through and she latched it behind me. "Not in the country. Life"—we started walking again—"is fine. The money sucks."

We spread the blanket on a small rise above the near corner of the pond, which glistened black and still in the moonlight. Knees drawn up, we looked down the hill at Jenny's house. A second line of hills rose beyond it, the other side of the valley; I dimly perceived there was a reason Jenny's road was named Hasting's Hollow.

I breathed deep. The stars wooed me. The wind blew, a demon in the trees, telling secrets. The moon disappeared behind a cloud, then reappeared, glowing brighter and still brighter. Sitting one leg up, the other straight, pulling grass with one hand, holding Jenny's with the other, smelling the pond, and when the wind blew, listening to it dance and scrape through the treetops, it hit me how far I was from the city, how good it felt to be here.

"We had the pond dug the first summer."

"You and Danny?"

She nodded. "Does it bother you when I talk about him?"

"A little."

"I don't want it to." She squeezed my hand between both of hers. "But I was happier here than I've been anywhere else. I was more than Bobby's sister. I felt"—she paused, and I could see her face in all its human perfection glowing midnight blue and white in the moonlight as she gazed across the valley—"I felt I finally existed. Not the girl whose mother had died, not Bobby's sister. Just me, Jenny, and I was safe."

"From what?"

"Wanting to make it in a world in which people got rich dropping napalm on babies."

She paused, and I could hear the wind, which was becoming part of the story sighing and sifting through the trees, the leaves shifting to make way.

"Since Danny was a big part of life here, part of the dream of living close to the land, I'm telling you about him. Not so you'll feel bad, but because I want you to understand what the country meant to me. To all of us."

"If it gets too painful, I'll yelp."

"Then you trust me? You don't think I'm trying to hurt you?"

"People don't have to try and hurt each other. It happens all the time."

"You're a funny guy, Potts. How about a kiss?"

I delivered a kiss with a side of hug.

"We stocked the pond with bass Danny was going to catch. Except it turned out we had too many dumped in so there wasn't enough food. Now there're hundreds of tiny, hungry bass in that pond, none of them big enough to eat."

I lay my head in Jenny's lap, and listening to the wind, I stared up at the night.

"Why things go wrong is as mysterious as why things go right. Anyway, it's very beautiful here."

"I'm glad you think so." Her fingers traced esses and eights on my forehead. "If it were summer, frogs would be singing to the crickets."

"Ribb-bitt."

"Crick-kett," she answered.

"Ribbitt."

"Crickett."

"Ribbitt."

"Crickett."

We continued for a while, then Jenny laughed and I reached up, guiding her cricket mouth down to my froggy tongue. We smooched, then she said, "I have to admit it. I really do like you."

I stared down the dark hillside.

"Is that all?"

"I love you Potts, I do. But you're probably better off with mild affection."

"I'll take my chances."

"You think I'm kidding, you dodo. With people I love I'm manipulative, demanding, I—"

"I'm a big boy."

"I know. I was there when you told Bobby."

I smiled. "Did you mind?"

She shook her head. Then I thought maybe she had minded, because what she next said was, "The first time I saw Danny we were both naked."

"Yelp. Yelp, yelp, yelp."

She laughed. "Just listen. There were forty other naked people at a pond about ten miles from here. That summer, I guess it was 'seventy-two, I still had an apartment in Ithaca. Danny, who'd just moved up from the city with Bird, also lived in town, and summer days, all the country hippies and some of us who weren't yet and wanted to be drove out to the pond on McKenna's hill and hung out. I had an allover tan you wouldn't have believed."

Her fingers began moving on my forehead again. Suavely, I said, "Uh-huh."

"There was a commune near the pond called the Glory Road. You ever hear of it?"

"No. You ever hear of Del Mar Pizza?"

"What about it?"

"Best pizza in Sheepshead Bay."

"People visited the Road," Jenny said, "from all over the country because it was one of the most successful, minimal-technology communes. What that means is horse-drawn plows, kerosene lamps, organic vegetables and a two-seat summer outhouse called Thunderbuckets, which had clear plastic walls because the Road believed that if people shared everything, particularly shitting, they'd be calmer and much happier."

"Were they?"

"For a while."

With my head in Jenny's lap, I peered up at her. My eyes had adjusted to the dark and I could see the small mole on the nether side of her chin and the sunset hair, subdued now, falling past her face. After a second she noticed I was staring and her eyes focused on mine.

"So what happened?"

"They began reading *Rolling Stone.*"

"The way to nirvana is to skip *Rolling Stone?*"

"Sit up," Jenny said. "My leg's falling asleep."

I sat up.

"People began to feel, maybe two years ago, that they were missing out. They realized they were becoming American farmers, which wasn't what anyone wanted. They'd all finished college and here it was three years they hadn't read anything except *Organic Gardening.*" She smiled; the moon danced on her freckles. "Anyway, the first symptom of 'What's happening man-itis?' was resubscribing to *Rolling Stone.*"

"I never stopped."

"Five years ago, I wouldn't have talked to you. And I certainly wouldn't have fucked you."

"Five years ago I thought you fucked everyone."

She smiled and her tongue peeked through her lips. "Okay, I might have fucked you. But I wouldn't have admitted I enjoyed it."

I watched the imp's smile shine on her lips, then I kissed her. Her tongue pirouetted around mine. The breeze began to blow. My penis, half erect since she'd mentioned suntanned titties, began throbbing the way it had when I was sixteen,

hoping against hope to get into Susie Blumenthal's pants.
"It'll be a little cold." Jenny leaned away from me, gazed
in my eyes. "But this is your official welcome to the country."
She slipped off the plaid jacket, and without standing,
reached cross-armed and pulled her blouse over her head.
"God, Jenny, but you're beautiful."
And she was, a statue in the alabaster moonlight.
"Hurry up. I'm freezing my bajoomies off."
I smiled. It was one of our favorite routines, and I delivered
the punch line like a proud poppa.
"Girls don't have bajoomies."
"A lot you know."
Afterward, stipple-fleshed but warm inside, I held Jenny in
my arms.
"That was my first time outside."
"You're kidding."
"Dogs'll piss all over you in Brooklyn."
"I got your cherry?"
"You're foul."
I rolled on top of her and sucked her neck. If she'd scored
my cherry I'd give her a strawberry, a fruit for a fruit.
"Okay, okay," she said. "It was a banana."
I released her.
"What I like about you," she said a few minutes later when
we were clothed and shaking out the blanket, "and don't be
insulted, is you think it's all right to make it. You think people
can be successful and happy, even good."
I didn't answer. We folded the blanket in half lengthwise,
then in half again, faced each other across the narrowing
length of Army green.
"Well, don't you?"
"You make me sound like Mickey Mouse telling the lemmings it won't hurt."
"What I'm saying is you're cheerful and optimistic, and I
admire you for that. You make me feel dreams can work out."

She came toward me, passed me her ends of the blanket, took the doubled middle, folded that and I hugged her across the wadded cloth.

"The Glory Road broke up," she continued, "because the people who made it special, a symbol for all of us because they dreamed of being self-sufficient, of a different life, they were pushed out by people who wanted to raise a cash crop of dope and buy everything else. The first group debated for months before putting in this incredibly beautiful skylight because they thought it might be too bourgeois. The others wanted electricity and an inside bathroom."

I didn't see anything wrong with an inside pisser. But Jenny could care less what I thought. Bringing her face up close, she said, "I don't want to be like everyone else, okay?"

And with the wind lifting and filling her hair, the moon sparking her eyes, Jenny looked like no one else.

"But I do want to be successful, commercially successful. I feel that's shallow, wrong, disgusting. But you don't, and I want to believe you're right." She paused. "And yes, goddamn-it," the words flying after each other like birds taking off, "famous, too. I know I can, Steve. And that makes me feel so fucked up I could scream."

She turned, walked away on the balls of her feet and stopped, facing away from me, arms crossed on her chest.

"So scream," I said.

Turning slowly back, her face catching the moonlight, she did scream. "Oh, God. *Oooh Goooooddddd!* Oh, *IIIIII!*" the sound ricocheting off the treetops before launching itself at the stars. "OH, GOD!"

She came toward me. "There's been so much to get through, Steve. The Road breaking up last year, which meant this life was ending. And I know you shouldn't let people become symbols because they begin to think of themselves that way, and in America symbols always become Christ figures. Bobby began to think he *was* the goddamn sixties."

She stopped and stared at me. Her eyes ran over my face as if she wanted me to do more than stand there and love her.

"I don't want to hurt him, but I feel like I've been shut up in a room not trying to make it because I believed it was wrong, you know? I came out here to get away from that world, and thought it was worth it even if it meant leaving my dreams behind, because I'd seen what that corruption could mean. My father's life and Vietnam, that's what Bobby was singing about. They were the same thing.

"I still believe that. I believe it's more moral to live here. But when Bobby almost killed himself, I realized I've been keeping myself pure for a life that's not me, that was never me. And I want out."

She swept her hair off her forehead and for a second time stared straight at me.

"Scream with me, Steve."

"What?"

"Scream with me. It was your idea."

I didn't answer, but my face must have showed how weird I thought the idea was, as if someone had asked me to pray with him, because loudly and very evenly she said, "If you can fuck me, you can scream with me."

"Sure." I couldn't think of what else to say. "Why not?"

"Oh, God," she began softly, ululating, then more loudly, "oh, God!" and I pitched in tentatively, then full-voiced, the two of us, necks bent, baying at the bright-eyed moon. *"Ooooooooohhhh God!"*

Our voices echoed, then faded. In the quiet of our not-screaming, she asked, "Do you love me?"

"Yeah."

"And we're really going to do this together?"

"We're going to be rich and famous, and still be nice to dogs and small children."

"I'm counting on you." She put her arm around me. "You're my magic charm."

And exhausted, the flashlight in Jenny's pocket, the blanket draped over my shoulder, we headed down the hill ready to face—whatever.

Wednesday we transformed Jenny's living room to practice space. Bird's drums filled the left corner near the bay window. I was barricaded into the corner opposite Bird's behind an ell of keyboards: Jenny's upright against the wall, my small electric perpendicular to it, facing the couch and stuffed chairs we'd pushed to the front end of the room near the doorway to what my mother would have called the foyer. Jenny and Danny were set up forward of and between me and Bird, Jenny closer to my side, their amps stacked behind them.

Wednesday and Thursday we practiced an hour or two, testing, you might say, the musical waters. Friday we submerged. Started at four, broke for dinner, were playing again by eight. By ten I was drowning, but at eleven we were still playing. We sounded, as we had all night, like a photograph looks when it's shot at too slow a speed: interesting but fuzzy, the kind you look at and think, Yeah, well almost.

I wasn't worried. Anxious maybe, but not worried. I'd been right. Danny and Bird were great, technically better than I or Jenny, whose genius lay in lots of places, but not in her fingers. Danny, on the other hand (that's a pun), was the best natural musician I'd worked with. His bass lines, and I kid you not, were so clean they shimmered. Rhythmically, Danny could break a tune down, make it walk on its hind legs and whistle "Yankee Doodle," all in the same measure. He was also a class guitarist, and by Friday I knew, though we hadn't discussed it, that Danny would overdub lead breaks on the demo.

If you haven't got this yet, Danny was a space case, a major cadet. After playing with him for only two days I was beginning to understand, I thought, why Jenny loved him and why they hadn't made it as a couple. For one thing, if I could play as well as Danny, I would have been doing sessions in the city and making fifty thousand a year in my spare time.

Danny wasn't interested. He didn't need money, he didn't care about being famous, and New York gave him the heebie-jeebies. His parents were Greek immigrants who'd left a small village and struggled hard, Jenny had told me, to become real Americans. They owned a small restaurant in Long Island City, having worked their way up from a lunch counter, along the way producing two sons.

The older boy was a stockbroker. Then there was Danny, special Danny, so talented but always out of place until he moved to Ithaca, where much to the horror of his parents, who'd spent their adult lives trying to bury them, the ancestral longings popped out. Within six months Danny Grabonus, child of the city, had become a confirmed country person. No bullshit, no affectation. He was simply there, one of the two or three best bassists I'd ever heard, living in professional isolation.

That fall, his choices made no sense to me. Later I understood. What Danny cared about, and this sounds silly and sentimental, was the thing itself. With a bass in his hands he was so involved in rhythmic patterns, so far ahead of the rest of us, that I'd want to shake him and say, "Don't you understand, you fucking dope?" but I never did because I was afraid he'd answer, "Understand what?"

Danny's indifference to his own talent and what it could mean to him intimidated me. By the third rehearsal I felt that for Danny, playing my music was like a world-class sprinter racing school kids. But I also knew his tunes, beautiful and intricate as Bruegel etchings, wouldn't sell. Not on a demo, not on a first album, probably not ever. Not because they weren't fine, but because, like Danny, they were too fine. I also knew that a live audience would ignore him, although it was clear to me even then that if Jenny Hall and Waterfall was going to succeed musically, it would be Danny holding us together.

Then there was the Bird. Playing, he kept his elbows high and away from his body. Perched behind his drums, nose addressing the ceiling, eyes alternately wide and squinched shut, he looked as if he were trying to take off. That Friday night he wore jeans, a Red Sox cap and a black Waterfall T-shirt. He'd done several lines of Grandpa Ziggie's cocaine, and while he drummed and sometimes when he wasn't drumming, he'd chant to himself: "Rue-bop, rubidy-bop, rubidy-rebop, rue-bop."

I got used to it. Which was good, because Bird spent more and more time chanting as practice wore on. We'd play a song, then Danny, Jenny and I would discuss it for half an hour. By eleven, Bird, who was expecting a painter named Anne, was cranky as hell and deep into the rubidy-rebops. Danny, Jenny and I sat on the couch discussing possible changes in "Where Are You Now, Babe?" the one song Jenny had written for the demo. Among other problems, I thought the bridge was too long. I'd just finished saying so when Bird, still sitting behind his drums, called out, "Hey, Potts, you don't know shit from Shinola, you hear what I'm saying?"

"What's that?"

"You couldn't find your asshole with both hands. What do you think about that?"

"I think you stuck too much coke up that enormous schnozz of yours."

"Ha! You got the biggest schnozz east of Mount Rushmore."

"Bird," Jenny said. "We're trying to work on my song. You remember my song."

Jenny, of course, had wanted both me and Danny to love "Where Are You Now, Babe?" We hadn't. She'd found a good hook, some good ideas musically, but the song needed work. Looking at her, anxiety crossing her forehead, I thought, Okay, she'll deal with it.

"Yeah, I know what we're trying to do," Bird answered. "I'm sick of the whole thing."

"Another run-through," Danny said, and that ended discussion because Bird would do what Danny asked. Really, Bird would do what anyone asked, as long as he got to discuss it first.

"Let's cut the bridge in half," I said, standing. "Just to see how it sounds."

Across the room Bird groaned. "Schlock, schlock."

From the corner of my eye I saw Jenny glance at Danny.

"Sure," Danny said, "let's try it. What'll it be, two figures?"

I crossed to the piano, fingered the chords. "Yeah."

"I hope you guys are having a good time diddling my song," Jenny said, but she was smiling. She strapped on her guitar, then tuned it, overtightening the E string, then correcting it.

"Everyone ready?"

We nodded. Jenny counted us in. "Three, four. One, two, three, four."

I began the intro. E-minor ninth, C ninth, D. After four bars the rest of the band filled in, Bird's snare leading into the verse. Jenny sang:

> *"You're going to be thirty soon,*
> *You look kind of scared, babe,*
> *You got those lines in your face,*
> *Looking for gray in your hair.*
>
> *"You used to think easy does it,*
> *Life wasn't real for you, was it?*
> *It didn't matter somehow.*
> *Well, where are you now, babe?*
> *Where are you now?"*

There were several more verses, some good, some not so good. We reached the bridge, which is the musical link between the final verse and the last chorus, a means of joining the body of the song to the closing. Everyone remembered to play it the way I'd suggested, Jenny singing only the first half of what she'd written. It sounded better, I thought, building the ending instead of delaying it, and I glanced over my shoulder at Danny. He smiled, as Jenny sang, "Well, where are you now, babe? / Where are you now?"

Suddenly there was a woman in the doorway, applauding and shouting, "Author, author."

Whoever she is, I thought, the painter, she's something. Tall, a long face, dark hair swept off her neck. She wore a floppy green dress; brown boots showed below it. She also wore a full deck of makeup: purple shadow, mascara, liner, the whole biz. I usually didn't care about makeup—Jenny wore little—but for this woman it worked. Her eyes were spectacular, and I winked; a reflex around sexy women. She didn't notice because Jenny was saying, "Thanks, Anne. It's mine."

"Terrific." Anne seemed to have some sort of an accent, English or Australian. "Is it new?"

"New as the night," said Bird, walking up to Anne with a strut I learned to associate with Bird and women. "How you doing, Good-looking?"

"Just fine."

She kissed him on the mouth. Women never took Bird seriously, but they couldn't resist him either. Anne hugged him, her eyes moving beyond him. Ours met briefly and I nodded. Then she focused on Danny, smiled, gave Bird another squeeze and stepped back.

"Anne," Jenny said, pulling the pickup from her guitar, which *kathumped* because she hadn't turned off the amp, "I'd like you to meet Steve Potts. We've been working together in New York."

I circled the electric piano, wondering what "working together" meant in Trumansburg.

"I'm glad to know you," said Anne.

We shook hands. Her fingers were long and thin. She was my height, and her jaw and chin were shaped so that on a bad day, someone might have described her face as horsey. It wasn't. Her lips were too full, and her eyes, under long lids dusted with purple shadow, were large, deep-set and artificially bright.

"Likewise," I said, letting go her hand. "I see why Bird's been eager for you to get here."

"Potts," Bird said, "has the biggest nose east of the Rockies."

"Big nose"—I grinned—"big humph."

"If you guys are going to discuss your noses"—Jenny winked—"I'm going to bed."

Several responses leapt to mind.

"The Greek's," said Bird. "Greek's beak is enormous."

"Mine," Anne offered softly, "is the largest of all. I can prove it."

Her accent, which I'd initially decided was English, I now thought more affected than anything else. Brooklyn-British, or British by way of Queens and Vassar College, like my cousin Debbie, who became Deborah and learned to drink tea with milk in it, a pinkie firmly up her ass as she moved from Poughkeepsie to a Madison Avenue art gallery, where she bullshits old ladies with blue hair.

"*How* are you going to prove it?" Bird asked.

"Measure," Anne said, her accent so good I couldn't decide if it was a fake or not.

"Distance from nose to lip," she added softly. "The basal nasal index. You first."

She placed her right pinkie against Bird's upper lip. Using it as a ruler, she marked off the distance from lip to nose tip with her left index finger.

"First joint." She showed everyone. "Jenny?"

Jenny's nose was straight and beautiful, an elegant Wasp nose, by far the smallest in the room.

"My nose is perfect."

"What you mean," said Bird, emitting his high ringing laugh, "is that it's a dwarf."

Anne measured Jenny's nose. "Half a joint."

Bird, triumphant: "See what I mean?"

I kissed Jenny's nose, smacked my lips. "Small but tasty."

"Now you," Anne said, facing me. Except for Danny, who was ignoring us, fiddling with his amp, we were gathered around Anne. Her cool pinkie touched my lip. Her index finger brushed my nose. Our eyes met, then she inspected her finger.

"First joint, same as Bird's."

"Nose brothers, all *right*. Hey, Greek, Annie wants to measure your proboscis."

Danny put down his bass and crossed the living room, blushing; I swear he was blushing. Anne put her pinkie under his nose, measured, then looked up.

"Joint and a half. What a nose, Danny."

"I demand a recount," said Bird.

Anne measured again, smiling as if she knew something we'd want to, if only we knew what it was. Bird bent over her shoulder, his hair sticking in her face, nose almost bumping Danny's as he watched her finger making sure it was all on the up and up. Anne displayed her pinkie.

"Joint and a half."

"Jesus Christ," said Bird. "Never turn your back on a Greek."

"Measure your own," Danny said.

Anne smiled, placed her pinkie under her own nose. "Joint and a bit," she announced. "Second place."

"Me and Potts are perfect," Bird said, and winked at me, "but the rest of you guys and your noses belong in a freak show."

"Good old Bird," Jenny said. "Such a graceful loser."

"Shows what you know. Come on," Bird added, leading us

out of the room and toward the kitchen. "Let's get fucked up and play Scrabble."

Anne was back the next night. The night afterward, too, and her arrival and presence helped shape our schedule. Jenny and I would get up around noon, work outside, walk in the woods if it was a nice day and often even if it wasn't. We'd eat dinner with Bird and Danny, rehearse until eleven or twelve, when Anne arrived, then play everything through for her; knock off, smoke dope and play Scrabble until everyone passed out, generally between three and four.

I learned it had been a red year, very intense, at least that's what everyone said. Which meant the leaves, or what was left of them, were more crimson than yellow, something to do with the ratio of fall sun to rain. The two weeks I was there were dry, but often overcast. As I looked across Jenny's front lawn to the neighbor's bare, plowed field, the woods beyond it brown, red and black-limbed, the still more distant hills rising with, then through, the tree line, it all seemed within reach. It must have been the dimmed colors, the bare trees and bleak sky, but that beautiful gray view felt two-dimensional, as if Jenny's farm were background to a ten-cent postcard.

I learned to split firewood. Not well, or quickly, okay, but without dicing fingers or pedal extremities I split and stacked my share for the woodstove.

I ran a chain saw.

I learned if you saw one deer on the road there might be others, so slow down. I learned many hunters, particularly weekenders from the city, were assholes. The afternoon after I'd met Anne, a Saturday, Jenny and I were walking in the woods behind her pond. Suddenly, *pop, pop, pop,* and we dived into a pool of dry leaves. A second later Jenny was on her knees and I was pulling at her.

"Get down."

The First Time I Saw Jenny Hall

"Hey, you assholes!" she screamed. "Hey!"

A voice answered, "Dad, is that you, Dad?"

And Jenny, trembling, I could feel it through her coat, we were both trembling, shouted back, "It's Jenny Hall. I own these woods and if you're not gone in thirty seconds, I'll have you arrested."

The hunters were too far away to hear, but they got the idea because a few minutes later two men, one around fifty, large and dark-haired, a gut like a swallowed half-keg, the other, I assumed, his son, seventeen or eighteen and still thin, both of them wearing red hunter's caps, walked up carrying rifles.

"I'm sorry, mister," the father said. He looked from Jenny to me, at my long hair, trying to guess how to play it. "You should keep your land better posted."

"Fuck you, you maniac. You're trespassing, you could have killed us."

The father's eyes got hard, but he didn't say anything. The boy looked at his boots.

"Now walk," Jenny said. "We're going to follow you off."

Until we reached the pond ten minutes later, we walked behind them. No one spoke except Jenny, who told me, loud enough for the hunters to hear, how two years ago, someone shot a deer on her back lawn, halfway between the house and barn.

"That brave sportsman heard our back door open and ran. Not only was he trespassing like these heroes, it's illegal to hunt that close to a house. Of course, the deer wasn't dead but the hunter didn't take time to find out. It bled into the snow moaning, until Danny got back with a neighbor's gun."

Jenny took a deep breath. "Fucking maniacs."

Again the father looked at us over his shoulder; again he said nothing. I felt sorry for him. Jenny was not only out of control, she was right. The rest of the walk the only sounds were the crunching of leaves and the echo of gunfire across the valley. At the pond Jenny and I stopped and watched them walk down her hill, climb into a station wagon and drive off.

"A lot of help you were."

"What?"

"You didn't say a word. Do you like hunting?"

She had the same crazed look as the morning I'd asked her about Danny. The pale-eyed rage she'd turned on Bobby in the hospital.

"I've never even shot a gun. Besides"—I smiled to cover how shaky I felt—"you were saying enough for both of us."

"Why don't you leave me alone? I'll meet you at the house."

I'd really thought it was nutty, but I said, "You were brave to do what you did."

"Please, leave me alone."

I realized she meant it and left her skipping stones on her pond. I walked down the hill, thinking how crazy and confused those pale eyes had looked, as if something inside had overheated and was still boiling; as if she was angry at those hunters for more than trespassing on her land. After that, we only walked in the woods on weekdays.

Other things I learned were as follows: We were going to be a fine band. While I was eating breakfast, chopping wood, melodies circled in my mind as if they were running laps. I'd wake up in Jenny's bedroom, which had windows in every wall except behind the bed, and wind would be gusting through the sugar maples, filling the room with low baroque music. And the light, it's hard to describe because it's all shade and nuance, but the light was a soft pre-winter gray that telescoped time and distance. Dreamlight.

I'd sit up looking at the neighbor's field and remember last night's Scrabble, the hours of practice that preceded the game, the four of us beginning to anticipate: one body, eight arms. And remembering, I'd get so excited I couldn't decide whether to slip off Jenny's nightie and melt into her blond dream or steal downstairs to the piano. Caressing her sleepy breasts, fingering the blacks and whites, my feeling was the same. We're going to make it. I know it. We are.

Most nights Bird slept in one of the upstairs bedrooms. Danny slept downstairs, love's martyr. On Monday he'd contributed his tune to the demo: "Lazarus," which stylistically was our closest to new wave. A driving bass line, simple chords and a screaming guitar solo Jenny now played, but which I knew Danny had written for himself.

The arrangement opened with Bird's solo, bass and floor toms that built to a crescendo as Jenny leapt to her mike. She wore jeans and a loose top, but I could imagine her poured into something tight, black and leather, her pelvis punched forward, mouth wide, blond hair shaking in a red spot, singing:

> *"Lazarus kicked back the stones,*
> *Shook his reborn bones.*
> *Coming alive, he said."*

The middle verses she half talked, half sang, not touching her guitar, both hands on the mike:

> *"Been where death can't follow,*
> *Come through shit and sorrow,*
> *Touched, yeah, felt all I could see.*

> *"Eternity, oh brought me down,*
> *The wheel of life circled round,*
> *Left me living but not free.*
> *Yeah, we're living but not free."*

Then we'd roar into the break, trading solos, and sometimes it would last fifteen or twenty minutes, the long lines paralleling the contradictions in our own lives, all of it captured reductively in Danny's phrase "Yeah, we're living but not free." The shapelessness of the music, the inchoate energy battling and bounded by the song's structure—verse, chorus, break, verse, chorus—just as our relations existed with the boundaries of who we were to each other, and the rules, undiscussed but sorting themselves out about what we were each allowed to do.

I learned, as much as I loved and was turned on by Jenny, it was possible to want someone else. Twice during the first week I dreamed about Annie. Playing the piano in an empty room, I'd begin to feel excited, and realize that Anne was sitting in a chair to my right, smiling the long-faced smile I found so mysterious.

I studied the keys, looked up at Anne; she'd slipped the green dress from her shoulders. Falling to her waist, it had gathered in folds. And beneath the half-circle of collarbone and bony shoulders, her breasts, three, no, four, a dozen of them, hung in the gray light. Then someone else was playing. Anne and I were in bed, my apartment, Anne riding me tall and spare, a half smile on her full lips and me lost inside her, grinning at the ceiling.

Once I woke up still hard, the other time just after I'd ejaculated all over my stomach. Embarrassed, the ocean smell of semen filling the room, my head swirling with the dope we'd smoked and Jenny beside me, I slipped out of bed, walked downstairs to clean myself off, the wood floor cold on my bare feet, wondering who I might meet and which bed, if any, Anne was in.

I couldn't figure out what she was up to. She'd arrive late, listen to rehearsal, play Scrabble. Then what? Sometimes she slept with Bird, sometimes she drove home. No matter where she slept she was gone before I rose in the morning—back to her studio to paint.

Her accent was a phony. Anne Peters grew up in Philadelphia, though she'd spent two years at the London School of Art, which was where, I imagined, she'd acquired the long *a*'s.

From Jenny I learned that Anne had lived in Ithaca about

a year. Though they were often at the same parties, Jenny
didn't know her well. She periodically ended up in bed with
Bird, but no one thought much about that since lots of women
slept with Bird and nothing came of it; though it was also true
that Bird's lovers tended to be younger than Anne, sexy in a
healthier, bouncy way, and a good deal less complicated.
Anne's paintings, Jenny said, the ones she'd seen, were sharply
divided between small exquisite watercolors, architectural city
scenes, and the weird ones. Women and trees made love, the
sky in skin tones, the earth on fire, cheering. Men did donkeys.
Leda embraced a giant black swan.

"As if," Jenny said, sitting up in bed one night, "she still
needs to proclaim her love for the country. Until she moved
here, she'd only lived in cities." Jenny put her arms around
me. "Like you, Potts"—she grinned—"my concrete lover."

"Like you, too. And Danny, the Greek boy from Long
Island City."

"When you're hot you're hot, lover."

I guided her hand downward.

"Concrete, is that it?"

I kissed her.

A week after Anne had first appeared, another Friday, actually Saturday morning, we were all playing Scrabble. Danny
was winning. He almost always won, averaging one and often
two seven-letter words per game, losing himself in intricate
patterns just as he did playing bass. He wasn't competitive, at
least not in the sense that I'd previously understood, but most
nights he not only won, he beat everyone silly. Didn't bang
down the letters like some classically aggressive male, just
played long graceful runs, *jonquil, heating, stylish,* and looked
up smiling, but just a little.

Jenny and I were seated to Danny's right at the green
kitchen table, sharing a rack. Anne, who was in second place,

sat opposite Danny, and Bird, mired in last, a position he both resented and deeply deserved, sat to Danny's left. We'd been drinking beer and smoking dope. It was maybe two-thirty and we were all waiting for Bird, who for the past ten minutes had been drumming his fingers, scratching his head, drinking beer, burping, but mostly, hoping for inspiration.

Suddenly a light flashed in his blue eyes and he surrounded a free *R* with an *F, A* and *T.* Then, because the square after the *T* was a double word score, Bird grinned and slapped down a final *Y.*

We sat silently, then I said, "Farty, what's farty?"

"Your breath."

"Farty." Anne began to laugh, then we were all laughing. "I challenge."

And still laughing, actually giggling, everyone stoned and tired, Anne repeating, "Farty," her accent making it sound like *fahrty,* "I don't believe it, fahr—ty," Anne reached for the Scrabble player's dictionary Jenny had bought Danny when they were living together. As her hand touched the volume in front of Danny, her small breasts rolling forward under her white silk blouse, the two top buttons undone, her nipples nearly scraping the Scrabble tiles, I saw Danny peer down her front. And I saw that Jenny, seated next to Danny, had noticed him peeking.

Who could blame him? I was jealous. Then Anne, her skin the bone white of some lucky dark-haired women, met Danny's eyes. Still bent over the board, she smiled up at him as if she were embarrassed, her white face flushing slightly, though I was pretty sure Annie knew what she was doing.

Just then, trying to sound outraged, Bird announced, "Farty, arty-farty."

"That's fartsy," said Danny.

Anne flipped through the dictionary. Jenny turned, and looking past me, watched Anne, her tongue showing at the edge of her lips, her eyes a little stunned, as if she'd glimpsed why Anne had been stopping by every night.

"Here it is," Anne said, and looked up. From hairline to nose to full lips she glowed with a smile that was a gift from her to Danny.

"No farty," she announced, breaking into a high giggle. "Not even a little fart."

After the game Jenny and I made love until we were exhausted, the house alive with ghosts, with moans and echoes. I helped Jenny to an orgasm, then came inside her. Later, nearly asleep, I heard Jenny returning from the bathroom. Footsteps, then her fingers summoned me back. The bed shifted and she had me in her mouth, sucking until I was hard. I reached for her. She sat up, saying, "Wait, I have an idea."

I grinned because I liked Jenny's ideas, and because it was all happening to me as I lay in the dark bedroom of a woman I loved. Jenny lay on her back, legs spread, a pillow under her butt. Reaching down, she wet herself, which I thought odd since she normally didn't need to. I climbed on top, started to enter her and she said, "No, wait," then guided me not into her vagina but into the next, lower and tighter hole.

"Easy," she said, lifting her bottom toward me. "Easy." Eyes clenched, her mouth open. "Eee-zeee."

Her muscles relaxed and I entered her. Her eyes opened as we began to move gently against each other.

"Is this your first time?"

"Yeah," I answered, concentrating on not hurting her. Millions of gays did it, but who knew what damage I might do? It felt awfully small, dark and intense down there.

"Got your cherry again."

She grinned. I plunged deeper inside her and the moans and cries in the echoing house were ours.

*   *   *

At breakfast Jenny told me what I'd already guessed. On one of her late-night trips to the bathroom, probably the last, she'd met Danny and Anne. Anne wore a man's button-down shirt, the buttons undone, nothing else. Danny was naked except for his ponytail spread across his shoulders.

"When he saw me he looked like he wanted to duck back into the john for a towel. Anne said, 'Good evening,' just like that, 'Good evening.' I said, 'Sweet dreams.' Then I pissed and came back to bed."

"Was that when we made love the last time?"

Jenny looked at me across her coffee cup. "Would you be angry?"

I thought about it. I felt tainted, a little dirty, but not much. "No, I had a wonderful time."

We sipped our coffee. Though only eight hours earlier she'd taught me what we came to call doing the devil, in the morning light Jenny always looked innocent; all her pixie highlights showed.

"I can't explain, but it was weird seeing them and how upset they were to see me."

"Were you surprised?"

Jenny stroked her hair, lifted it off her forehead with her left hand, then let it fall, one of her unconscious beautiful-girl twitches.

"No."

"As much as he loves you, Danny is almost human."

"What does that mean?"

"It means Danny and I look at each other from a million miles away with you in the middle."

Her eyes narrowed, the lids did, then Jenny said, "I suppose you think I should be happy about Anne."

"Depends how you feel about me."

Jenny lifted her hair again. Released, it tumbled past her cheek. "Things with Danny are over."

"Tell him that."

"He knows."

"Then you ought to leave him alone."

Jenny raised her coffee cup until it covered her nose. She set it down empty. "You think I'm horrible, don't you?"

"No, but I sometimes think you do. You know, Jenny, there's nothing wrong with wanting to be successful, just the way some people go about it."

Jenny stood, came to my side of the table and put her hands on my shoulders. "You keep me honest, okay?" She kissed me, then smiling she said, "Let's go for a walk. We can use it."

Maybe I should have repeated, *Leave him alone.* Maybe I should have said, "Let's keep each other honest." Instead, always looking for the easy way out, I said, "Sure you're up to walking after last night?"

"Try me."

"I'd love to."

I drained my cup and followed Jenny out the door and past her barn. Up the hill and into the woods, where the wind whispered of dreams, of destiny, the leaves crying, Oh, no. Too soon. Not me.

· PART TWO ·

To the Country

Chapter Five

•

MONDAY BOBBY CALLED from New York to announce he'd been released from Payne Whitney. Also, a friend's studio had gone sixteen-track, were we interested for the demo?

"Does this mean," Danny said, "Bobby's going to produce?"

Jenny dangled the phone from her hip. "Should I ask?"

"Ask him," Bird said, "if we get a special rate. Who is this bozo in Jersey?"

"I will not."

"Hey, this is business."

"Tell him," I said. "If he's involved, tell him yes."

Anne slept with Danny every night, and Bird stopped flirting with her. Bird. When I think of him, jargonized phrases bubble up from a dimly remembered semester of Anthro 101. Kinship groups, male–male bonding. Quicksilver, quirky Bird, a complex man who lived, or tried to, by simple rules. Friends, he'd say and wink, never let a woman come between them. Clean your clothes every two weeks whether or not they need it.

Always tell the truth, even if you have to make it up.

Two days before the five of us left for New York, five because Anne came, Bird and I were running errands. Marketing at the P & C, then beers and pinball at the Rongovian Embassy to the United States. The Rongo's dark wooden tables, brick walls and archways connecting the two large rooms, Mexican food, mounted sailfish, stuffed cat, forty brands of beer and mixed drinks with names like Blind and Dead Bastard made it a T-burg landmark. Wednesdays and Sundays live bands drew Cornell students. Other nights it was the fixed point in the hip universe north of Ithaca.

Around five, which was when Bird and I descended, it was deserted except for Todd, the balding, bearded bartender, a couple of drinkers bellied up to the long bar, a few early eaters, and Nan and Kay, the sexy waitresses. The Rongo was too hip to have a jukebox, and recorded music blared from overhead speakers. Dylan finished the note-bending harmonica intro to "Visions of Johanna," then began singing, as Bird and I, bearing mugs of Pryor's dark, settled in behind the pinball machine, of which Bird was a master. By which I mean he could simultaneously talk and play, bells ringing, lights flashing, jaws yapping.

Of course, Bird could and usually did jabber no matter what he was doing. When I think of him it's not Bird drumming I see, but Bird talking, his nose a bony question mark. I didn't know him well then. In some ways, no one did. For all his chatter he rarely mentioned his family, his pre-T-burg existence, what his parents thought of his drumming, or what growing up a crazy man had been like.

But whoever Bird had been as a kid in Boston, Bird was *there*. And maybe it was because we were shadows, me the small dark reflection of his blond height, but I loved Bird Murphy. As I sit here writing this, he's beside me, grinning, has been for months, his sharp chin on my shoulder, the tip of his nose bumping my pencil's pink eraser.

Bird pumped fifty cents into Armageddon, which sported upper and lower flippers operated off the same set of buttons, tabs to knock down, lights to light and spinners to spin which activated numerous star-spangled bonuses, because like most things at the Rongo, Armageddon was a fair deal.

"Potts," Bird said, after he had the first steel ball pinging across the board, the bonus value already 3x, "what do you think of Annie?"

"I like her."

Bird caught the ball with the lower left flipper, then spun it through the right spinner marked *Eternity,* which routed the ball to the top of the board and the bank of roll-over lights.

"Interesting, sexy."

"You got a hard-on for her?" Bird winked, but refocused in time to save the silver ball speeding down the center alley.

"Nice move," I said.

"Misspent youth."

"If I do—"

"Since you do," Bird said, banging the board with his hip.

"I'd ignore it. You think I'm crazy?"

"Nuts," Bird said as he lost the ball, and lights flashing, the board totaled his bonus. "You're up."

"What about you?" I put a ball in play. "You mind about her and Danny?"

My eyes on the game, Bird's voice floated at me unfaced, on faith. "Me and Anne had good times. But she always loved the Greek."

"You weren't jealous?"

"They might have something real. With me, my man, it was just yuks."

"Sounds tragic." I smiled at him and the ball zipped between my flippers.

"Hey, your playing's tragic. My life's a comedy."

The machine totaled my bonus, making the score Bird 62,000, me an inept 7,200.

"Danny," he said, "carries a flaming torch for Jenny. They lived together three years and she's still a fantasy woman for him. I mean, the Greek oozes suffering and devotion."

Our eyes met.

"What about it?"

"Be cool, little man. Jealousy doth not become thee." Bird grinned, stepped in front of the machine, put a ball in play.

I drank some beer.

"Listen good, while I enlarge your mind. There's two kinds of people. Nice guys like you, me and Annie. Ask me something, you know what I'm going to say. We compromise, give and take"—Bird banged the machine with his hip—"we're reasonable."

"You're reasonable?"

"In my own way. You, too. You can be a shithead, but you're a reasonable shithead. Then there're cranks. Nice guys and cranks. Jenny and Bobby Hall, they're cranks. Once they decide something, they're like a dog with a fucking bone. Bobby was politically effective in the sixties because he and that dude Ethan turned rudeness into an art form."

I found myself wishing Bird would miss the ball and shut up before he said something about Jenny I would have to be mad at him about.

"What are you saying?" I asked.

"Guerrilla theater."

Bird caught the ball on his bottom right flipper, balanced it motionless, then snapped the ball toward the bank of tab-activated lights on the top left, which when completed would spell *Armageddon*.

"Don't get me wrong," he added, as the ball pinged off the second *d* and lights flashed. "I love Jenny, and Bobby Hall was flying kamikaze, lonely and visible long before it was hip. When little farts like you and me are puffs in the wind of history, people'll remember Bobby Hall." Bird looked up and grinned. "But he'll still be a crank. And when people start expecting cranks to act like nice guys, there's trouble."

Bird looked down, banged the machine with his magic hip, but lost the ball anyway. I stepped forward and played. My ball flashed down the top slot, lit the *m* and began to attack bumpers and light lights as if I knew what I was doing.

"Hey," Bird shouted, "you got it hotted up. Go with it," which is when I lost it.

"The point," Bird said as he put his last ball in play, "is Danny. The Greek looks like a nice guy, those suffering eyes, right, but he's a crank. Three years ago he and Jenny had this thing out of a fucking Ivory Snow commercial. Every afternoon they'd pick berries and make a pie. He'd show at parties and she'd braided his hair with ribbons. You'd visit them, and either they'd be naked or wearing each other's clothes. And you probably haven't heard this." Bird grinned and fired the ball at the bank of lights, scoring the *o,* which left only the final *n* of *Armageddon.* "Two years running they were runners-up to Bambi and Snow White as hippie couple of the year."

"You're kidding."

"I kid you not."

Bird flipped the ball toward the top of the board, trapped it with his top left flipper, knocked it toward Armageddon's final *n,* and the machine oohed, ahed and flashed as if experiencing sexual ecstasy. Bird trapped the ball with his bottom flipper, shot it through the Eternity spinner and began to rack up free games. Before he returned the board to me he'd won four.

"Anyway," Bird began, as I watched my ball ping dully from cushion to cushion, the game almost over and less than half of *Armageddon* lit, "my point, and I've got one this time. Keep your pecker in your pants around Annie, and remember what I said about cranks. I've got a feeling we're going to hit. I want us all to be talking a year from now."

"Of course we'll be talking. You and me, Bird, we're blabbos."

Instead of flipping the ball through Eternity, I hit a bumper to its right and lost the ball and game on a carom down the side exit lane. A little relieved—if I couldn't beat him, I could lose quickly—I watched the machine total my score. Then I faced Bird, who was finishing his beer. He looked at me over his mug. I felt he was angry at me, trying to read how seriously I'd taken what he said. The moment lengthened. I hadn't taken him seriously, and I think Bird knew that. But it wasn't the sort of thing Bird would call me on. Instead, he grinned.

"Sure, blabbos with big noses."

"Big nose," I said, "big humph."

"Pottsie, haul your big nose to the bar and buy us some beers. Let's play these free games, what say?"

I retrieved the beers. Which Grandpa Ziggie paid for, which Bird and I drank. Buddies, one and all.

The next two days, Tuesday and Wednesday, I called everyone I knew in New York to pitch them on the Friday and Saturday night gigs at Discovery. Ziggie said he'd get Arnie to take him. Rosemarie was working. Most other friends said they'd come. I called managers, booking agents, independent producers, A & R men for the major labels. I called Sean to make sure everything was happening. *No hay problemas.* The *Voice* ad was out.

I asked if he'd ever heard of The Big M, which was the name of Bobby's friend's studio in Jersey.

"Is that where you're doing the demo?"

"Next week."

"Doehr's a loony-tune. Worked at Electric Ladyland when Hendrix was recording, and I think he did a couple"—Sean paused, the line hissed—"of Bobby Hall's albums for Apex."

He paused again. Sitting alone at Jenny's kitchen table, everyone else in the living room, the November night blowing cold and stormy, I felt my heart begin to pound.

"He didn't work a couple years. Word was he did so much crystal he almost checked out."

"Meth'll do that."

Sean didn't answer. Without straining my mind's eye I saw him at Discovery's bar, sucking a Reddi-Wip nozzle.

"Potts, how'd you hear about Doehr?"

"A friend."

"Jenny's friend?"

"What's on your pea brain?"

"I may be dumb, but you want to keep a secret, don't have Ethan Marks acting as your manager."

"Ethan's been in to see you?"

"Jews have big noses?"

"Not funny, Sean."

"Not funny, Stevie, keeping secrets. I could have run it up if I'd known in time."

I didn't answer. Sean obviously knew, and why not? I listened to the scritch of long distance, more excited than anxious, and Sean's teeny fuse popped.

"You trying to tell me she's not Bobby's sister?"

"I'm not telling you anything unless you can keep a secret."

Sean snickered. "You must be high. The only ones who don't know are the fucking bag ladies. You didn't know at first, didja?"

"I suspected."

"You know, Potts, sometimes I think you're a bimbo, then you pull something like this. What are you, a hustler?"

"Wanna buy a bridge? What's Ethan been in for?"

"He and Bobby have been inviting Bobby's old friends. Hershkoff, Hammond, Landau, the real juice. Ethan's been checking on tables. Half the place Friday"—Sean laughed— "he or probably you're paying for. He's also been checking who's doing sound, lights, manager shit. The story I hear is Bobby's getting you an album deal with him as producer." Sean paused. "You need a backup singer, remember, I introduced you."

"Don't worry," I said, feeling sorry for Sean, who must be desperate to ask for something he knew I'd never give him. "I remember."

Driving to New York the next day, Jenny beside me in the front seat, Bird squeezed in back between his bass drum and accessory case, the rest of his set stashed in the trunk with

The First Time I Saw Jenny Hall

Jenny's guitar while the amps, my Rhodes and Danny's gear rode with Danny and Anne in Jenny's Volvo, I turned to Jenny, who was gazing out her window.

"Tell me about Ethan."

When she faced me, Jenny's expression was what I think literary men call baleful.

"I told you. I didn't know Bobby was hustling, so I certainly didn't know Ethan was."

Eyes on the road, I flipped on my blinker, pulled into the passing lane to circle a milk truck.

"Are they a team or something?"

"You should be flattered," Jenny said. "Bobby's never done this before."

"Hey, Big-nose," called Bird from the back. "You're the grease this act needed."

"I know," I said, "I know," adrenaline speeding through me to D.C.'s eight cylinders. "If Bobby gets us a deal with Hershkoff, I'll kiss his feet."

"Don't bother," Bird said. "You're not his type."

For anyone who's been in the Gulag for the past twenty years, Sol Hershkoff signed Bobby to his first contract in '64. For those same twenty years, actually thirty, Hershkoff was one of the majordomos in the industry, signing and producing jazz and blues players in the 40's and 50's, then the first wave of singer-songwriters in the mid-60's. Now that Hershkoff himself was in the midsixties, he'd been made some sort of senior vice-president as a way of easing him out. But he was as active as ever, and when people said Apex, they meant Sol Hershkoff.

Jenny said, "Hershkoff's been after Bobby to produce since his voice went. He wouldn't."

"You've met him?"

She grinned. "He reminds me of Ziggie."

I thought about that while passing a green Subaru with a man, woman and small baby in the front seat. Bird said, "Now that Bobby's tried to off himself and didn't make it"—Bird leaned forward, propped both elbows on the front seat—"he figures he might as well produce pop-rock. What else is left?"

"Disco," I said. "What if they package us as white disco?"

"I've got standards, ya fucking sleaze." Bird began to drum the back of the seat, singing, "Shadow dancin', ooh-ooh, shadow dancin'."

"After what's happened"—Jenny turned, faced me across the front seat; wheat-blond hair, the Huck Finn nose, *my lover*, and I thought, What's happened is fifteen years of American history—"Bobby's willing to accept some changes."

Jenny paused, and I knew from her voice she was either wetting her upper lip or pushing the heavy sweep of hair from one side of her face to the other. One eye on the road, I peeked at her. She was doing neither.

"But disco," she continued, her voice brightening, "not bloody likely."

"You really think," Bird began, "and don't get me wrong, Jenny-O, but a star like Bobby, the kind of ego he was supposed to have. Of course, I'm drowning in clichés, I'm flailing in them. But a star like Bobby, you think he's ready to be in the background? He does a good job producing, you'll replace him as the family star."

"What am I supposed to do, spend my life protecting Bobby's past?"

I turned, smiled to reassure Jenny, but it was wasted motion. To Bird she said, "I never asked for his help because I was afraid he *would* think I was trying to replace him."

"That's because you are."

We started up a hill, circling toward the summit. A light rain was falling and I flipped on the wipers. For thirty seconds their *swish-swick* was the only sound in the car. Then I said, "If Bobby gets us a deal, okay, we'll worry. I'm still waiting to hear about Ethan."

We crested the hill, and a dark valley, squeezed between

green knuckled hills like a giant's finger, extended below us to the left. A lone chimney sent up smoke into the gray mist.

"What's this about you and Ethan?" Jenny asked. "You got some kind of thing for him?"

I knew what I wanted to say, but decided I shouldn't. Then it burst out of me anyway. "The thing I'm worried about is you and Ethan."

"Whoa," Bird said as we started down the hill. "Just us chickens in back and we ain't listening, right, Mister Rooster?" Bird imitated a barnyard.

"You got something to say," Jenny said. "Say it."

I peered at the bright and future star sitting stiff-backed against the passenger door. "I'm not trying to make a scene," I began, and Jenny shot back, "It comes naturally, huh?"

Bird laughed, a short harsh burst.

"Look, babe," I said, "Bobby gets us a deal, Ethan will probably manage us."

She didn't answer.

"I've met Ethan once and thought he was an incredible asshole." I tried to catch Jenny's eye. "I'm willing to believe he was having a bad day, but you got to help me."

"I don't want to."

Arms folded, Jenny stared out the window. For two, maybe four or five dark minutes we drove in outward silence. Inside I was roaring. Goddamnit. Goddamn her. Fighting was bad enough. Fighting in front of Bird was fucking unacceptable, and if we hadn't been doing sixty-five down the side of a mountain, I would have bolted, bam, out the driver's door, and every man or bitch for him- or herself.

What was I supposed to do, apologize with Bird listening? Apologize for what? Tell Jenny to be reasonable, I was just asking, which I had every right to since she'd gone behind my back before? Or continue to sit, teeth knitted, breath ragged, fingers clenched so tightly the car was filled with vaporized steering wheel?

Bird said, "What if I tell him what I know about Ethan? It ain't much."

"What if you don't? You think because he made his question sound reasonable, it wasn't pure shit?"

"Now look, Jenny—"

"Look yourself. I met Ethan when I was seventeen visiting Bobby and thought he was Lord Byron. What happened then isn't your business. If I were fucking him now, that wouldn't be either."

I felt intricate, unnamed knots tighten in my gut. My head filled with wind. My body screamed for air. I choked out, "I think it would be."

"That's where you're wrong. I'm not answering to you every time we deal with a good-looking man. The business is full of them."

The knots snapped, my lungs filled and I screamed, "I don't care if he's fucking Robert Redford. Just tell me why I should deal with the asshole."

That hung, sizzling. Realizing I was around the bend and deep in the woods, I flipped on the blinker, and hands shaking, pulled onto the shoulder.

"Oh, great," Jenny said, "great." The red Volvo braked and pulled onto the shoulder two hundred yards ahead of us. "How big a scene do you want?"

"I'm trying"—I glanced at Jenny, who looked absolutely furious—"to keep from running into someone."

We stared at each other, then Bird said, "I'm going to take a leak."

Leaning across his accessory case, Bird opened the door. Climbing out, his hand on the frame, he leaned back, looked first at Jenny, then me. "You're both being incredibly uncool. You ought to think about that."

The door closed. We scowled into space. Jenny said, "Why are you being so mean to me?"

"To you?"

She flicked her bangs out of her eyes. "I could kill you for throwing this scene in front of Bird. If you're really worried about Ethan, why didn't you ask last night?"

That got through, but I was damned if I'd show it.

"Is telling me you want to kill me your idea of how to end a fight?"

"At least I tell you what I feel." She cocked a blond eyebrow. "What are you feeling, you repressed son-of-a-bitch?"

"I'm angry and jealous because I find myself with a manager who doesn't like me, and has the hots for you."

Jenny's mouth opened, but before she could defend herself, I said, "Listen, Ethan may turn out the world's best manager, but he's going to look after his and Bobby's interests first, yours second, and mine right after Mister Dogsqueeze."

Jenny laughed, and the happy sound rolled around the car. Then, her eyes a calmer, lighter blue, she said, "Keep making me laugh, can you do that?"

"I'll try."

Jenny hugged me. Lips to my ear, her voice breathy, dreamy, she whispered, "We're so lucky. We love each other, the band's going to work, things are good with Danny." She leaned back. We looked in each other's eyes, and she asked, "Don't you think?"

I didn't know what I thought except I was upside down inside and wanted her to love me.

"I think."

"Don't worry, I'll look after your interests." She smiled and fondled Mister Johnson. "The band's, too. And I'll tell you everything you'd ever want to know about Ethan."

I kissed her, and with Jenny's lips soft on mine I thought, We are lucky. Kissing her, eyes closed, my ears began to function and I realized the drumming I'd been hearing wasn't just my ambivalent, yearning heart, but rain against the roof. I opened the driver's door and spotted Bird talking to Danny a hundred yards up the shoulder in front of an oak which had lost its leaves to winter.

"Hey," I shouted. "Hey, Bird!"

He turned, mouth open, blond hair dull in the gray light. Danny said something, Bird nodded, then came running back to us down the asphalt shoulder, rain falling, arms pumping, his face streaked and wet.

The showcase went like a dream. Both nights the room was packed. Friday we did one encore; Saturday three. Ethan, Bobby and Anne sat in the center rear of Discovery's small showroom in front of a black-tinted wall mirror where Ethan could greet important guests, Bobby could have his hand pumped by fans and starseekers, and Anne could beam her sweet smile at all of us onstage.

Friday, okay, we had equipment trouble. Never got the monitors right, which, because speakers point away from the stage and sound comes back garbled, meant we couldn't hear ourselves. The audience didn't notice, but Bird and I were upset half the night, around our notes instead of really on them.

Saturday we played like stars. An hour set, all of it original, and they loved us. Halfway through I could feel us settling into the music. One by one we seemed to swell into larger-than-life versions of ourselves looming above the stage like parade floats, invisible wires keeping us off the ceiling. In short, we became a band.

Afterward Jenny, Bird, Danny and I drank free Rémy Martins in Discovery's bar, still putting out the assured vibrations of the blessed, while some poor schlub of a comic tried to follow us in the showroom. We'd been there about ten minutes, wondering where Bobby was, when he pushed through the glad-handing crowd leading a short, older man. Sixty, maybe sixty-five, he looked tough; make that self-contained.

His chest was broad and powerful, but he barely topped Bobby's shoulder. His eye sockets were paunchy, his full cheeks sagged, but anchored by a small chin and pugnacious jaw, his face still battled gravity. White at the temples but dark on top, his hair was cut short, almost a crew cut. He had bright, humorous eyes and looked, in a way that was both comic and impressive, like a miniature of a much larger man. He wore a dark blazer, white shirt and narrow tie. Seeing him with Bobby, however briefly, you sensed they were protective of each other. Father and son, but also a grown-up son with an aging dad.

"Sol, you remember Jenny." Jenny and Sol Hershkoff smiled. "And this is Danny, Bird"—Bobby turned and I was terrified he'd forgotten my name; then he finished—"and Steve Potts. He wrote those tunes you liked."

"Great," Hershkoff said, pumping my hand. "Great."

He repeated it over and over, *Great,* a dynamo in an Abe Beame body. Sixty-five for sure, but with a younger man's strong, fleshy grip. He shook Bird's, then Danny's hand, for a moment covering Danny's with both of his, saying, "Beautiful work, son, just beautiful."

Then he stepped back and his eyes darted from me to Bird to Danny to Jenny, all of us ringing him and Bobby as if we were ghouls, a Greek chorus, scared school kids.

"I want you in my office first thing Monday."

His voice retained the slight nasality of Brooklyn, an ethnic wheeze which never quite damped out even if—as I learned later—you've shaken the hands of kings, queens and what's known in the trades as legends in their own time.

"And get yourself a good lawyer." Hershkoff turned toward Bobby and looked up, his square chin even with Bobby's shoulder and aimed at his nose, Bobby who'd lost some of the excess weight and now looked like a slightly puffy pinup of his old heroic self. "Maybe you can hold on to more money than this *meshuganah.*"

Bobby seemed to stiffen, then he grinned. "That shouldn't be hard."

Meanwhile pint-sized Hershkoff, heavily jowled spark plug, had noticed no one from Waterfall had said a word.

"You want to sign with Apex, right? Whatever you've heard about crooked contracts, and record companies not keeping up their end of a deal"—he turned toward Bobby and they laughed—"it's all true."

I looked from Danny to Bird to Jenny. What we felt, at least what I felt, was stunned, and we stood there, a stunned circle in the noisy bar. Then the spell collapsed and someone was pumping Bobby's hand. A voice called, "Sol. Sol, you old dog. Aren't you dead yet?"

Hershkoff was surrounded by a fat man who looked sixty, but a man that big it was hard to tell. Bird, Danny, Jenny and I huddled, our eyes bright, and Bird, who was flying on a combination of coke and free cognac, whispered, "This guy's really Hershkoff?"

"Of course," said Jenny. "What are you, crazy?"

"Pinch me," Bird answered. "Fucking pinch me."

"Why don't—" Danny began, and laughed. "Why don't—" He laughed again, loose as I'd ever seen him. "Why don't we tell him yes and sign tonight?"

Bobby leaned into our huddle: the coach sending in a play. "Tell him maybe, that there's other people interested."

"Maybe," Jenny said, when Hershkoff escaped from the fat man. "Maybe," she repeated, for a second looking as lost as I felt in the sea of chaos and possibility we found ourselves afloat on. Then she smiled. "Which songs," she asked, "did you like best?"

"Wait a minute. Maybe what?"

"Maybe"—Jenny glanced at Bobby, who nodded—"Maybe we'll sign."

"Oh," said Hershkoff, and I thought the grinning old man was going to chuck famous radical Bobby under the chin. "Big brother's been coaching you. Well, this is no place to do business. Ten-thirty in my office, Bobby knows where." Then he looked, I hoped, straight at me. "You kids were great, you hear? Great."

On Monday Hershkoff signed us for Apex Records. Bird began buying his cocaine in half-ounce Baggies from a Colombian named Juan. I grew two inches. Danny permed his pony. Not to be outdone, Jenny produced a third tit.

Okay, Hershkoff didn't sign us Monday. What actually happened was he repeated his intention to sign us. A week later our lawyer, Constantine Stamos, a plump bearded Greek Bobby knew, spoke to their lawyer and set up a lunch meeting at The Four Seasons for the following week. Bobby, Ethan, Stamos and their lawyer each downed two martinis, ate their way through a hundred-dollar expense account lunch, then chewed over Apex's terms.

After dinner that night at a Thai restaurant on Eighth Avenue, Stamos, an ex-Movement, currently an entertainment lawyer whose claim to fame was springing Huey Newton not once, but twice, Stamos said that between him, Bobby and Ethan, the Apex man never had a chance.

"Bobby made it sound"—Stamos paused to pick his teeth, Stamos was a toothpicker—"as if you had so many offers you needed an accountant to keep track."

"Yeah, offers," Bobby said, his mouth and still plump cheeks grinning around one of the big cigars I'd seen him photographed with in the 60's. "Ya wanna pay your rent before I hit you in the fucking head?"

We laughed.

"I told him"—Bobby took the cigar out of his mouth, flicked the ash—"we were signing only out of loyalty to Sol, and unless he wanted Hershkoff kicking his butt up and down the thirty-first floor, he better stop quibbling over nickels and dimes."

"Will he?" asked Bird. Bird was also smoking a cigar. We

all were, Jenny included, purchased from a startled four-foot-high Thai woman at the front desk.

"No problem." Ethan leaned close, his head high in the cloud of cigar smoke shrouding the table. He smiled, which made him even better-looking: Ethan Marks, the luxury item. "It's in the bag."

"I wish he'd throw some nickels my way," said Bird. "Ever since I got discovered, I've been starving my ass off."

"Yeah, Bobby." Jenny sat on my right. Smoking a cigar, her hair a blond shadow crossing her face, she looked especially sexy; also, slightly green. "When are we going to see some money?"

"As soon as the contract's signed," said Lawyer Stamos.

"And when's that?" asked Anne.

Danny smiled at her. She'd taken over their business arrangements.

"When it arrives," said Ethan.

"Provided"—Stamos, who was plotzed, discarded his toothpick, sat up straight and tried to look dignified—"everything's up to—"

"Snuff," Ethan finished, glancing at Jenny.

"Thank you," said Stamos.

"And when's that?"

"Could be soon," Bobby said. "Could be two thousand and one."

"Trust me," Bird said, "the check's in the mail."

"Don't worry, girlie. I won't come in your mouth."

"Ooh," Jenny said, and draped herself over my shoulder. Laughing, she coughed cigar smoke. "That's disgusting."

"Potts," said Bird, "you are one gross fucker."

Jenny's arms still wrapped around me, I raised the glass I hoped was mine. "Here's to Bobby, Brother Stamos"—the fat Greek smiled; overcome with good feeling myself, I added—"and Brother Ethan, who are doing such a fine job."

Grinning, we toasted our new lives.

*   *   *

The contract that arrived several weeks later called for one album and two sides to be recorded and released within twelve months, or Jenny Hall and Waterfall, hereinafter known as Artist, was absolved of further contractual obligations. A 14-point production deal against which we would receive a $30,000 advance, half upon signing, half when we'd finished in the studio. A six-week tour behind the album's release, scheduled for June and July, or July and August, which Apex would subsidize up to $50,000 for publicity and promotion, band salaries, travel expenses (food and recreational drugs not included), the salaries of the lighting and sound men, road manager and any side musicians. A 50–50 split on royalties, with Apex retaining administration.

If that sounds like mumbo jumbo, it is; in a minute I'll explain. But first, here comes reality. It's January again, a year after we signed with Apex. I'm not in my new, stylish apartment. I'm not in the Seventh Street slum, either.

Give up? I'm gazing out my boyhood window in Sheepshead Bay. Craning to see around the blue spruce blocking the view, I stare at the back of the brick row houses where my best friends lived. The day is clear, cold and so bright, so momentarily pure and untouched, that the smoke rising from my Camel disgusts me, but not enough that I put it out. At dinner last night I heard from my mother, who hears from their mothers, that my old friends are happy. Rick, a doctor, lives in San Francisco. Jerry repairs computers in the basement of a bank on Madison and Thirty-eighth. The last time I stayed with my parents was early September, shortly before I began recording this tale of guilt, glitter and woe. I was in the kind of beat-me, whip-me mood I'm only now trying to leave behind.

Ruth and Arnie were worried, and with a zeal that was both touching and simpleminded arranged little outings to distract me. Which is how I ended up in Jerry Haas's living room, for me virgin turf since 1968. Jerry's mother opened the door,

and big as life behind her, Jerry Haas sat on the couch beside
his father, wife and new baby, bald as his old man, Harvey the
Cabbie. Harvey Haas, baldest man in Sheepshead Bay. The
funny thing was the baby was bald, too, so lined up on the
couch in front of a full wall mirror were three generations of
bald Haases, light shining off their skulls, then reflecting so
brightly in the mirror it brought tears to my eyes, I swear it.
I sat between Jerry and Harvey, Jerry's new baby on his lap,
no more hair on the middle of Jerry's head than on a hard-
boiled egg.

"Who would have guessed, you know? Who would have
guessed?"

And Jerry, who was never real smart, but always sweet—as
a kid I stuck up for him and I believe he loved me for it—Jerry
said, "I don't know, I always thought you might get famous."

Then he wanted to know what Jenny was like.

"A bitch on wheels. A dream. Take your pick."

Right about then, the baby began spitting up and I left. And
you know, my mother was right. Jerry, his bald head shining
like a beacon, Jerry seemed happy.

The contract was a good one, better than we would have
been offered without Bobby. Fourteen points refers to 14
percent of the record's retail price. Of the 14 points, the band
kept 8 and Bobby, as producer, got 6. Fine. Without Bobby
we wouldn't have received more than 12 points (with at least
4 to the producer), so if Bobby took 6 instead of 4, we still
had eight.

I'm sure having Bobby deal for us also sweetened our advance. General wisdom is you have to pay musicians enough
to keep them comfortable during recording or the product
suffers. Since our advance was $30,000, less 20 percent to our
managers (Bobby and Ethan), we would each receive three
thousand up front, three thousand more when we finished.
Figuring two to three months in the studio, we were going to
be extremely comfortable.

The First Time I Saw Jenny Hall

Anyone snappy with numbers will have noticed that we shared the advance among us. We also divided the band's 8 production points equally, 2 apiece. Jenny's name was up front, but she didn't want or expect more than the rest of us. She was hungry in a way that only an innocent or someone who has watched, waited and decided it's finally her turn can be. But she didn't want money. What Jenny needed was to prove she was as good as her heart whispered she was, which meant better than Bobby. But to be recognized as better, in her own mind she had to be worse. Tune out and drop in. Abandon the upright country life and chase a dream which she believed was cheap and dirty. All those years on the farm she tried to be good, but always knew in her heart the ambition was there, a disease not cured but merely in remission.

I want to be better than Bobby.

Bad Jenny, he's your brother, bad.

I want to be famous.

But fame meant money, making money was immoral, and if Bobby was anything, he was moral. Oh, my, was he moral, a generation's conscience.

And there was Jenny, his sister. It's easy to imagine her late at night on that farm, dreaming her dreams and hating herself for it. She went round and around until Bobby unraveled and the rope broke, giving them each a second chance. Bobby, if he wanted to, could start his life again—he'd killed the singer. Jenny was finally free to pursue her dream, but not yet free to believe it was okay. As a result, I soon realized, she was neurotic about money. Until I took over her finances, she spent what she earned as quickly as possible, it didn't matter on what. Beggars, drugs. Twice she lost her wallet. The one time Ethan hinted at a band meeting that she deserved more money than Bird, Danny or me, Jenny not only said no, she raged at him, crying hysterically, as if some deep psychic button had been pushed. It was the only time, except when we were alone, that I saw Jenny cry.

The aspects of the deal that made me want to cry, and I really had no right to since they were standard, were sharing royalties with Apex, and more important, allowing Apex to be named administrator. For each song, royalties come to approximately four cents per record sold. Composers also make money from sheet music sales and indirectly, each time a song is aired on radio or television. (This money is collected by ASCAP and BMI, organizations which monitor airplay, then divvy up funds established by radio and television stations.)

Splitting royalties with Apex meant they'd take half my money. Unfortunately—the euphemism is "publisher's and writer's share"—that often happens to new writers. What was worse, since Apex retained administration all royalties would be paid to them, which they'd subsequently divide into two "halves," a big one and a little one. Record companies typically skim 10 to 20 percent for "administration," which consists of cashing one check, dividing it in two, then keeping track of how much they're not giving their writers.

Understandably, record labels generally succeed in retaining administration on first-time deals. But because of Bobby, we weren't getting a "first deal." What griped my ass was that as principal writer, I was the only one seriously hurt. Now maybe I've got a jealous heart, but if Jenny had been principal writer, I felt the deal would have been different. Maybe that's nuts. Maybe, as Stamos claimed, Apex insisted and I was a twit to resent it. But our contract, good as it was, convinced me that for Bobby and Apex, Jenny and only Jenny mattered.

The key was Bobby. How much our deal had to do with Apex being hot for Jenny Hall and Waterfall, and how much was Sol Hershkoff helping Bobby, I couldn't begin to guess. Our total package, counting advance, studio costs, pressing, distribution and tour guarantees, easily topped $150,000, so maybe Apex did love our music. But Bobby had made millions for Apex; Hershkoff, who was childless, considered him a son; and what could be a more perfect way to help the old star who'd embarrassed his friends by ending up in the gutter than paying him to produce his sister's band? Particularly since we need a write-off this quarter. And you say she's good? In that case, maybe not. Just kidding, Sol.

Before we started recording, we drove to Trumansburg for two weeks of intense partying and rehearsal. We'd go to bed after first light, waking after the short day had ended, breakfasting on crunchy G in the dark. New snow sometimes covered the old, but I stopped paying attention because in two weeks I never saw bare ground. One night I woke first and walked downstairs to stoke the woodstoves. Venturing into the unheated mud room for split wood, I felt particularly cold and I checked the outside thermometer: 24 below. Jesus Christ, I thought, and hustled my citified butt back to bed.

Most nights starting at ten, we practiced in the living room. Bird, Jenny and I slept upstairs. Danny, when he wasn't at Anne's place, used the downstairs bedroom, so physically, nothing had changed. But the echoes in the house were different. Danny and Anne were a solid couple. Instead of dreaming of a contract we had one, the future secure in our hands, signed and legally sealed.

During rehearsals, which often lasted six or eight hours, it snowed almost as much inside as out. Bird, Jenny and I had chipped in for a quarter ounce of cocaine, which disappeared up the band's collective nose during those two weeks and no doubt helped account for our weird hours.

Danny, however, used very little. The second night back, we were sitting around Jenny's kitchen table after dinner, watching Bird lay out lines on a small mirror.

"Everyone want some?"

"No, thanks," said Danny.

Seated opposite Danny and to my left, Jenny said, "Why not?"

"If I'd wanted it, I would have bought some."

Jenny brought her right hand to her mouth, drew sharply, blew the cigarette smoke to the ceiling. "I assumed you forgot."

Without looking up, Bird, who was carefully dicing the coke with a razor blade, said, "The Greek's saving his money."

Bird snorted his lines through a two-inch plastic straw, first the left, then right nostril, his nose making a wet sucking noise much like the one produced by a dentist's saliva tube. Bird looked up, grinned happily, passed me the mirror and the straw.

"Who cares who paid," Jenny said. "Do some."

I snorted up, right, then left. When I raised my nose, Danny was saying, "It wouldn't be fair."

"God, Danny, what are you talking about, fair?"

He didn't answer, and listening to Jenny's *sniff, sniff, Ahh,* I could feel the tension. I could feel, too, that old wounds were bleeding. From the little Jenny had told me, I knew they fought about money. Neither had made much, but Jenny's father occasionally sent her some, which Danny wanted her to return. His solution was to spend less. Disconnect the phone, cut back on food, on going out, on electricity—ideas which made sense for Danny, since he needed less to be happy. Jenny's choices were to spend as little as Danny, or spend more and feel guilty, which was what she did, usually on luxuries and as quickly as possible. It was complicated, Jenny had told me, because she believed Danny depended on her to buy things he couldn't afford and wouldn't admit to wanting.

His voice very low, Danny said, "It's not fair because I could have paid for it and didn't."

"I don't care who paid." Jenny pushed the mirror at him. "Do some."

"No."

They glared at each other, the two lonely white lines and their mirror images taunting everyone. Then Bird said, "What are you guys, nuts? I'll do them."

Whoosh, up the beak, which left us still sitting there, Jenny furious, Danny immobile, his dark eyes fixed on Jenny's, the air in the room vibrating like a struck drum, when Bird broke into his crazy birdsong banter.

"Couple a fucking lunatics. One of them likes coke and won't snort it, the other is going to make him snort it or else. And me, I'd generally give my left nut for a line, I'm listening. You believe this, Potts?"

"I believe it."

"Old lovers. I can't believe I'm working with old lovers and her new one. I'm the nut."

"Enough," Jenny said. "That's enough."

"She never even fucked me, what am I, a leper?" Bird paused, and an evil grin spread across his lips. "Well, not more than once or twice."

Danny looked up wild-eyed.

"Just kidding."

Bird laughed. I laughed, too. Jenny smiled, and at last so did Danny.

"I like my men dark."

Bird leaned across the table. "Turn out the lights—" he began, leering, and Jenny kissed him loudly on the mouth. For a second Bird didn't know what to do, and pleased she'd flustered him, Jenny smiled. Bird's leer returned.

"Turn out the lights, Momma, and I'm plenty dark. Huzzah, huzzah."

"Ah, Bird," Jenny said, then smiled at me, "it's my blond blood, only boils for Jews, Greeks and Italians."

"Turks," Bird offered. "Chicanos."

"The entire third world," said Danny.

"I'm glad to know," I said, trying to join in the fun, but my heart wasn't in it, "there's some means of selection."

"Oh, oh," Bird said, and sniffed. "Junior's getting jealous."

"Don't worry," Jenny said, and smiled at me, then Danny. "I like Greeks and Jews best." She put her arms around both of us. "What a world of riches I have."

"I'll dye my hair like Superman. You ever notice the dude's hair is blue?"

"I'm saving my money," Danny said, "to buy land with Anne."

For a second no one spoke. Then Jenny said, "Oh." Just like that, *oh,* and slipped her arms off our shoulders.

"You got a place picked out?" Bird asked.

"I figure"—Danny looked straight at Jenny, who was suddenly staring at the tablecloth, palms supporting her chin—"we'll look come spring."

Neither Bird nor I spoke. Then Jenny raised her chin, and sitting beside her, I could see her eyes had filled with tears.

"That's a good time."

"Between recording and the tour. We'll move in afterward."

"I see," Jenny said, and I've always loved her for it, she smiled. "Now why don't you do a line or two?"

Chapter Six

•

BOBBY HAD PROMISED to visit the farm, but didn't
show. Instead, our third night back, we met in his loft to
discuss arrangements. Since the songs weren't charted yet,
there wasn't much to discuss, and I found myself staring at a
huge exposed beam which divided the south wing of the loft
into living space and two bedrooms.

"Yeah, there but for fortune hung I."

When I realized what Bobby meant, I felt something go
cold inside me. Jenny said, "Way to stop conversation, big
brother."

I still couldn't look away from the beam, which was rough-
hewn, a foot square and, like the building, at least a hundred
years old. I could see Bobby hanging from it, neck twisted,
mouth and eyes jerked open in a shout of pain.

"Did it hurt?"

For a second, I couldn't believe I'd asked. Then I was glad
because even before Bobby answered I realized, He brought
it up, he must want to talk about it.

"It hurt less, then more than you can imagine, as if I were
being burned and choked at the same time. But I was so
drunk, it was a while before I felt anything."

Bobby looked at me, and for the first time, I think, saw me
a little.

"Then there was pain, but because I was so fucked up, it
wasn't happening to me. Then it was. I woke up on the floor

and couldn't remember where I was. I thought, It was you, you idiot. You've killed yourself. I decided"—he turned toward Jenny—"I should look for Mom, and because I was home in a way, I felt happy. Then I saw the broken rope and my throat began to burn."

Sitting on the couch beside Jenny, the rest of us around them in straight chairs, Bobby looked dazed, unformed, like a full moon lost in clouds. I couldn't tell if he was going to scream, cry, pass out, who knew? Then his features coalesced.

"This keeps up, they're going to lock me up again, right?" He laughed; no one else did. "I'm sorry," he said, and his eyes brightened with shame.

"No, no," we all insisted. "No."

"It's all right," Jenny said, and hugged him. He held on, and for a while, no one spoke.

Bobby's friend, Dickie Doehr, was a 60's figure who'd soared on giddy prophetic wings, flying around, as Jackson Browne sings, in the rain. Then he crashed so badly, for a year they couldn't find the pieces.

"Got so bad," Dickie liked to say, "my old lady, amazing Grace, used to send me shopping with my address pinned to my shirt.

"People said, 'Hey, Gracie, aintcha worried about him?' Gracie, she'd laugh and say, 'He can still make change.'

"Then I started coming home with the wrong count. When you're high, nickels look like quarters, dimes like pennies, and wow, man, the bills"—Dickie, who was five-three and still looked like the needle speed freak he once was, a sparrow's chest, wire arms, ecstatic curls he parted in the middle and combed over his ears, Dickie would roll his eyes—"wow, the bills were the same color, old Gracie headed back to the Coast, where she found true happiness as a nurse, no shit. When I heard that, I moved back in with The Big M, and began getting the studio together."

Watching Dickie diddle dials, levels and gains, small hands moving like the feelers of a hyperkinetic ant, was an impressive, even inspiring sight. Someone so good at what he did, it was a joy to be in the same room.

But that first morning, Groundhog Day, on which we all saw our shadows because we met in front of Jenny's apartment at the unheard-of hour of 11 A.M., we didn't know about Dickie's master hands and furious patter. All I knew was that any day now, any way now, my record was going to be released, and I'd stop being Stevie Potts and be reborn Potts the Hero of 45's and L.P's. And that's *my* song shining above the goddamn wall, you got that?

We set out, Jenny and I in D.C., Bird and Danny in the Volvo, both cars necessary because we were hauling our equipment. At his loft the night before, Bobby had given us directions because he wanted to arrive first and talk to Dickie. He'd also been evasive about the studio's layout, which I hadn't questioned; Bobby was often evasive. But driving across the G.W. Bridge, then west on Route 4, which is a suburban four-lane lined with stoplights and record stores, shopping centers and Burger Kings, it occurred to me we might be in trouble.

When Jenny, who was in charge of the directions—Bird and Danny were following—said, "Right," and we turned off 4 onto Woodfield Avenue, which was mixed residential and Mom-and-Pop stores, I began hoping we were lost.

When she said, "Left at the light," and the turn took us past —*Oh no!* What's this?—a Jewish community center, a grammar school, then a pizzeria and a beauty parlor, I knew we were hurting. I glanced at Jenny. She was studying the directions and looked worried. Suddenly there was an old woman wearing a pillbox hat in the way.

"Steve!" Jenny screamed.

I spun the wheel, swerved right and slowed down. My hands were shaking, only partly because of the old lady. No one, I was thinking, no one gets their big break in Fair Lawn, New Jersey.

"Turn right."

I nodded, read the street sign and wanted to cry.

"Happy Homes Drive? You're kidding."

"I wish I were."

"You think Bobby wants this record to work out?"

"That's a mean thing to say."

I didn't have time to answer because she said, "Turn left on Bennett Cerf Court," and started to laugh.

I turned left. There were twelve identical ranches on Bennett Cerf, each with a large bay window in a false brick front. To me, it looked as if the houses were winking at each other, and the joke was on us.

"Fourth on the left," Jenny said.

I parked, slid across the seat and hugged her.

"I'm sorry."

"Don't worry." She hugged me back. "I'm sorry, too."

Bird bounded up and I rolled down my window.

"Tell me I'm hallucinating."

"You're hallucinating."

"For a second I thought our studio was inside one of these babies." He grinned. "So what are we doing here?"

Before Jenny or I could produce a snappy answer, a front door opened across the street and Bobby stepped onto the front porch dressed in jeans and a blue flannel shirt.

"You're late. Where you been?"

Bird looked from Bobby to me, then back to Bobby.

"What are *you* doing here?"

Bobby walked down the cement path which led from the front door to the sidewalk. By the time he'd crossed the street, Jenny and I were out of the car, standing next to Bird and Danny.

"What are you talking about?"

"You mean," Bird said, his breath frosting as he spoke, "the studio's really inside that?"

Bobby grinned. "I guess I forgot to tell you."

"Forgot," said Jenny.

"The Big M is named for Dickie's mom. This is her house."

"I hope she's happy in it," Jenny answered. "We're not going in."

"According to your contract, I choose the studio."

"You're not pulling that kind of shit."

"If I have to."

"Be reasonable," said Bird.

"Reasonable," Bobby repeated, his eyes anything but reasonable. "I'm freezing my ass off."

"At least," Danny said, "you have to tell us why."

"*Touché.*"

Bobby's eyes moved over all of us, from Danny to me to Bird, then stopped at Jenny. "Dickie's the best engineer I know, and he needs record work so he can stop doing demos and break back into the bigs." Bobby lowered his voice though there was no one nearby to hear us. "Now no one look, but Dickie and his mother are probably watching this little scene through the window, so let's get going."

"This is bullshit, Bobby."

Sister and brother glared at each other, and I remembered what Bird had said about cranks. Our breath froze and hung.

Bobby said, "I've already guaranteed him a week's work."

No one moved.

"Dickie's the best, and he needs a break."

Bobby's eyes, which now glowed deep and soulfully brown, traveled from Jenny to Bird to Danny, then rested on me.

"Trust me."

I was ready to follow him. But I knew, we all knew, the next move was Jenny's, so we stood another fifteen seconds, noses reddening, fingertips burning with cold. Then Bobby snapped, "Fine, get a slick asshole to produce you in the city," and started back across the street.

Jenny sprinted after him, blond hair flapping on her blue parka, a flag against the sky. She caught him on the sidewalk and without breaking stride kicked him in the ass as hard as she could. Bobby whirled, saw Jenny and grinned.

"You think I deserve that, huh?"

"You could have told us."

"If I'd told you"—he grinned wider—"you wouldn't have come."

We tested mikes, got to know Dickie, and the next day, starting at three, we ran through our material. More than anything, I wanted Bobby to say, "Your tunes are great." Instead, sitting with Dickie on the far side of the glass, Bobby watched, listened and took notes on a yellow pad.

Inside the main sound room, which was barely large enough for the four of us and our instruments (two pianos for me, my Rhodes and a small acoustic grand separated by baffles), we were high, rocking and wearing headsets known in the biz as cans. The sound from our instruments (except for Bird's drums, which were miked) went out through pickups to the main board, where Dickie adjusted the faders, then fed us the mix through the cans so we could hear each other and, most important, ourselves.

If we'd been recording, we would have played just the basic tracks, which are called the floor. Afterward, listening to the floor through cans—ain't jargon groovy?—you add the lead and backup vocals, then any sweetening you want. Strings, woodwinds, synthesizer, congas, flute, and in our case, the lead guitar tracks Danny would do later.

Since we weren't recording, but merely letting Bobby and Dickie hear the material, we rehearsed with vocal mikes. This is *never* done. Playing while singing, you can't do either well enough to record. As a result, even on "live" albums, artists cover their mistakes by editing in alternate tracks from other concerts or done afterward in a studio.

But that Friday, not worried about how it would reproduce, we simply wailed. Bird would count us in: one, tap-tap, two, tap-tap, three, tap-tap, and wham, we'd fly into the music. And despite the confines of the room, the newness of the event, it sometimes felt so good I'd forget about Bobby and his judgmental eyes.

Periodically Dickie or Bobby would press the cue button on the main board so we could hear them in the sound room, and ask, "What do you need more of?" Which meant, How's the mix in the cans?

And someone, generally Jenny, would say, "More me," or "Push up the vocals." But Bird, it was always Bird, Bird would object, saying, "Jesus Christ, Jenny," or "Jesu Cristo, Potts, all I hear is you."

Then we'd argue and laugh about whose ego and eardrums were most distorted. Dickie would adjust the dials and we'd continue playing. And playing. We'd worked up ten tunes, Bobby wanted them each five and often six or seven times, so between setting up, playing, sending out for a pizza and horsing around, we didn't finish until eleven-thirty.

"What do you think?" Jenny asked her brother when at last we were done, exhausted and smoking a joint for the road on the couch and chairs in what had once been the Doehr family basement, but which now served as a buffer between the studio (originally a two-car garage) and the lived-in portion of the house.

"Yeah," I said, "what do you think, Kemosabe?"

"Will it play in Peoria?" Bird asked. "I got an aunt in Peoria."

Bobby toked the joint, made a small characteristic move with his eyes, as if squinting into a bright sun, then passed the joint to Dickie. They were quite the duo, an ultra-hip Laurel and Hardy sitting together on the couch. Bobby wasn't fat anymore, but still looked as if his edges needed defining, while Dickie disappeared when he turned sideways.

"I like it," Bobby began. "Up to a point, I like it a lot. Maybe six, seven tunes can go on the album." He paused, took the joint from Dickie, toked twice, passed it this time to Jenny. "But I wish, you know, they were about something."

Silence.

"Don't worry, I'll produce the songs you want the best way I know how."

"No problem there," said Bird.

Bobby smiled. "But we all know what an asshole power freak Bobby Hall can be. I mean, I dragged you out here without telling you you'd be working in Naomi's garage."

Dickie snapped to life. Even his curls bristled. "You didn't tell them?"

We shook our heads. Dickie cocked his at Bobby, shook it back and forth.

"No wonder they walked in yesterday like they were smelling gas. Fucking-A, Bobby. Not exactly The Hit Factory, eh, boys and girls?"

"It's fine." Jenny reached past Bobby, squeezed Dickie's hand, then hugged him. "I bitched loudest but I wouldn't be anywhere else now. Really."

Bobby grinned. "Didn't I tell you? Anyway, it's well documented what an asshole Bobby Hall can be, and how difficult he is to work with."

"You know," Jenny said, "it really gives me the creeps when you refer to yourself in the third person."

Bobby's jaw tightened. Then he said softly—and I believed he meant it; I grieved for him—"I'm trying to keep public and private lives separate. I'm sorry." He turned to me. "Aren't there any issues you care about?"

"Sure."

"Besides making it."

"Nukes," Dickie said. "That's a big one."

"Cocaine," Bird added cheerfully. "I care about cocaine."

"I want to live honorably," I said. "Understand the world before I cash out."

"Nice," said Bobby, "but I'm talking about social change. Making a record is a public act and carries public responsibilities. Except for beating up his old lady Bobby Dylan lived honorably. But if he hadn't abandoned politics, we might have stopped the war years earlier."

"Heavy guilt," Jenny said. "You're making me mad."

"You asked what I thought."

"Remember Mom used to say, 'If you've got nothing good to say, don't say it'?"

"I remember," Bobby said, while the non-Halls in the room made believe they weren't there, "we both thought that was bullshit."

No answer, then Jenny said simply, "Why don't we drop it?"

Monday, walking up the cement path to The Big M, Bird pointed at the green Porsche in the driveway. "I bet that's Ethan's."

I turned to Jenny, who was behind me next to Danny, hands submerged in her parka pockets. "Is it?"

She smiled. For someone who hadn't gotten much sleep— we'd been out partying—she looked awfully good.

"Is what what?"

"Is that Ethan's car?"

Her smile vanished. "How should I know?"

"Hey," I whispered, slipping my arm around her waist. "Bird wanted to know, not me."

Jenny dropped her head on my shoulder. "I feel like the DMZ between the band and Bobby."

"Don't worry," I said, "the war's over."

I kissed her, then we followed Bird and Danny into the house. Ethan and Bobby were at the kitchen table; the woman who'd let us in was serving them tea and noodle kugel. She wore a blue dress, and her gray hair, done in beauty parlor waves, shadowed a small oval face.

"Who wants tea?" she asked. "And who wants coffee? There's plenty."

No one answered and the woman, who was at most five-one but had large breasts which merged in a friendly way with her midriff, announced, "I'm Naomi Doehr." Her face, made-up to cover wrinkles, creased in a wrinkled smile. "The Big M."

Stunned, I was stunned, we found ourselves sharing coffee and kugel with Naomi, who turned out to be a Jewish Momma with a capital *M*. Twenty minutes later, we descended to the studio, where Dickie was waiting in the control room with Ethan and Bobby.

"Let me guess," Dickie said. "You're too stuffed to play."

"Hey," said Bird. "Your mom feed all your customers?"

"Having a skinny kid warped the Big M's soul. But she'll calm down."

"Keep it coming," I said. "That was great kugel."

Ethan, who'd been sitting in a director's chair next to Bobby at the far end of the control room, stood and came toward us.

"You guys are in this week's *Billboard,* you know that?"

"Have you seen it?" asked Danny.

Ethan grinned. He was as well tanned as when we'd met in August. "Hell, I arranged it."

Ethan handed Danny a *Billboard* open to page five, and we crowded around. The article was boxed in black:

> Apex recording artists Jenny Hall and Waterfall have begun work on their debut album. Lead singer Jenny Hall is the younger sister of 60's star Bobby Hall, who will produce. The legendary Sol Hershkoff, who signed the group for Apex, declared, "We believe that Jenny will be as big a star as Bobby."

The album is being recorded at Dickie Doehr's The Big M. Doehr engineered several of Bobby Hall's albums, so it looks like reunion time at Apex. Inside sources say that Hall and Waterfall will receive a 50's "wall of sound" production of the sort recently used by Jon Landau and Bruce Springsteen on the Boss's Number One L.P. "Born to Run." Look for heavy promotion and a midsummer release for this big debut album.

"Hey," Bird said. "I got my name in the paper without getting my name in the paper."

Ethan smiled. "She's better-looking than you are."

"No argument there." I met Ethan's eyes. "Better-looking than you, too."

I couldn't help it. He was too tall, too smooth. Too committed to putting down everyone except himself, Bobby and by extension Jenny, whom I suspected he wanted to put down somewhat differently. His position—I'd finally learned the details from Jenny—was that anyone who hadn't gone through the 60's as Bobby Hall's best friend and constant companion except for the two years he'd spent in a federal pen for draft resistance (thereby accumulating even more cool points) wasn't worth talking to.

"It's not looks," said Jenny. Ethan and I stopped scowling at each other and turned toward her. "The point is we're equals in this band, and publicity should reflect that."

Bobby grinned. He was standing between Ethan and Jenny.

"That's sweet, but you're the hot body fronting the band, baby sister, and you better get used to that. This ain't Ithaca."

"Does that mean," Bird asked, "that when I get my picture in the paper, my picture won't be in the paper? How will my fans know it's me?"

"What fans?" I said. "Your mother?"

"Your mother sucks farts out of subway seats, Potts."

"How did you know?"

I peeked at Ethan. He looked as if he were doing his best to tolerate our puerile wit. Fuck him.

"I thought," he began, "you'd be more impressed with the article."

Jenny laughed. "We are impressed. We're trying not to let our feelings run away with us."

"Why don't we start working," said Bobby. "Between Naomi's kugel and this bunch of jokers"—he turned his head—"Dickie, what are we paying you, ninety an hour?"

"Nah, I gave you a package deal."

"That's right. Let's get to work."

Bird, Jenny and I moved toward the sound room. Danny, who'd either been savoring or trying to memorize the article, looked up.

"What's this about wall of sound?"

Ethan turned to Bobby, who shrugged; and Ethan, looking as if he were in the middle of a pond listening to the ice crack, said, "I thought that's what you and Bobby had worked out."

"When?" I said. "You must have fed them this piece weeks ago."

"What's wall of sound?" asked Bird.

"High gloss," said Danny. "The music sounds like it's coming at you all at once, then the vocal's laid over it. The Phil Spector sound."

"Bobby," Jenny said, "what's going on?"

Demons began to sing.

"Don't believe everything you read in the trades."

Five feet away from them, I could see Jenny was about to lose control, if she hadn't already lost it. Her eyes shone with the enraged light which meant no one should expect anything calm or conciliatory until she'd vented what she liked to think of as the truth.

"Look, Bobby. If you were listening at Discovery, you know we want a straight-ahead rock feel."

Six inches from hers, Bobby's eyes, brown to her pale blue, shone with the same dull glow.

"If *you* were listening, you would have heard me say I'll produce you the best way I know how."

"Is your best what we want?"

"Sometimes yes, sometimes no."

"And when it's not?"

"We modify."

"That's what a producer's for," Ethan said, trying, as befitted his role as manager, to calm the muddy Hall waters. "You're a first-time group."

Jenny ignored him. "Friday you tell us our songs aren't about anything, although they're about love, living honorably and the loss of innocence. Diddly-shit, right? Today we find out you don't like the way we hear our own music. Well, goddamnit, Bobby, what do you like?"

His eyes blazed, but he didn't answer. Then he did, his voice remarkably soft, almost calm. "I'd like you and your band to get in the goddamn sound room."

"I bet you would. You write meaningful songs. You know how ours should sound." She paused, then the finale roared out of her. "Why don't you get in there, that's what you want anyway."

In the horrible silence, I heard blood beating in my temples. I heard the wind moaning above Jenny's pond.

"Come on, Jenny," I said.

Her pale eyes withered me. "Fuck you, too."

I listened to her footsteps on the stairs, then ran after her. Climbing the half flight to the basement, racing through it, then up the six stairs to the kitchen, I wondered if Jenny remembered she had the keys to D.C. In which case, I thought, opening the kitchen door to discover Naomi sipping coffee as if the world weren't blowing up, Jenny was probably outside and on her way. Legs still spinning, gulping air, I met Naomi's gray, savvy eyes.

"What have you boys been doing to her?"

"Where is she?"

"Locked in my bathroom." Naomi smiled. "Where would you be?"

The Doehr household was small. Stairs to the bedroom corridor led off the kitchen, so knocking on the bathroom door, I was at most fifteen feet from Naomi's eager ears. Mouth pressed close, I whispered, "Are you okay?"

No answer.

"Please, let me in."

"Go away."

"Please."

More silence. Why, I thought, couldn't she have kept her mouth shut? I flashed on Danny, Bobby, everyone waiting in the studio and felt, still feeling it, the blood which had scorched my cheeks when she swore at me. And why, goddamnit, for trying to help?

I breathed deep, then whispered, "I love you, Jenny. Open the door."

"No."

Not feeling it, but knowing it must still be true, I repeated, "I love you. I want to talk."

Footsteps, the lock's creak and anger soared within me. I was going to slug her. Suddenly we faced each other, and framed by the doorway and pink walls, hair falling over her face, Jenny looked almost vulnerable. Her blue eyes, their anger vented, were wide, moist and frightened. She collapsed in my arms.

"It's all right, babe. It's all right."

"It's not."

I maneuvered us inside the bathroom, kicked the door shut.

"I meant it," she sobbed, then began to cry for real. "That's the worst of all, I meant it."

I held her, murmuring, "It's all right, babe. Shh, it's all right."

After crying a few minutes she stepped back, rubbed her cheeks and eyes with the palm of her right hand, painting her face with spirals of mascara.

"I look terrible, don't I?"

What she looked, I thought, was eight years old and wrung out by her own tears. I brushed our lips together; hers were warm, chapped and salty.

"You've looked better."

"That's what I like about you, Potts. *Très gallant.*"

She blew her nose in wadded t.p., pushed her hair behind her ears and ran water in the sink. Soaping her face, she seemed to revive. Cheeks white with lather, she said, "It's always been like this. Bobby makes me madder than anyone except my father, so I guess he comes by it honestly."

Rinsing, she added, "He has very weird feelings about my career. When I moved east he promised to help, but never even got me an audition. Now that he needs me"—our eyes met in the mirror over the sink—"here we are. What's that about? Not that he *had* to look out for me, that's not what I mean. But I would have for him."

"I believe that."

"Thanks."

I smiled at her. "You're welcome, babe."

"What really makes me mad is that before he'd deal with me at all, he tried to kill himself. Maybe I should have paid more attention. But goddamnit, he should have called me."

Jenny braced herself, elbows locked, against the sink. Her eyes, sometimes so pale they seemed to lack substance, looked straight into me.

"I'll never forgive him for that. I don't even want to."

I felt Death flutter in the room, her crappy little wings brushing up against me. I felt the loss of their mother, the inheritance of anger, and there was nothing to say, no hopeful sentiment seemed worthwhile. Jenny turned off the water, dried her face on one of Naomi's pink towels.

"When he acts like the big star and treats you and Danny like dirt"—she smiled—"like Mister Dogsqueeze, then I really get crazy because I brought you into this."

"*Hey,* I don't know about Danny, but I came running fast as my little legs could carry me."

She hung the towel on the rack. "Well, sure. But you know I feel responsible, like I have to do all the arguing."

She was right there. Me *argue* with Bobby Hall? I nodded and she finished, "That's why I got so mad. I felt you were siding against me."

Blood rushed to my cheeks.

"Don't worry," she said, and placed her head on my shoulder. "Don't worry, everything's going to be okay, remember? Bobby and I are fighters, that's all."

We kissed, then slightly worse for the wear, I followed Jenny out of the bathroom and down the two stairs to the kitchen. We crossed it, then Jenny opened the door to the basement. Reaching back to close it, I looked up and Naomi, who was stirring a stockpot on the stove, caught my eye.

"Swedish meatballs," she said.

"You're not kidding."

I pulled the door shut.

No matter when we arrived, Naomi would be holding court at her kitchen table. She seemed to divide time between cooking, phone calls, novel reading and sixteen versions of solitaire, but Naomi's true gift was hanging out. Since you not only had to cross her kitchen to reach the studio, but pass back through it to use The Big M's one bathroom, in three months we all became good buddies. Because I was the band's one Jew, I think, she singled me out, and Naomi, if you let her, could bend your ears back. In particular, she liked to discuss jazz and what my parents thought of my relationship with a *shiksa.*

"Mrs. Doehr," I'd answer, munching cookies or noodle

kugel in between takes, "I don't think they notice. They certainly don't say anything."

"They don't say anything, but *inside.*" She'd sigh and lean close. "That no-good Grace who abandoned Dickie when he was so sick, may she have varicose veins and children who don't love her, she was half Irish, half Italian."

Then she'd pin me with her gray eyes. I'd say something like "I understand you might resent her, but that doesn't—"

"Have some more kugel."

What Naomi thought about the drugs and weird goings-on downstairs, I don't know; she probably thought about them as little as possible. But one afternoon as I was getting ready to descend into the studio, quite stoned, my mouth full of chopped chicken liver and Ritz crackers, I asked Naomi didn't she mind having all these freaky musicians around.

"Mind? I love all these creative boys—" I eyed her, and she added, "and sometimes girls using their talent. I was talented when I was young. I even had scholarships, but somehow—" Her voice suddenly abandoned her. "It keeps me alive to know young people with such talent."

Pierced, I stayed in Naomi's kitchen, eating chopped chicken liver until I heard subterranean voices, mainly Bobby's, screaming, "Where the fuck is Potts?"

"Go," she commanded.

I went.

Bobby at that time was almost always depressed and difficult to talk to. My sense is that he'd realized his career had prevented Jenny from having one, and he felt he owed her. He produced us not because he wanted to, or yet had any hope for his own future, but because if he had to be alive—he took the broken rope as an omen—at least he could help Jenny.

But a part of him resented her for tying him to life and he took it out on her. Maybe she understood. She seemed able to fight and forget, or fight and go on until the next fight as if all that pain and anger were perfectly normal. For me they weren't, and I was regularly grateful for The Big M's down-home atmosphere. Escaping to Naomi's overheated kitchen to discuss current events, Coltrane or her latest bridge club triumph over coffee and kugel was the best way Bird, Danny and I had to pop the balloon of tension that hovered inside The Big M. How Dickie survived, I don't know. He and Naomi seemed to have worked out strict rules for peaceful coexistence: She never set foot in his studio, he never left it. What he did about pissing—the only bathroom was upstairs—I never did figure out.

Making records is a funny business. We spent most of our $600-a-day studio time relaxing, smoking dope and cracking jokes that would have embarrassed most fourth-graders. Not us. Bird's favorite, which he told whenever we had visitors, went like this. "Hey," he'd say, and his eyes would glitter. "What's the difference between dark and hard?"

The latest victim would answer, "I don't know," and everyone would shout, "It stays dark all night."

Dickie, no doubt from years of experience, was a master of studio humor. His bit was cartoon voices. He did a brilliant Porky Pig, Elmer Fudd and Yogi Bear, but his triumph was Popeye. Adjusting dials, coiling mike cords or giving sophisticated advice, he'd slip into one of his voices, and suddenly Popeye would announce you were flat. And a fifth, Olive, was better than a thurd, anyways.

What was going down wasn't drug-induced presenility, but an attempt to reach a calm enough space so that you not only hit the right notes—small mistakes could be punched in—but you arrived on the mythical edge. The jazz player's out *there,* where linear perception, the connection between consciousness and talent, falls away, and the music explodes the way a movie screen does when it's graced by a face like Garbo's; so that you not only get an acceptable take, but the one you're willing to go with.

By Saturday everything was done on "Waiting for Love"

except the vocals. We'd finished a set of basic tracks we liked. I'd done a couple overdubs, called punches, to correct mistakes. Danny had added the lead guitar tracks, I'd done some synthesizer fills, and with my electric Rhodes I'd doubled my part on the bridge—played the same notes—which is a technique for adding depth and musical texture.

Jenny's turn. Bird was in the kitchen with Naomi. (They were lovers of sorts. She loved to cook, Bird loving eating, and during those twelve weeks he rarely ate anywhere else.) The rest of us—me, Danny, Dickie and Bobby—were in the control room when Jenny opened the door to the small sound room and stepped inside. The room was maybe ten feet square, empty except for a top-of-the-line Neumann mike on a stand.

Standing beside Dickie at the control board, which faced the main sound room glass, I watched him rewind the black two-inch-wide sixteen-track tape by remote control until the strip of white warning tape flitted by. Dickie reversed the machine, cued it so the marked section lay just before the recording heads, then turned the dials on the first twelve pots to Sync so that the tracks we'd previously recorded would play. Then he pressed Record on track thirteen, which was for Jenny's voice.

As I stood, back to the control board, the door to the small sound room was on my left. Bobby said, "Go for the feel, okay? Come down on the consonants, especially at the beginning of a line."

Looking past Bobby's left shoulder, I could see the top half of Jenny's face, her eyes intent on Bobby's.

"Remember, you're trying to sound bitchy and sweet at the same time."

"I ought to be able to handle that."

"I'm not worried about bitchy. Try keeping vulnerability in there, too."

Jenny just laughed. "I'd scratch your eyes out, but I love you too much."

"Perfect."

Bobby kissed her cheek. Jenny closed the door behind her, but because the wall of the sound room nearest me included a large window, I could still see her. Jenny pushed her hair behind her ears, and put on her headset. She tugged the sleeves of her turtleneck up her forearms, then stood behind the mike, eyes closed, concentrating, hands on her hips. She wet her lips. A small vein trembled on her forehead, and I suddenly felt as if I were peeking into a stranger's bedroom.

Dickie rolled the tape. Jenny's eyes opened; but focused on the door (I was to her side), she didn't see me. I glanced across the control room at Bobby and Danny seated side by side in the director chairs. Bird's sticks tapping us in came through the control room speakers, then the cascading sixteenths I played, Bird's high-hat, the cowbell he'd added later, Danny's note-bending lead which built to an early crescendo bursting when Jenny began singing:

> *"Many men have tried.*
> *They didn't understand.*
> *Stare into my eyes,*
> *Swear they were my man.*
>
> *"Waiting, waiting,*
> *Still waiting for love."*

I glanced at Jenny through the glass. Her eyes were closed. A hard smile iced her lips, and I remembered writing the song with Danny, the eerie sexual energy that had been in the room when we composed resurfacing as Jenny repeated:

> *"Aching, shaking,*
> *Still waiting for love."*

There was a short break, another verse, then Jenny broke into the center verse:

"Don't want no fantasy lover
Coming down for me."

She thrust her right index finger at the blank door, bouncing as if she were onstage. Beneath the swelling music, I could pick out my doubled octaves, the tinging of Bird's high-hat.

"Loving dreams'll break your heart.
But dreams won't set me free."

Out of the corner of my eye, I saw Bobby signal Dickie. The music stopped, and a beat or two later Jenny quit singing. Through the glass I watched her face cloud. Then the door opened and Bobby's head appeared.

"You got the feel, but I'm hearing thump, thump, thump. Either you're dancing or I'm going crazy. Which is it?"

"Shit."

"Hey, Danny," I called, "we could do a dance number, Jenny and the Jives."

I broke into a Motown routine I'd been saving since high school and Dickie joined in. Ass swirling, hands slapping; not bad either.

"Hey, Potts," Bobby called. "Can it, wouldja?"

I canned it.

"And the last part, I said vulnerable, not whory." Bobby imitated Jenny's phrasing. "Luv-in' dreeeems," making it sound as if he were about to come in his pants. But even hacking around, his voice thrilled me, the first time I'd heard him sing since we met.

"Okay, okay," Jenny said. "I got it."

Bobby shut the sound room door, sat again in the director's chair beside Danny, shot me an odd look. I didn't understand. Then it occurred to me that in his mind—mine, too?—we were fighting over who meant more to Jenny; anyway, who most influenced her. I thought about that, and glanced from Bobby to Danny. Typically, he hadn't said a word. But he looked troubled, as if he'd caught what was going on. Something that used to happen to him?

Dickie recued the machine. Black tape spun through the heads. The white marker flashed through, and Dickie switched the machine from Reverse to Play, Jenny's track to Record, and I was again listening to Bird's tapping, my high cascading sixteenths. Then live, Jenny was singing:

> *"Many men have tried.*
> *They didn't understand.*
> *Stare into my eyes,*
> *Swear they were my man."*

Practicing the back-up vocal I'd add later with Bird, watching Jenny through the glass, her voice hard, pure and bitchy but with enough cry in it you wanted to end her waiting for love right away, I forgot about Bobby, Danny and what I might or might not have imagined. Madman lover, lost one more time in the music.

Chapter Seven

·

AFTER A PARTICULARLY MADDENING SESSION during which Jenny and I were supposed to record lead and backup vocals for "Fall in Love Again," I drove home frustrated and enraged. Bobby made us sing the parts four and five times, then threw out all the takes.

"The arrangement sucks, you'll have to redo it.·'

You're wrong, I thought, you old man, but I didn t say anything. Instead, driving home with Jenny, I sulked, hallucinating in my own anger. The weather didn't help. Six-fifteen and the sky was midnight gray. Diamonds of a cold rain fell through our headlights as I eased D.C. off the G.W. Bridge. Below us, a stripe of orange arc lamps cast a Halloween glow on the West Side Highway. Jenny hunched against her door, looking out her window. All in all, it was a grievous wet winter evening.

"Why don't you sit closer?"

She turned and a band of light washed over her face, then swept on.

"How're you doing?"

"Bummed."

"So am I," Jenny said. "What's bothering you?"

I braked. Judging from the ocean of stopped cars up ahead, the trip home was going to be slow.

"I'm worried that Bobby's attitude, his ambivalence, okay, is going to screw up the record. I could have killed him today."

I glanced at Jenny, whose features were in shadow.

"Then I worry he's right, that the songs are second-rate and I ought to redo them."

"That's crazy."

We crept forward ten, fifteen miles an hour. Jenny said, "I wish you'd known the old Bobby. Right now, he's half dead and takes it out on us because we're not only alive, it's obvious we want to be." Our eyes met. "He knows he's impossible. And I'll tell you this. He'd respect you more if you fought with him."

"I guess."

"He also knows you probably won't."

I could now see what the problem was. Some poor bastard was changing a tire in the rain, and cars had to merge around him. We inched forward, passed, and traffic sped up.

"I'm also worried these, uh, problems, will screw things up between us."

"So am I, so don't worry."

"I'm worried."

Jenny slid across the seat, kissed me below the ear. "What happened to Steve Potts who didn't worry about anything?"

"You mean the whizbang?"

"That's right, success and happiness."

"*That* Potts. He's driving down the road, feeling a little better."

"Good, I can't bear it when he's sad."

Brake lights suddenly gleamed alarm red again, traffic slowing to exit at Fifty-sixth Street: last stop and everyone out since they'd begun "repairing" the road surface.

"How about," I said, "we eat at Oscar's?"

"You eat oysters."

"Lobster and oysters, what the hell?"

"And afterward," Jenny said as we bumped toward the exit ramp, "no shoptalk. What record, huh? Just ficky-fick."

"Think we can manage that?"
"Let's try."

On a scale of one to ten, give us a five. Don't misunderstand. We had good times. Ate good food, drank good wine. Lots of good. And word of the record deal had spread. When we went out, people treated us differently. Rod Stewart smiled at me. The doorman at Studio 54 learned my name, a dumbfuck he was. One of the Kennedy kids bought me a beer. Some lunatic, an ad exec, offered Jenny a thousand dollars to do him and his four German shepherds. Incredible, but true. Disgusting modern times. Stardom.

The truth, however, is that through the end of March we were too obsessed with the album to notice much else. War could have broken out. The President could have launched a peanut into lunar orbit, the nut of the Unknown Soldier, and all that would have interested me was whether I could get a song out of it, and once I had it, how to keep Bobby from messing with it too much.

Listening to the album now, I believe Bobby wasn't worried about our music as I thought then, but about his own ability to produce it. He felt, and I sympathized, that working as a producer meant his singing career had ended in failure. What I didn't understand was that his deeper fear, more terrifying because he couldn't admit to it, was that he'd fail as a producer. The reason for the superfluous strings in "Time Stretches Out," which Jenny is singing to me in my dark living room, my own words bringing tears to my nitwit eyes, was that Bobby was proving he could manage high-tech production. The reason for the sax solo on Danny's "Lazarus," the reason for our high-gloss production despite the simple ones on Bobby's albums was that Bobby Hall was worried about his own talent.

Me, all I wanted was for him to respect mine. I wanted

Bobby to treat me as if I were a real person. Most of all, I wanted him to phone and say, "Hey Potts, how about we write a song together?"

Instead, one of my Tuesday nights away from Jenny, a new arrangement so I could write the final songs, I called him. Don't laugh. The heart is a dumb, lonely hunter and mine, mine's as dumb as they come.

"Sure, Potts," his voice came back. "You talking tonight?"

"Why not?" My voice quaked. My hunter heart percolated between my mouth and throat. "I've got some—"

"Jenny with you?"

"No."

I assumed his next line was "In that case, Potts, buzz off." Bobby asked, "You remember how to get here?"

"Uh-huh."

"Okay, then."

A minute later I was rocketing through the cold Village streets to the indoor garage off Third Avenue (Arnie's orders) where I stored D.C. As always, walking up the west side of Second Avenue, I approached the black focus of my earliest dreams and ambitions, the Fillmore East, and my heart began thumping like a dog's does when Mr. Dog smells blood. But instead of scurrying past, the superego murmuring, "Those days are over, Potts, over," I paused, succumbed, stopped and dreamed under the dark marquee.

After a moment, I pressed my nose to the one remaining pane in the wood-and-glass panel door. A gray runner led up the hall floor to the ticket-taker's post at the inside door. A burly gray-haired freak guarded it, a storm of green tickets swirling past his eyes and bearded cheeks.

Suddenly, the street boomed with bodies; police barriers sprang up like demon warriors. Sixteen, I waited to hear Traffic and an unknown opening act from England. A third-row ticket, awaiting its destiny, had been searing a hole in my jeans for two weeks since the morning I cut school to get on line at 6 A.M. Stoned, dreaming, a face in the crowd, I gazed into the dead smile of a blond boy my age, a beard of weeds sprouting on his chin. Passing me on the far side of the barrier, he whispered, "Acidgrass, acidgrass, who's buying?"

We all were. Later, slight, dark-haired Cat Stevens, unknown then, performed solo to a packed rowdy house. In the first row, a thick-necked yahoo I've remembered since as Dogbreath, rang a cowbell through the second half of the Cat's soft, lyrical set, shouting, "Traffic, we want Traffic," while stunned at the unexpectedly beautiful music and furious at the yahoo, I sat in stoned silence.

When Traffic's lead singer, tiny Stevie Winwood, followed the band onstage, his fine-featured face opaque under the bright lights, the crowd leapt to its feet. The music began and from the third row I could see Winwood's face stayed white under the rainbow of stage lights. Could see from the way they swayed, grinned and lost time that the entire band was too fucked up to stand straight. But there they stood, ten feet away, their eyes holding no light, while I watched the sweat bead above Winwood's eyes, listened to his mistakes, my heart crying to my gaping mouth: I can do it. They're just like me!

A tiny body raced across the gray runner as fast as four mouse legs could carry it. Rubbing my hands against the cold, I turned, continued to the parking garage and drove to Bobby's. I buzzed, was admitted, climbed three flights and knocked.

"It's open."

I pulled the brass-knobbed door shut, and it boomed down the loft. Walking toward Bobby, who sat fifty feet away in front of the hanging beam, his face illuminated by a reading lamp, I listened to my heart and lungs whooping to each other; to the soft music coming from the stereo. I stopped near him, unzipped my parka, and he got up from the couch.

"How's it hanging?" he asked.

"Froze solid."

He grinned. Then I recognized what was playing, and the rest of me froze. The title cut from Bobby's best album, "No More Dying, No More Lying," recorded in '68 during Bobby's high prophetic period. In this cut, his voice was mixed over a simple melody and the subliminal beat of drums and exploding bombs. The final verse was just beginning.

We know the Man's been lying,
We've heard the children crying.
Please, please, they don't understand
Why the bombs are falling,
Why the Man's been calling
Foreign death into their land.

No more dying, no more lying,
No more murdered children,
Stop this useless bloody gore.
No more dying, no more lying,
No more crying women.
Today's the last day of the war.

I faced Bobby when the music stopped. Eyes wide, he stood, walked to his sound system, lifted the tone arm off the disc.

"I've always loved that song," I said, sitting in the chair kitty-corner to the couch. "Unfair to Potts."

Bobby sat again on the couch, fixed his famous brown eyes on me. "What's that?"

"I'm intimidated as hell." Then my pride broke and a tidal wave of hero worship, held back for months, rushed out. "I mean great songs, songs like that which live in other people's lives, it's hard to believe one person wrote it. It's like the song was always out there waiting, but you heard it first."

"Not I, but the wind that blows through me, huh?"

" 'White Guns,' " I said, recognizing the line from another of Bobby's best-known songs.

"I worked three months on 'Dying,' threw out a dozen verses. And the bomb bit. I came up with that in the studio, then had to fight Sol to keep it in because he said it would offend people. I told him that was the idea, and we fought until I threatened to quit him."

"I know better," I said, "but always believed you wrote it the way it sounds."

"Ten years ago, I must have been your age when I wrote it."

"It changed a lot of lives."

"It changed mine. I never wrote anything as good again. Twenty-fucking-six and washed up."

" 'White Guns' is as good."

"Written before."

"In fact," I hurled into the gloom, "I thought your next album—*Refugees,* right?—was as good as 'No More Dying.' "

"Worship me no heroes, Potts. Don't bullshit me."

Bobby turned, eyes glowing with the vulnerability of the suicide, with the pain which was sometimes so close to the surface you could see it shimmer and dance like a candle flame. Then it went out, replaced by Bobby's who-gives-a-fuck smile.

"So," he said, "you're two years younger than Jenny?"

"Eighteen months."

He grinned. "Didn't mean to get personal. You wanna drink or smoke something?"

"Sure."

"Which?"

"Both."

"Bourbon?"

I nodded; he headed for the kitchen, returned carrying two stubby glasses, ice, an ashtray and, stuck under his arm, a bottle of Jack Daniel's. He dropped two cubes in each glass, covered them with J.D., handed me one, followed a few seconds later by a lit joint.

"So, Potts, what kind of song are you and me going to write?"

I considered polite, evasive answers, then flashed on Jenny's advice. "You don't like me very much, do you?"

Bobby toked the joint, met my eyes across a gray cloud. "Don't take it personally, but not really."

"How do you want me to take it?"

Bobby toked the joint a second time, passed it. "Any way you want. When you're down you loathe everyone. Haven't you been there?"

I suddenly felt his pain was my fault, that Bobby had sacrificed everything to stop the war, but had been given nothing in return.

"Nah, why should you? You're twenty-six and everything's going well." He groaned, sipped his bourbon. "Listen to me, will you? Hell, maybe you're a great guy. Jenny seems to think so."

"You trust her?"

"Most of the time."

"She believes in my tunes."

His eyes said, "Go away, kid, you bother me," but I plunged on anyway.

"For two months you've been making me feel what I do is dog shit. Since you're not only my producer but I grew up loving your music, I'm kind of confused."

He stood, and arms folded across his chest, Bobby paced. I drank. A minute later, words piled on words piled on sound, he said, "Look, you don't write what I did, but if it makes you feel better, your stuff's right for Jenny, or I wouldn't be involved."

"Thanks."

"Another thing. You dig your tunes, Jenny does, ignore what anyone else thinks, including me. The business is full of sharks, you hear what I'm saying?"

"I memorized too many of your songs not to trust you."

Bobby's heels beat against the oak floor. I finished my bourbon, poured another. At the sound of whiskey Bobby turned. From where I sat, his eyes were awful to look into. God knows what they were like from his side. Standing above me, he said, "This business goes on talent, okay? No one knows where it comes from, why or what happens to it. Short people have it, fat and stupid, white and black. Talent's the great equalizer and guys like Hershkoff and Clive Davis get rich because they can tell maybe from the real thing."

Bobby bent, snatched his glass from the coffee table, drained it, added bourbon, sat on the couch.

"Now my talent's gone, that happens. The business reeks with ex-phenoms, most of them working as producers."

I tried to say something, Bobby wouldn't listen.

"Shut your mouth. Maybe it *was* the wind blowing through me. Maybe I had talent for only one thing and that's over. Maybe I used what I had"—he took a deep swallow of bourbon, looked straight at me—"but if you can tell the difference, you want to die. Wordsworth spent his last thirty years writing shit poems and found Christ. Me"—Bobby grinned—"I'm an atheist."

Almost in unison, we raised our drinks and drained them. I refilled our glasses, not bothering with ice.

"Those writer assholes—" He paused, made his voice high and affected. " 'If he'd only change with the times. The sixties are over, Bobby Hall, Bobby Hall.' " Bobby sipped his bourbon, spoke normally. "I used to fantasize about inviting all the shit, hip New York critics to a party and blowing us up."

Booze-brave, I said, "You can't still want to die."

"Don't fuck with me."

"Jenny would never forgive you. She hasn't forgiven you for the last time."

Bingo. His left eye made that funny move, almost but not quite a squint into some cosmic or moral sun, a muscle tensing from his temple down to the corner of his mouth.

"You know, you're right. Losing Mom like we did, it's unfair to Jenny to kill myself. So I give myself pep talks. 'Hey, schmuck, if you were meant to die that rope wouldn't have broken. Hey, schmuck, stop feeling sorry for yourself. Help Jenny or write a song about it. Everyone will remember what a hero you are.' "

He smiled, actually smiled at me.

"Anyway, don't ask me how or why because you're pretty ordinary, a spoiled boy from Brooklyn, but you've got talent. You combine words and music and they're more than you could have known or meant in any conscious way. And frankly, my dear"—he paused; I remembered the quote, Rhett Butler—"that pisses me off. So I wouldn't trust me. I have to watch out for Jenny, but I got no obligation to you."

"Thanks." I sipped my bourbon. "I guess."

"Don't expect to hear this from me again."

"Believe me, I don't want to."

He grinned. "So, you want to write a song?"

"What am I supposed to say?"

"Whatever you want."

I stood, grinned and my dumb hunter heart beat triumphantly.

"I've got some ideas."

"To the Country," written that night, focused on the breakup of the country hippie life. Like all my better songs, it grew out of imagining I were Jenny long enough to compose, while knowing subliminally that the real Jenny would soon sing my words as if they were her own.

Bobby felt that doubleness, too. We were drunk, relaxed, and for the first time nearly honest with each other, burying our love and resentment in the act of imagining words to place, some might say like phalluses, in Jenny's mouth. God knows, as he watched her sing, no cool citified Blondie, but the proverbial country girl busting out of her calico, his love must have bumped over the edge of what nice boys were supposed to feel for their sisters.

And my hero-love for Bobby, a constant since my bar mitzvah, there's no one in this empty apartment who wants to analyze what wanting to *be* Bobby Hall or Bob Dylan means. Let's just say that working late in Bobby's loft, trying to imagine words Jenny would not only sing but feel about her life, as well as the music to express that emotion, was an intense happy time for us both.

The result, which opens the album, contains my favorite lyric:

> *Dust rising from the road,*
> *Blue horizon where it showed*
> *Summer meadow, turning yellow*
> *In the country.*
>
> *The pond upon the hill,*
> *We lay naked in the sun.*
> *All the kids had come*
> *Dreams on the run*
> *To the country.*

Anyone who knows the album remembers the strings and lush harmonies Bobby suggested and I eagerly agreed to, part of a flawed attempt at a panegyric in song to the lost country life. Listening now, I realize that although my original inspiration was to write a song about Jenny's life, "To the Country" 's beauty, its feel of loss and high romantic ideals conjures Bobby: how drunk we were that night, how intimate and close we felt for the first and, in some ways, last time.

"Don't you know," begins the verse Bobby wrote, "it feels so strange / but life and love will change, / deals are made, / reasons fade. / How I wish I had stayed / in the country."

The First Time I Saw Jenny Hall

*   *   *

That same week, with help from Bird, Danny composed "Wrong Number Lovers." A duet between Danny and Jenny, the second-best rocker on the album, "Wrong Number" tells the story of Rozzie, who's getting calls for some other girl. Roz falls in love with the voice of a stranger named Mike.

> *Love at first voice,*
> *Everybody's choice!*

They arrange to meet, and following the wonderfully bent logic of Danny's and particularly Bird's sensibilities, the song builds to a punch line.

> *Mike was small and skinny,*
> *Roz was six-foot-four.*
> *When she came through the door,*
> *Man, what a sight*
> *On that hot Friday night.*

> *They were wrong number lovers,*
> *Met on the phone.*
> *Wrong number lovers,*
> *Didn't want to be alone.*
> *Wrong number lovers,*
> *Wrong number lovers.*

Because Danny, whose real love was rhythm and blues, had written it, "Wrong Number"'s first principles were opposite to those of my songs, which typically grew out of a few lines of lyric or theme. Even the song's humor is achieved not so much through words as by juxtaposing rascally, funky music with romantic truisms.

"Wrong Number Lovers" was easy to arrange, communicated Danny's feelings about my relationship with Jenny (or, to grant him deeper reserves of self-knowledge than is probably justified, his own relationship with Jenny), and except for an occasional twinge of jealousy on my part, was a positive, joyous event from start to finish.

I wrote the album's last and ultimately title cut a week after Bobby and I had composed "To the Country." That makes it the first or second Tuesday in March, a strange, awful, exhilarating month. That Tuesday night, wandering through the Village with my coat open—springtime!—I knew as surely as if there had been a wizard at my ear that I was going to write our last song. I'd had it in mind for weeks to do one about the wind as I'd experienced it the first night with Jenny above her pond. Wind as fate blowing through the trees, yet always in them. The wind which touches our lives, then gusts on unconcerned with human existence. The soulless, guiltless amoral wind: Maria, a real mother.

I never wrote that one. Instead, wandering up and down Bleecker and its crosses, closemouthed but already beginning a silent yowl like an Old Testament prophet who can see His arching dazzle but doesn't yet know when the bolt will strike, I saw images of Danny and Jenny earlier in the day. Lips parted, necks bent to the same mike, teeth flashing like dimes, and the idea popped into my brain full-developed like Athena squeezing through a zit on Zeus's forehead. I'd written "Fall in Love Again" as a love song for Jenny to sing to me. What was needed; anyway, what was skating in circles inside my skull like a pat of butter in a hot pan as I hurried east on Bleecker, what was needed was a song in which Jenny sang about why things hadn't worked with Danny. They'd loved each other, they still did, but that wasn't enough. Christ, it happened all the time. The true love who breaks your heart. And right there on Bleecker, mouth open as my coat and blinded eyes, I heard the hook: love is no reason.

I walked faster. Except for the fall, when I worked every afternoon to have something for Jenny in the evening, I'd often found my best ideas walking or riding the subway, short bursts when a demon nerve in my gut plugged into the cosmos and I'd hear snatches of words or melody I knew were the real thing. Then, like a dawn-dazzled vampire, like Clark Kent intent on a phone booth, I'd have to drop what I was doing and hustle my ass to my apartment or, in a pinch, to a friend's piano.

That warm March night, words and melody exploding into my Potts and Pan noodle kugel of a brainpan, I felt, I imagine, like a woman does after her water has burst. "Help," cries the baby. "Help!"

I began to jog. Pretty soon I was sprinting east on Bleecker to the Bowery, the wind in my hair, a song in my heart like Julie Andrews in the Hollywood Alps. I turned north, ran up the Bowery past Cooper Union to Seventh, turned east and raced the half block to my apartment. Wheezing up the five flights, lungs burning, eyes spinning like tires on ice, I had the entire chorus, the melody, too, if I could only get to the piano before I keeled over.

> *Love is no reason, you say,*
> *Love is no reason, to stay,*
> *Love is no reason, this way*
> *Running our lives in circles*
> *Day after day.*

I won't describe the odor a man's body produces during a three-mile run under a down parka; or my six-minute piss, the tinkling of water on water which sounded to my crazed ear like a flute, congas and an oboe.

You won't get the artist at work. Chord changes tried and rejected. Rhymes gone astray. There's a sequence in *Bound for Glory* in which David Carradine is seated atop a freight train or maybe in the back of some Okie's pickup. He plucks a guitar. "This land is your place, / this land is my place." He rubs his chin, mutters, and as the camera dollies in, a holy light sparks in his eyes, and you know Woody is going to get it right this time.

No. What matters is that after two hours I was exhausted but as excited as I'd ever been about a song and wanted to play it for Jenny. I dialed her number, wasn't surprised there was no answer. It was just one and she'd planned to be out at uptown rock clubs—God and His angels knew when she'd get home. I showered, whacked off fifty push-ups. Still no answer. I played the song through and was so overcome by its sad, dark beauty and by my joy at having written it that I needed to play it for her or they'd find me in the morning eating the wrong part of an egg, shell-shocked.

I dialed her number. She didn't answer. I threw on a coat, ran out the door and down the stairs, headed for D.C.'s garage with just enough time to get there before the one-forty-five closing. Passing the Fillmore, I blew the ghosts a kiss, kept going. Jenny might not be home until three or four, but I'd had my own keys since January. Besides, she *might* get home early. Moving, driving, I thought and looked at my feet flapping up and down inside their new Bass floaters as if they were attached to someone else's legs, a sight which made me realize I was trotting again; in motion, I thought, and slowed down, in motion I might not end up batshit.

I drove east, then north on First Avenue. I cruised the U.N. to kill a little extra time. I passed the chic-chic shops in the low fifties. I turned left on Fifty-seventh, which even at 2 A.M. ran with traffic and cabs hustling fares. I turned south on Ninth Avenue, then left again on Fifty-sixth Street, pulled into a spot I waited for a pink-and-white Pimpmobile to vacate. Walking to Jenny's front door, I sang the first verses two, then three times.

> "Long before I left you,
> Long after the end,
> I'd hear the same questions
> Time and again.
>
> "Through broken, lonely, fearful nights,
> Watching the morning sky grow light,

The First Time I Saw Jenny Hall

Where did our love go wrong?
Was it ever right?"

I let myself in the locked lobby door, rode the urine-and-rotten-peach-scented elevator to the second floor. Careful not to sing or whistle, I walked down the quiet hall to Jenny's corner apartment and opened the door, a little surprised both locks weren't thrown. I covered the short dark hallway to the kitchen counter, heard it and died: the whimpering, animal sound of Jenny impassioned, love patois oozing from the bedroom.

I told myself she was masturbating. Schmuck, I knew better. The moans grew louder and more frequent until she was either coming or about to. Then I knew she wasn't alone because I could hear the *thump-thump* of belly against belly, of ass against mattress, and a deeper, more guttural moan which had to be male.

Suddenly, I understood. She's fucking Ethan. The nights we're apart I'm writing songs and dreaming dreams for both of us while she's doing that dildo.

I marched six paces to the half-open bedroom door and considered peeking in to see whom she was with. But once in motion I was afraid to stop. I knocked twice, threw the door open so hard the inside knob pummeled the wall, which spit paint.

She was underneath him, and I'm pretty sure that when I burst in he was still inside her. In the half-light cast by one shaded bulb, her face looked as beautiful, as seamy and sordid as any you've ever seen or imagined.

"Oh, God," she screamed. "Get out of here!"

She pushed Loverboy off her. Maybe he was dripping semen. Maybe he hadn't come yet, I sure hope so, the bastard. But I don't know and had no time to find out because when she screamed she also pulled the sheet up. All I focused on before I backed out of the room, Jenny screaming, her breasts hidden by the sheet, was that it wasn't Ethan. It wasn't Danny, Bobby or some black superman with a dick big as a pony's. Just some guy with long hair a little lighter than mine who'd seemed terrified, then embarrassed, and hid his vile body beneath the sheet.

I waited in the living room until Jenny appeared, wearing her blue bathrobe.

"Give me fifteen minutes, okay?"

I nodded, crossed the living room and let myself out. I hit the street, realized I needed a drink or a lobotomy and ended up at McCann's Irish House, where the crowd was what you'd expect that time of night. Old men at the bar, nursing beers. A couple guys my age, also nursing beers, hoods in T-shirts who flashed me the macho eye. A black-and-white movie played on an overhead TV: Clark Gable looking tough on a rubber plantation. I downed two quick bourbons, told the bartender, an old Irishman with a pancake face and mashed-in nose, to make the next one a triple over ice in a tall glass. He wiped his hands, squinted at me, trying to decide if I were a nut case. Apparently not. I tipped him a dollar, retreated to the back of the bar, and for the next half hour pumped quarters into a pinball machine.

"I'm sorry, Potts," Jenny said, a body-length away on her couch. "What can I say?"

"I called. I called till I left my apartment."

"I heard the last one but didn't answer." She paused; my lip curled. "It's not what you think. I've been getting crank calls."

"Not when I'm here."

"It's not important."

"That's for sure."

"I'm sorry."

I nodded, ran my hand across my forehead, through my hair and heaved a huge sigh.

"Oh, God," she said. "Stop acting so wounded."

I looked up. She smiled and for a second I feared she might touch me.

"I *feel* wounded."

Jenny stood, walked to the window end of the room, peeked out through the venetian blind. She turned and said, "What do you want me to say? I was fucking someone. Sex relaxes me."

"Who is he?"

"A sax player."

"Is that what you've been doing the last couple weeks, picking up guys to relax with?"

Jenny crossed the room and sat beside me. Hand on my thigh, eyes searching mine, she said, "I love you, Potts. I'm sorry I hurt you. I never saw him before."

I hugged her, but it wasn't over because I didn't want it to be. My breath began coming in short, shallow bursts till I felt if I didn't let go of her I'd suffocate. I stood, walked to the window, bit off clouds of air. Then I sat beside her again.

"Why?" I asked.

"Why what?"

"Why did you fuck him?"

"Why didn't you leave? I told you, I'm under a lot of strain, and purely physical fucking helps. It makes me feel sexy."

"And I don't?"

"You. You're a big part of the strain."

I looked at her mournfully.

"Please. I'm sorry, I couldn't be sorrier. But who I fuck is my business, I told you before."

"You did this with Danny, not just between lovers?"

Her eyes asked, Where have you been the past ten years?

"Yes, with Danny."

I no longer felt cool or grieving. "I thought at least you loved him."

"I do. And I love you, you silly ass. Don't make this into more than it is."

"What is it?"

"I think it's incredibly bad timing."

After a beat, a pause, I smiled as I knew she wanted me to. Jenny smiled, too, then walked to the kitchen and returned with a pack of Marlboros. She'd promised not to smoke during recording because it thickened her voice, but I didn't say anything. We smoked in the half-dark of her living room, not looking at each other while outside madmen blew horns and gunned their engines waiting for the Eighth Avenue light. After a few puffs I noticed the cigarette was stale, as if it had been sitting unsmoked for weeks, and my heart lightened toward her. Feeling that, perhaps, Jenny said, "What are you doing here anyway?"

I thought a minute and remembered. "I wanted to play you a new song."

She pivoted on the couch, faced me. "You still want to?"

"Let's smoke a joint first."

"Sure."

She disappeared into the bedroom, returned with a joint already rolled, which turned my distress juices on again because I knew she'd had it ready for him. Halfway through the number, I said, "Didn't Danny mind your other lovers?"

"Ask him."

"It's only human."

"Making love is human."

I drew on the joint, watched that dazed inhuman glow come over her eyes and turned away, sucked down smoke until my lungs burned.

"Sure it's human. But if lovers are in the same town, they sleep with each other. That's what it means, lovers."

"Why don't you scream you hate me instead of this guilt shit?"

"I don't hate you." I watched her chest heave. Her hair scaled peaks as if there were wind rushing through it. "I just don't understand why you did it."

"You don't?" Her right hand fumbled on the coffee table, seized a small ashtray. "Maybe you'll understand this."

Jenny wound up, fired the ashtray across the room. It skimmed the TV, hit the wall and shattered with a shriek; shards arced and disappeared into the carpet with a *shush* of pebbles hitting grass.

"Nice shot," I said. She was berserk, mangling her lower lip between her teeth, and I thought, Hey, I'm the injured party.

"What I'm saying is, no matter how it was with Danny, it's not okay with me. Maybe it's stupid, but that's how I am."

"Listen, I'm still who I was with Danny. That's who I am."

"Hey—" I began, trying to pacify her.

She grabbed my hand, shook it as if hers were a dog and mine were a cat's neck it was trying to break. "Hey, yourself."

She released my hand, and slowly her eyes lost their inhuman glow. Her shoulders dropped two inches, and she said, "I love you, Potts. You may not believe that now, but I know it's true."

I wondered what was the use of being loved if it meant seeing her legs wrapped around some guy's ass as if she were straddling a fence.

"And I love you," I said, "or this wouldn't be so awful."

Her smile ignited. "I've been waiting for you to say that." She hugged me. "Look, if you can't be with me and sleep with anyone else, why don't you be faithful? I'll be very flattered."

"I can't believe you."

I grabbed the other ashtray, threw it against the wall. Instead of shattering it *dong*ed loudly, then spun itself still at our feet.

"Brass." She winked. Then, before I could laugh or answer, she said, "As for me, I'm not making any promises, but not counting tonight, I've slept with one other man since we met. And if you've slept with anyone, I don't want to know. We love each other, and that's what matters."

I relit the joint, inhaled, then passed it. In between tokes, she said, "You're not convinced."

"Not completely."

"Enough to play me your song?"

"Maybe later." I considered the song's theme and decided later would be morning. "What I really need is a shower."

"Can I join you?"

"Better not."

"You all right?"

"I will be."

She nodded. I walked to the bathroom, pissed and climbed under the spray.

· PART THREE ·

Waiting for Love

Chapter Eight

•

THE HUMAN HEART is an amazing piece of work.
Standing in the shower, I tried to dissolve who and what
I was in the damp darkness, but Jenny's face kept coming back
to me. Jenny pushing the guy off her. Jenny covering her
breasts. Jenny begging me to leave.

Okay, I could have knocked, told her to get rid of him and
waited in the bar. Not me. What did I expect, arriving at
two-thirty? What did you fucking expect?

Not that.

I soaped my armpits for the third, maybe fourth time.
Schmuck, dingus, dicknose. You acted like a puppy, a
wounded puppy.

I rinsed, then soaped my armpits again. I felt wounded.
Because I *felt* wounded. And the spray continued, hot and wet.

When I entered the bedroom naked, Jenny was sitting up
in bed, smoking.

"Damn spot out yet?"

"You're not supposed to be smoking."

"You missed my allusion."

"I ignored it."

"That's worse." She smiled. "Okay, last puff."

Jenny exhaled, eyes closed against the smoke. Sitting up
nude except for panties, her sprite/beautiful woman's face
gray and drawn, Jenny looked small, almost fragile. And I
admit it, that turned me on.

"Can you stay?"

"Do you want me to?"

"Very much."

I crossed the room and sat beside her.

"If you're worried, I changed the sheets."

"God, you're crude."

"Don't." Her eyes were wide and very pale. "I'm doing my best."

At first she felt like a stranger. No, an enemy, and I held back. I could feel her lips caressing mine, her breathing, her small, tight body beneath me, the need and affection in her arms, the *need*—and the ice in my heart, which had outlasted one of history's longest hot showers, melted and I began to sob.

"Oh, God," she whispered. "Do you know how much I love you?"

When my tears had stopped, she murmured, "Can we make love, would that be all right?"

As such things go, it was fine.

A week later, Wednesday night, the phone rang in Jenny's apartment just after eleven. We were in bed, oddly enough, watching the news.

"Should I answer it?"

"Don't stay on long, babe, okay?"

After a second, she palmed the mouthpiece. "It's your mother. Want me to leave?"

"No. What's up, Mom?"

"I'm sorry to call so late. I didn't interrupt anything?"

"Don't you wish."

"Wait a minute, the other phone's ringing."

She put me on hold. For the most part, Mom kept her opinion of Jenny to herself. Instead, she and Arnie dropped hints. They generally disapproved of my musician friends, but months had passed, Jenny and I were still together, in fact cutting a record, so they'd concluded she must be a good influence. But that sort of parental approval didn't mean much. If Jenny did something they judged unkind, six months of lived life to the contrary, they'd decide she was another of Stevie's mistakes.

"That was your sister."

"What's wrong?"

"Why does something have to be wrong?"

"You said you were sorry to call so late."

"As a matter of fact, it's Grandpa."

"What happened?"

"Nothing happened."

My mother, a sharp, talented businesswoman, to paraphrase Dylan, the brains behind Arnie, was a master of torture by omission. Her love for me had never reconciled itself to having to track me down in the apartments of slightly suspect young women, often blond and gentile.

"If nothing happened, why'd you call?"

"He says he won't have the operation."

"What operation?"

"That's right, I haven't told to you. His good eye, the left one, isn't so good anymore. He has cataracts."

"Let me talk to him."

"It would be better in person."

I covered the mouthpiece, asked Jenny, "Are we busy to-morrow?"

"I don't think so. How's Ziggie?"

"I'm not sure."

"Can I come?"

"If you want."

"Mom, Jenny and I will be there around six to take him out to dinner."

"You really think it's appropriate?"

"Yes," I said quickly, "I do."

The next night Jenny and I drove from The Big M straight

to Brooklyn. We spent a half hour with Ziggie and my mother —Arnie was still at work—then Jenny, Ziggie and I left via the front door. Climbing the steps to the gate in the hurricane fence, Jenny on one side of him, me on the other, I took Ziggie's arm, the first time I'd ever treated him as an old man. Jenny closed the gate behind us, Ziggie turned, and I wondered if he'd seen it or just heard the sound. Then Ziggie faced me, and eyes twinkling as if there were nothing wrong, thick eyebrows reaching for the straggly gray tent of his hair, he said, "Mister Boy Scout, it's my eyes, eh? I can still walk."

He grinned; I released his arm. A few minutes later, after we'd settled into D.C.'s front seat, Ziggie said, "You came to see me because I won't have the operation." He smiled. "It's all right, I know you're busy." He turned to Jenny. "Maybe I should have stopped crapping weeks ago. Who knows what might have happened?"

"Your eyes would have turned brown."

"Eh," said Ziggie, when he'd finished laughing. "If I was sixty years younger, I'd steal her away."

"If a pig had wings, Grandpa, it could fly."

"So drive, Mister Pig, I'm hungry."

I pulled out of the parking place and turned left on Bedford, heading for a seafood restaurant facing the Bay.

"We brought a tape," Jenny said. "It's a rough mix, but you'll get the idea."

She slid a gray studio cassette into the in-dash unit and the opening of "Love Is No Reason" filled the car. Halfway through, Ziggie asked, "You write it, Stevie?"

"It's the newest."

"And you're singing?"

Jenny nodded and we drove to the Bay. At Emmons Avenue, I turned left and we cruised the party fishing boats tied up at the piers which reached into the Bay like fingers: my happy childhood. We passed Stella Maris, the bait shop; the

song ended and Ziggie said, "It's beautiful, but sad. You're
not happy?"

"We're happy." I glanced at Jenny, who met my eyes, then
looked away. "It's a song."

"Song, schmong," the old man said. "My heart hurts."

"People like that," Jenny began. "It makes them forget
their own pain."

"Eh," Ziggie said. "I guess. Making a record is hard work?"

"It can be. Tension, deadlines, and my brother, who's—"

"The rock star."

"That's right, he can be difficult."

"And Stevie here, is he ever difficult?"

Jenny laughed. "He is, but he doesn't think so."

"Hah, just like his father, Mister Potts and Pans."

"And I know where we got it." I pulled into a parking spot.
"Why won't you have that operation, you want to go blind?"

"Listen to him. Persecute me after I eat, Mister Nazi."

I started to answer him, then noticed Jenny shaking her
head.

"Sure, Grandpa."

Jenny and I ordered lobster, Ziggie a broiled fillet of red
snapper. We ate, laughed and chatted. Ziggie's eyes never left
her; and watching them eat, Ziggie neatly and precisely, a
skinny old man who had never cared about food, Jenny attacking her lobster, dismembering the carcass, then sucking each
feeler clean, Ziggie taking it in and beaming at her, I felt a
rush of love and connection, of the three of us forming a
family. It was then, if ever, that I forgave Jenny her relaxing
lover.

At one point Ziggie said, "You're a happy eater," and
Jenny, who'd been alternately sucking at the narrow end of a
lobster claw and poking it with a small fork to extract the
last shred of meat, stopped and looked up. She swept the hair
off her forehead with her forearm because her hands were

too greasy. Then, smiling—she flirted outrageously with the old man and he loved it—she asked, "Why, is there lobster on me?"

"Three pieces." The old man raised his eyebrows and shoulders, a gesture that for me was a distillation of Ziggie Potts, eighty-two years of being alive and funny. "But who's counting?"

Jenny wiped her chin. "I've always been a messy eater. I've gotten used to it."

"She means"—I laughed—"that she wears a bib."

"Your grandson didn't want me to meet your son and daughter-in-law because of my bib. Can you imagine that?"

"My wife was messy," said Ziggie. "Potts and Pans was embarrassed to bring his fiancée, your mother, home from college."

"I didn't know that."

"Everything a pile." Ziggie pointed at the saltshaker, the pepper, then the water glasses with his fork. "This pile, that pile. You couldn't walk for Bessie's piles. A little one like you, she never got fat because she missed her mouth so much."

"She should have used a bib."

Ziggie laughed. "She did."

"I don't remember piles. I thought you owned lots of things."

"*You.*" Ziggie cut a small rectangle of white fillet, inserted it between his false teeth. "You were still making cackie in your pants when she died."

"I was seven, I was not."

"You've been alone since?"

Ziggie wiped his mouth, set the cloth napkin in his lap. "Not so alone. I had the store, my books, Mister and Missus Potts and Pans to amuse me, great-grandchildren and now, in my declining years, Stevie the rock star to be proud of." Ziggie smiled, ate another square of fish. "Not so bad, eh? You live, you get used to things. You wake up and thank God for another day, for everything still working." He winked at me, then added, "And for not making me a woman."

"What?"

"It's a Jewish prayer," I said. "Jewish men thank God for not being women."

"That's disgusting," Jenny said. "Don't you think, Ziggie?"

"My whole life I've loved women, which I might have missed being one. So maybe I'm a piggie Ziggie, but I'm happy."

"Lousy jokes," Jenny said. "They run in the family."

Ziggie shrugged his world-beater of a shrug.

"Potts," he said, "I peddle."

"And pans," I added, inserting a soft *t*, "*pants* remind them of me."

"How's your eye?" I asked after Jenny had excused herself, ostensibly to powder her nose. "And no bullshit."

"Sometimes it's good, sometimes bad. When it's bad, it stinks."

"So have the operation."

Ziggie sipped his coffee, shook his head. "When I was a little boy in Poland—"

"Still named Potzgovitz."

"That's another story." He grinned with pleasure; Ziggie liked stories. "My mother took me to the fortune-teller. An old woman with a wart on her chin, I've never forgotten, that grew red hair, eh? She said it was fine to send me to America, and I would live till eighty-two."

"I never knew that."

"I only told Bessie."

I sipped my coffee, which was still hot. "You believed her?"

"When my younger brother and sister died of pneumonia their first year in America, and I had it too but lived, then I believed her." Ziggie gripped my right forearm, which lay between us on the table. "When Bessie died young, and I was unhappy, so unhappy, Stevie, Bessie came to me in a dream."

"You're kidding."

"As I sit here, it was Bessie. And she said, 'Zig, you're young, you're going to live till eighty-two. So you must be happy. Be happy.' "

Ziggie paused, sipped his coffee, all the energy in his long face concentrating in his dimming eyes: points of light. "What's the matter, Mister Rock Star, you think only you have a life?"

I didn't know what to say, and looked past him out at the dark waters of the Bay. When I turned back, Jenny was entering the dining room. She'd brushed her hair till it shone.

"Do you mind discussing this in front of her?"

"Isn't she lovely?" Ziggie said, and stood, held her chair. Then we were all seated again, Ziggie in the middle.

"So what have you boys been talking about?"

I glanced at the old man, who was smiling at having been called a boy. "When Ziggie was little, a fortune-teller predicted he would live till eighty-two and he's always believed it."

I drained my cup. The waitress materialized with a fresh pot of coffee. When she moved off, I said, "Ziggie's eighty-two now."

Jenny added milk, and I watched her coffee swirl black, cream, then mocha. She placed the spoon beside the cup. Her tongue appeared briefly, moistening her upper lip.

"And you're afraid the operation will kill you."

"Kill me," Ziggie answered, "or make me blind for what little time remains. A dead man, I'll be able to see again."

No one spoke, then Jenny asked, "When will you be eighty-three?"

"Next February."

"And if you're still alive?" I asked.

"I'll be very happy."

"Will you have the operation?"

"First I'll have a party."

"Great," Jenny said. "Steve and I will perform."

I thought for a minute. "Will it be too late for the operation?"

"The doctor says it could still be corrected. But there's a good chance by fall, eh, by Christmas, I'll be blind."

"Doesn't that scare you?" Jenny asked. "It would scare the shit out of me."

"For that," Ziggie said, "I use prunes."

We finished recording a few days later and began mixing. Think of mixdown as a football coach directing his team through the Super Bowl. He has wonderful athletes. They've worked hard for months, assembling a complex playbook. But unless he orchestrates the game plan correctly, the right play at the right time, each decision made once and once only, the result is disaster. Fans don't watch practice games or listen to rough cuts. All that counts is the final score.

Working generally with the engineer, a producer creates the final mix by deciding among alternate tracks, and by pushing up or toning down the volume of the different instruments and voices, thereby giving the mix a particular feel or color. There's also a tremendous amount of outboard equipment used these days. Echo, digital delay, frequency compression, noise reduction and equalization, technologies which allow the producer to emphasize certain frequencies and phase out others.

Since the band and Bobby had very different ideas about what to phase out or emphasize, we battled during mixdown, especially at first. One afternoon early on, Bobby threatened to burn the masters unless we calmed down.

"You wouldn't," said Jenny.

"Just keep telling me what to do."

"Punch up my vocal over that useless shitty organ."

Bobby produced a small red lighter and headed for the

sixteen-track console on the other side of the control room. Before he could get there, Dickie, all five-foot-three-skinny-inches of him, rushed forward and spread his arms in front of the tape recorder and shelves of stacked tapes.

"No one burns nothing." Dickie's frizz hair stood straight out like the fur of a raccoon defending her kittens. "What's wrong with you fucking Halls?"

"Get out of my way."

"I'm warning you. No one fucks around in my studio."

Bobby stepped toward him. Dickie reached up to the tape shelves, came down with a black revolver.

"Put it away."

"Shut up," Dickie answered. "Bird, you got a joint?"

Bird nodded.

"Good. Relieve Mr. Hall of his lighter and fire it up."

Eyes on Dickie, slightly crouched, Bobby reached behind him, handing Bird the lighter.

"Smoke that mother."

Lined up against the control panel, the five of us smoked the joint while ten feet away Dickie watched us, eyes glittering.

"You got two choices," he announced when the joint was gone. "Calm down or get the fuck out of here."

He squared his jaw. Then, almost faster than my eyes could follow, he flipped the gun from his right hand to his left and back again. Jenny ended up on the floor, so did Danny. Bobby and I finished humped over like boulders. Bird alone remained upright, face hidden behind his forearm. When my heartbeat had slowed to a roar, I said, "It'd be easier to calm down if you put that gun away."

"Oh, yeah, Potts?"

Dickie aimed, and a stream of water flooded my right eye.

"Bang, bang," he said. "You're wet."

After that we fought less. The momentum of finishing seemed to take over, and we abandoned the mix to Dickie and

Bobby. Sol seemed happy, and the band, at Bird's suggestion, voted unanimously to call the album *Love Is No Reason.*

For the front cover Jenny was photographed in a white dress. The full moon, another White Goddess, glowed above her. Wearing black, Bird, Danny and I were arranged in a semicircle behind Jenny, our faces in profile. We're all gazing at a small bird meant to symbolize lost love, flying across the midnight sky toward the moon.

On the back of the album, in addition to the song list and credits, there's another picture of the group. In it we smile straight into the camera, which is quite different from what we'd planned: another mysterious, incredibly hip shot. Instead, Bird made animal noises, and told a long story about his older brother, who'd forced Bird and a still smaller Murphy to accompany him for years on his paper route, storing rubber bands around their ears, flattening the papers against the tops of their heads once they'd been folded. So we laughed, and used it.

In April, Apex gave us the barest outlines of our tour. We'd go out in June for six to eight weeks, mainly in the Northeast. But we'd play as far south as Atlanta, and there might be a week's work in the Midwest: Chicago or Kansas City. Primarily, we'd play midsize clubs in cities like Poughkeepsie, Kingston and New Haven, but at least once we'd open for an established Apex act in a large venue, fifteen or twenty thousand people, minimum.

A warm Thursday night in April found us in a French restaurant off First Avenue, Hershkoff's treat. Anne was in from Ithaca, and Grandpa Ziggie, who'd become a surrogate band member—Bird wanted him to play tambourine at our New York gigs, claimed he'd get the old man laid in return for the cocaine he'd bought us—was also present. So were Bobby, Ethan, Dickie, the Big M, a half-dozen execs and publicity people from Apex, as well as Rock Isaacson, the lead guitarist who was going to tour with us. Unlike most of Bobby's old friends, Rock (né Roger) wasn't down on his luck. A legendary session player, Rock had sat in on albums for Dylan, Joplin, Bobby, the Stones. You name them, Rock had been there.

Part of the legend, though, was that Rock preferred puttering in his apartment, reading Kierkegaard and watching the Mets to working, so he left home only when he had to, meaning when broke. He entered Bobby's loft on a Monday, two nights before Hershkoff's party, dressed in jeans, a blue pea jacket and sock hat, carrying a black electric guitar case. A big man, maybe six-two, 220, he looked familiar. Typically, Bobby hadn't told us who we were auditioning, preferring the power that came with surprising us. Did he need to pull that kind of shit? No, but try to tell him that.

When Rock took off his coat and sock hat to reveal a gut pressing against his shirt like the closed end of a six-quart mixing bowl, and a long bald forehead, a hairless dome which looked as if he were wearing a football helmet of his own skin above huge, heavily browed brown eyes, I knew him for sure. Before Bobby introduced us I walked up, shook Rock's hand.

"You're Rock—"

Measuring me with his enormous orbs, Rock answered, "That's right."

"For those of you who don't know," said Bobby. "This is Rock Isaacson."

Rock shook our hands, then Bird said, "So I'm a fucking dummy, but who are you, Rock?"

"Best session man and TV hound in the city," Bobby said, and laughed.

Rock didn't. Rock, it turned out, rarely laughed, though he was funny, and for a big man, for any man, I guess, sensitive and gentle. Instead, in jeans and flannel shirt he stood in the kitchen area of Bobby's loft, large hands holding his guitar case upright in front of him, the moment growing awkward.

Then Danny asked, "Didn't you play on *Blonde on Blonde?*"

"Yeah," Rock said, looking neither impressed nor engaged by his own fame.

"And *No More Dying,*" Bobby added, never able to hear Dylan mentioned without thrusting his own work forward.

"Wait a minute," Bird burst out, "you're the dude who won't leave home."

"Hey, Bobby," Rock said, "you didn't tell me there were whiz kids."

"Yeah, right." Bobby lifted Rock's guitar case. "Come on."

We followed Bobby to the loft's main living space. Jenny asked, "Did Bobby tell you we're looking for someone to tour?"

"He told me. You must be the kid sister."

She smiled; they shook hands. "The other whiz kids are Danny Grabonus, bass; Bird Murphy, drums and coke; and Steve Potts, keyboards and writer."

We shook hands, then Danny, more forthcoming than usual, said, "I've admired your work for years. You were with The Electric Flag."

"Yeah."

"Fucking Bloomfield," said Bobby. "You hear from him?"

"Nothing good."

For a minute we fell quiet, thinking about Mike Bloomfield, one of the 60's great guitarists. Bloomfield, who'd organized The Electric Flag, was the original high-energy man, the Jewish Prince, the soulful comet. Then he burned out on junk, but unlike Hendrix and Joplin didn't die. He now lived, wasted, his chops gone, a pillhead somewhere near San Francisco.

"By the way," Rock added. "You look pretty good."

Bobby looked at him, eyes narrowed, and I thought he was going to say something like "Compared to what?" But his heart was healing. "Thanks," he said, and smiled. "You, Rock, you look like a fucking mountain."

Rock looked down at his gut. "You want me to play?"

The First Time I Saw Jenny Hall

A lot of murmuring, then Bird said, "I'd dig that. But you got to tell me something. You're the guy who has food delivered so you don't have to go out. I mean like yogurt and potatoes."

Rock nodded.

"We'll be gone seven weeks."

Rock knelt, opened his guitar case, strapped on an old white-faced Stratocaster. Standing, he said, "I ain't left town in eight years. Bobby convinced me it was time."

"Why not the Riviera?" asked Bird.

"I been there."

"Ya dig Poughkeepsie? We're playing Poughkeepsie."

"Poughkeepsie." Rock strummed his E string, tightened it, strummed again. "That's my hometown."

"No shit," said Bobby.

Bird tried once more to figure it out. "We're paying what, six-fifty a week? You could do better in the studio. You'll be on the road in a ratty-ass van, eating fries. What, are you crazy?"

Rock finished tuning up, played a bar chord C, A minor, then a short, lightning-fast run on his E string. "Bobby said you were his sister's group, good kids, and you wouldn't ask a lot of dumb questions."

"Boy," I said, "was he wrong about the questions."

Rock's face widened in a rare smile, lips opening over his teeth. He nodded at Bobby, who put on a cassette of "Where Are You Now, Babe?" Rock began to play, and God, he was something. His musical lines, like his face, were sweet and sensitive without being sentimental. Rock played up on his toes, a 220-pound dancer, knees slightly bent, his belly thrust forward. He held the guitar away from his body, large hands caressing the neck as if it were flesh.

And his eyes, Rock's eyes. When most players take a solo, their lids seal or at least narrow with concentration. A reflex, turning inward. Not Rock. His forehead remained smooth and his eyes widened until they shone like lanterns. But instead of emitting light, Rock's eyes absorbed the energy, the emotion in the room, and glowed with feeling. Girl's eyes, I thought, watching him play, the eyes of a woman you've just entered. So beautiful and precious, they're almost painful to look into. God, I thought, can this big fucker play.

Rock was with us at Hershkoff's party. Wine flowed. Hearts soared on the wings of tiny quail, the internal organs of milk-fed veal while the two old men, Ziggie and Hershkoff, outdid each other telling funny stories.

We all wore our Sunday's best, even Bird and Danny. (Bird's was kind of a Thursday's best. Clean T-shirt, tie, a canary-yellow sports jacket.) Anne, who'd been in Ithaca the past month, arrived on Danny's arm, wearing a long dress, her hair gathered off her neck. Bangs edged her forehead, and as always, her eyes were elaborately made up: liner, white highlighter, purple shadow. During the fruit, cheese and wine course—every course was a wine course, this one a good German Riesling, a Rheingau—Annie, seated to my right, put her hand on my shoulder. In her soft voice, the accent both silly and somehow charming, she asked, "How are things between you and Jenny?"

"Fine."

She couldn't know, and yet— No. I looked at Jenny diagonally across from me, seated between the two old men at our banquet table in the private room Hershkoff had catered, charming them both. She said something about marbles, then laughed, and light flashed on her bare throat.

"Why do you ask?"

Annie raised her glass; the pale-gold wine sparkled. She sipped, set the glass on the white cloth. "Why don't you knock her up?" Annie giggled.

Laughing, I answered, "What, are you nuts?"

"That's it." She laughed again. "Crazy."

Lightly, she touched my wrist with her long nails. "Look at him," she whispered. "Just look."

Peeking past her, I watched Danny, his ponytail halfway down his gray thrift-shop special sports coat, stare across the table at Jenny.

"Talk about crazy, that's the man I love."

My heart beat fast; I didn't answer. Ethan kissed his date. At the same end of the table, nose skyward, mouth open, Bird hugged a redhead who worked in publicity for Apex.

"Danny asked me to tour with him. Should I?"

I looked again at Annie. She was painfully pretty and her nails still pressured my wrist. She was drunk. So was I, but at least I knew it.

"Why ask me?"

Her eyes widened in their lavender caves. "Feels like we're in the same"—she smiled—"same pickle."

I didn't say I thought the pickle was pretty much one-way. Or that when I worried about Jenny, it wasn't Danny's gherkin that came to mind.

"The more the merrier."

"You think so?"

Annie looked straight into my eyes. Women, I thought. Then Hershkoff tapped his water glass and stood up, Bobby to his left, Jenny on his right. His face glowed; his eyes never rested. No matter how often I met him, Hershkoff reminded me of a toy bulldog. At sixty-eight and after three heart attacks, he still put in ten-hour days, arriving each morning before the younger men who worked for him, dressed, rumor had it, in one of an identical set of blue blazers, white shirts and narrow ties he bought by the half dozen.

"This is a great occasion." His eyes moved around the table. "Just great, and not only because I'm picking up the tab."

Hershkoff grinned, puffed his cigar; a few of the younger execs applauded.

"Fifteen years ago when I signed Bobby, people on the outside asked, 'Who is this bum, this radical?' while the young turks I worked with then"—he eyed the Apex end of the table—"whispered, 'The old fart's done it this time.' "

"Well." Hershkoff sipped his wine; I smiled across the table at Jenny. "We all know what an important figure Bobby became both in the industry and in this country. And you probably know Bobby became a son to me. A son of the very best kind. He may have been a pain in the ass"—everyone laughed—"but he kept me and this country honest."

More applause. A look of embarrassed pleasure lit Bobby's face.

"I may be out of line, but at my age why shit around?" Hershkoff nodded in Naomi's direction. "Excuse me, Mrs. Doehr.

"Until last fall, I'd been pretty worried about Bobby. Everyone who knew him was, and with good reason. When he called in November to say he wanted to produce his sister's group, I was torn between saying yes without hearing them play a note, and asking if he was up to it.

"But Bobby, with his usual charm, saved me the decision. And this is a quote, Mrs. Doehr, you'll have to excuse me again. 'Sol, this isn't a fucking handout. Just listen to them.' "

Hershkoff paused. I sipped my wine, remembering the night at Discovery. Sean, whom I hadn't seen in some time. How nervous we'd been. Hershkoff coming up afterward like Tony the Tiger. *Great, just great.*

"So I listened and here we are. The single will be out in a month, the album in what, two?"

"That's right, Sol," someone sang out from the Apex corner.

"And they're going to be hits. The music and the times are different, but when Jenny sings there's the magic of a young Bobby Hall." Hershkoff touched Jenny's shoulder. "Sexier, though."

We all laughed. We were obligated to laugh. I looked at Annie, who smiled. I looked past her at Danny. He was staring at Jenny.

"The other kids all have that special something, too. Danny, Steve and Bird. And they're nice kids, which is why, as I was saying, this is such a great occasion."

Hershkoff's eyes moved over each of us, and I'll tell you, smiling at Jenny, who smiled back at me, I *felt* special.

"This is my family. Sure we fight, who doesn't? And here's Ziggie, even older than me, who put up the first money and tells me he has ideas what happened to it."

"Bird's nose," we all shouted. "Bird's nose."

Quite drunk, Bird stood up and announced, "Big nose, big humph."

"And Mrs. Doehr," Hershkoff went on, "the famous Big M, who's reputed to be the best cook in New Jersey."

"Come out and try, Mr. Hershkoff," a beaming Naomi answered. "For you the door's always open."

"Mom," Dickie called. "Think of your reputation."

"Reputation. I could entertain two Mr. Hershkoffs, our reputation on Bennett Cerf wouldn't get no worse."

"Bennett Cerf," Bird and I howled from opposite ends of the table.

"The other day," Naomi began.

"Mom," Dickie said, "later."

"As I was saying." One hand behind his back, Hershkoff puffed his cigar. "It's a family. Maybe the wounds of the past are healing, I hope so." Hershkoff again puffed his cigar. "But now, with Bobby launched in his new career, I can stop worrying and maybe think about retiring."

"No," we all shouted, a cry which rose loudest from the Apex end of the table. "No, no, Sol."

Hershkoff grinned. "Okay, not for a few years. So with the family doing well, and *Love Is No Reason* headed for *Billboard's* top ten, well, maybe top fifteen, mark my words"—Sol rested a hand on Jenny's shoulder, another on Bobby's—"you understand why this is such a great, great occasion. So here's to everyone here, but especially to Jenny Hall and Waterfall. *L'chayim.*"

Hershkoff sat down to applause.

The next morning, woefully hung over, Jenny and I were jetbound for Cozumel. At home, Bird and Danny were set to move out of their sublet Tribeca loft, Bird into my hovel on East Seventh, while Danny, driving Jenny's red Volvo, was returning to Ithaca. In three weeks we planned to rendezvous, rehearse and work out a show with the sound and light men Ethan was hiring, but until then, I thought, we were free.

Sore-eyed, groggy, I looked out at the sunlight flashing on the jet's wings and considered what Anne had said. No. Thinking about Anne was upsetting. We weren't in the same pickle; what an awful expression. That she believed we were made me angry.

A blond stewardess, her cheeks highlighted with All-American Beauty rose, passed on the aisle. Perhaps because we formed such a pretty still life—Jenny's legs were curled on the empty aisle seat to her left, my shoulder supported her cheek —the stewardess smiled. I smiled, too, but the exchange enraged me, which was when I admitted something was wrong. Schmuck, someone smiles, that's friendly.

I watched the sun grinning on the wing, and reminded myself we were going to have a great time the next ten days. Maybe two weeks. Fun, fun, fun.

The glare hurt my eyes. While Jenny and I were vacationing, the first expensive trip either of us had ever paid for, Danny would be squirreled away in T-burg, saving money for the farm he and Anne planned to buy after the tour.

We flew into clouds. My head hurt. My throat ached. My mouth was dry. Anne bitched about Jenny, but didn't complain about the rent money Danny had been saving since

August. And Danny; he probably had the first dime he'd ever made. Spending money around him I felt like a bourgeois toad.

Jenny shifted on my shoulder. "Can I put my head on your lap?"

"Sure, babe."

She lay across all three seats, cushioned her cheek on my thigh. I stroked her hair. Bird, I thought, was indifferent to Danny's admittedly unspoken disapproval. The wild man's money disappeared up his nose as fast as he made it. What was left he spent on friends, lovers and anyone who might some-day fit into either category.

But Bird was Bird, one of five kids, a poor boy, I thought then, from South Boston, a natural force, the Bird; Jenny and I were heir to all the doubts and guilt of children of the upper middle class who were making money for the first time. Bobby, after all, had given his to the Movement. Jenny had dropped out to avoid temptation, while I'd fled Potts and Pans, the whole commercial schmear for the world of art, man. Then, creative giants, or trying to be, we spent our lives worrying about unpaid bills.

So when Danny looked at us accusingly, dark eyes filled with disapproval the weeks we snorted a couple hundred dol-lars of coke; or when he smirked, not much but enough, because we were flying to the Caribbean while people starved, nations suffered and yea, the poor who are always with us really needed that cash, I wanted to tell him to fuck off. I made it, Jack, I spend it. I don't have to defend my life against your eyes and sainted dreams for forty acres with an old house and maybe a barn or two on it. I could have made more as a lawyer or helping Arnie sell pots. And where's the great virtue of being poor? Living on pizza in a fucking closet? Telling your-self you don't mind as time passes and dumbbell college friends move to Fifth Avenue, fly to Europe when they want, but until three months ago the only car you could afford was your old man's and the only money you could raise for a demo was begged from your grandpa?

No, I thought, there's nothing wrong with making money, with being successful. Money wasn't corrupt, success wasn't immoral. People were. You had to be careful, that's all. And my eyes were wide open.

But another voice, small, nasty and insistent, was with me as I looked out at the sunlight on the jet's silver wing. Danny's right, it said. Be careful. Give it away.

For a week Jenny and I had a wonderful time. We'd booked an excursion rate at one of the island's new hotels, and our terrace overlooked the Caribbean. We ate melon for breakfast, mangoes for lunch. In the afternoons, after returning from the beach, we'd shower, then oil each other for long massages. Leaving the air conditioner off, we'd make love in the still heat. Jenny danced nude. I sucked her twenty digits, kissed her in places the Pope and my rabbi wouldn't know names for. There were times, covered with a patina of oil, sweat and each other's sexual fluids, that we seemed to dissolve, how sweet it was, in a moist funk of the purely physical.

We fell in love again. After a few days we were tanned and able to relax, the winter's tension apparently behind us. We ate dinner downtown at Pepe's. Tequila, beer, *camarones*, fresh fruit, fresh fish and homemade coconut ice cream topped with Kahlúa. Afterward, we cruised the *zócalo* and the shopping streets. Jenny wore one of the simple, nearly sheer cotton dresses she'd bought, and her skin golden, her hair streaked with sun, Jenny turned heads. If I left her alone, I'd find her surrounded by Mexicans trying out the six English words they knew, or by a crowd of pubescent, black-haired boys whispering, "*Guapa, guapa.*"

Señoritas didn't follow me. But I was tanned, sexually charged; and one happy gringo, I trooped around in drawstring trousers and a Mexican wedding shirt. At night, doing the six miles between downtown and our hotel on a rented moped, both of us in white, the velvet Caribbean sky pricked with stars, Jenny's arms circling my waist, she'd put her lips to my ear. Usually she'd kiss it, nibble a little, but once she whispered, "Ain't we grand, Potts?" and began to laugh. "Ain't we grand?"

We returned from the beach one afternoon, from the white sand, azure sky, from the frozen threads of high clouds around the sun, to find our telephone's message light flashing. I rang the front desk. *Call home. Dad.*

"Don't." Jenny's skin shone with health, her eyes with worry.

"What if it's Ziggie?"

"I know, it's just—"

"I know."

Her eyes searched mine. "What can you do from here?"

"I can stop worrying."

I reached for the phone. Ten minutes later the call went through, and thousands of miles away, a modern miracle, I heard Ziggie.

"*Nu,* you're back?"

Heart racing, Jenny watching me, I said, "Are you okay?"

"Sure I'm okay." The line whistled; his voice came through angry, suspicious. "You're calling from Mexico, Stevie?"

"There was a message from Dad."

Ziggie cursed in Yiddish, then he said, "Your father, Mister Shit-for-brains."

"What happened?"

"Hershkoff died yesterday. Bum-bum, the heart. Tomorrow's the funeral."

I covered the mouthpiece, told Jenny, and her eyes swelled with tears.

"I'm sorry."

She nodded, walked to the window, and crying, her bathing suit sky blue, Jenny stared at the sea.

"Her brother called last night, asked when you'd be back."

"What time's the funeral?"

"Two. But what's going to change if you come, eh? Better to send flowers."

I looked at Jenny sobbing against the blue sky.

"Hug her for me, eh?"

"I will."

"Your father," Ziggie continued, "he probably thought he was doing the right thing."

"Sure. Good-bye, Ziggie." I almost hung up, then asked, "Hey, how's your eye?"

"Today, not so bad. Tomorrow, who knows?"

Chapter Nine

•

W E SENT FLOWERS, stayed another week, and Sol
   Hershkoff, one of the great names in the industry, a fine
man and "shining light," according to the *Times* obituary, was
laid into the ground with tears, sorrow and the love and
respect he deserved. We would miss him, more than we then
knew.

Five weeks later, the band was on the road. Opening night
—ta da!—in Poughkeepsie, New York's Last Chance Saloon.
Poughkeepsie, City of Sin.

Tour personnel, in addition to the core group, Rock, Anne
and sometimes Bobby, were as follows: Ethan would be road
manager, which meant he'd attend to the practical details of
getting us from point A to B and set up once we arrived. Ike
Thomas, sound. Tall, black, wickedly funny, he wore his hair
in a raked Afro like the black cop's on "The Mod Squad."
Steve Rankin, lights, was short, squint-eyed and generally
disagreeable. A twenty-four-year-old old pro, he'd been in the
business since he was sixteen and kept to himself except when
Bobby was around. Last and very least was Tony Two, Rosemarie's juvenile delinquent son, who at Jenny's insistence
we'd signed on as roadie and general roustabout, fulfilling her
earlier promise, a good deed.

In the dressing room of the ominously named Last Chance,
the whole band plus Anne minus Bird were smoking a number. *Wham-wham,* comes a rap at the door, which opened to

be immediately filled by Ethan's well-tanned puss, his long body.

"Show time in five, boys and girls."

Bird followed him in. He wore jeans, a blue Jenny Hall and Waterfall T-shirt. His eyes glowed. His elbows banged invisible walls.

"My man," he said to no one in particular. "There's a blonde in the first row who's going to improve my social life."

"Oh, yeah?" said Rock.

"I was onstage, you know?"

Bird was buzzed, wired, wacko, but no more than anyone else except Rock, who per usual seemed rocklike.

"I adjust the high-hat, look up and this little chick smiles. I smile and she licks her eyebrows."

Everyone laughed. Fucking Bird.

"Okay," said Ethan, "this is it."

He grinned his elegant grin. One cheek dimpled. I was so excited I almost liked him.

"Break a leg, huh?"

He kissed Jenny, who stood and hugged him. Dark eyes glittering, Anne kissed Danny, then me, Bird and Rock. They left and we had maybe two minutes.

"Fucking-A," Bird said. "Someone shoot me."

"Everyone know what we're playing?" asked Danny.

Greek humor. We'd rehearsed the opening set so much we didn't need a set list. I turned toward Jenny, who wore black skintight pants, a loose black silk blouse. Watching her, I thought, Wow, Jenny, and winked. Self-absorbed, she didn't notice. Her hands grasped the opposite arm's bicep; tugging them, she breathed deep, trying to relax her back muscles. A look almost of prayer sealed her features, and I moved to her side, kissed her cheek. Her eyes opened and Jenny smiled, threw her arms around me as Bird opened the dressing room door.

". . . proud to welcome Jenny Hall and Waterfall, whose

single, 'Waiting for Love,' you've been diggin' on the box. Jenny is Bobby Hall's younger sister, and Apex Records predicts great things. So we're glad they're here, while we can still afford them."

We began moving single file through the door, Bird first, Danny, Rock, Jenny last, me in front of her, Jenny holding my hand like an elephant holds its buddy's tail in a parade. We walked past Anne, past Ethan, past Tony Two, who with his dark brows, chipped tooth, weight-lifting muscles and black, wavy hair looked as hoodlumy as ever despite his beautiful, his magnificent Jenny Hall and Waterfall T-shirt.

"So without further ado"—and I thought, They all like ado, a fancy word for shit—"I give you Jenny Hall and Waterfall!"

My heart roaring in my ears, my chest, damn dumb hunter heart roaring, I followed Rock onto the black stage. I squeezed behind my right-angled keyboards, the house acoustic, my electric Rhodes. Bird settled behind his drums. The others strapped on guitars, played a few notes to make sure they hadn't gone out in the two hours since sound check.

Now, I thought, heart thumping, and looked toward Danny, set up front left. He nodded, caught the others' eyes and Bird began the count. Flash, flash, the tap of sticks. Fingers suspended over keys, trembling; my foot on the pedal, heart racing cool, now cool. Bird tapped one, two, three—and the stage exploded in color. I began the high runs, the cascading Waterfall intro, and Jenny, golden Jenny, burst into view. Playing, thinking yes, thinking yes, I watched her, her voice leaping the wall of sound.

> *"Many men have tried.*
> *They didn't understand."*

We were flying and gone.

We didn't play either set as well as we might have opening night. Still, we were okay or good enough, because the next night the club was sold out, word of mouth, and we were better.

I remember flashes, strong images from early in the tour of Jenny singing love songs. She'd often do these standing beside me at the piano. I see her singing in the follow spot's circle of light, smoke rising through that bright column, and beyond her the audience in seats or at tables, faces blurring in the distance like crowd faces in a Rembrandt. As she sang, her eyes for a moment all mine, I'd feel time stop, anyway stumble. Jenny sang, face in the light, and the smoke curling to the ceiling hung, suspended in the extraordinary energy that poured off her, proof of the talent Bobby worshiped, had lost and could never describe as well as I could see, feel, even touch in Jenny singing to me.

Then she'd stop, bow, and smoke would rise, second hands ticking, the world drawing breath.

After the second set Saturday, we returned triumphant to our motel, and having no gig the next night, began some serious partying. Bird had scored Friday night with Shelly, the little blonde who'd caught his eye by licking her eyebrows, and she'd returned on a free pass he'd given her. Bobby was up from the city, planning to spend the night in the band's extra room. Ah, the extra room. Officially, it was mine or Jenny's, provided for in our contract. But since we slept together, everyone thought of it as the band's party room. And it was there, Saturday night, that we consumed the case of champagne Bobby had brought with him.

Around three, the party got interesting. Sniff, sniff, the sweet smell of grass, the snort of toot; pop, pop, the roar of bubbly. I sat on one of the room's two beds, my arm around Jenny, and watched Bird do a snake-hipped shimmy with little Shelly. The Bird. Joyous, an animal spirit dancing in his life's spotlight, big nose and blond brows jabbing the air, scraping heaven. Lovely, fucking Bird.

The music changed. Aretha began singing "Respect," cour-

tesy of the FM radio Mr. Binders had inserted in each room's
bedside commode below the Magic Fingers coin box, two bits
for three minutes. A class act, Mr. Binder's place. Rock got up
to dance, cutting in on Bird. Jenny and I stood, me remembering the first night at Discovery. Sandwiched by the two beds,
we danced dodging bodies, engulfed in the weird happy vibes.

Beside us, Ethan danced with Anne. On the bed to my left,
the one farther from the door, Ike the sound man was kissing
a woman he'd picked up. Or maybe she'd picked him up.
Roxie or Doxie her name was. Ike's hand was down her pants.

On the other bed, the one we'd been sitting on, sourpussed
Rankin was snorting coke with Tony Two, who glowered at
me from under his adolescent brows, the little shit, while
managing at the same time to smile goofily at Jenny. On the
same bed but worlds apart, Bobby explained something to
Danny, who nodded, both of them grinning.

Amid all that lovely chaos, as Aretha sang, *"R E S P E C T,"*
I pulled Jenny to me, one hand palming each of her flat buttocks.

"Remember that first night at Discovery?"

She smiled, clasped my buns, and with my hands still pressing hers, we joined groins like Siamese twins. She arced her
back so that I could see her face, then shouted above the
tumult, "Who would have guessed?"

"Me. You were as good then as tonight."

"Ah, Potts."

Eyes closed, we kissed, grinding sure and slow against each
other, our beat a third as fast as Aretha's. I considered whispering, "Hey, babe, let's head for our place." Jenny tapped my
shoulder, pointed at Rock.

The big man was blasted. His eyes mirrored the room; his
bald dome shone like *la luna,* while Rock, the placid man,
did indecent things with Shelly the long-tongued girl. Hands
crooked behind his neck, Rock gyrated his beachball belly like
a dancing girl, like a snake with no bones, like a woman in-

side a pasha's tent with bells on her fingers and Arabian eyes. Except it was 220-pound Rock, the all-star session pro, bumping and grinding his amazing grace and girth to Aretha's beat, while little Shelly, who on tiptoes reached Rock's shoulders, danced like an island girl going under a limbo stick, as if her body also knew no bones or bounds. Back parallel to the floor, groin under his knees, she shook her breasts at his belly while her happy tongue traced circles on her cheeks, eyebrows, and once, as I watched, flitted up to his belt buckle.

Man, it was obscene.

Wild with joy, Bird clapped and whirled, flamenco-bird. Then the three of them danced a sandwich, hinting, I thought, at what might come later this wild and sexy night.

The song ended. Rock, Bird and Shelly bowed; everyone applauded. In the midst of the cry and tumult, my arms around Jenny, I glanced at Ike, who'd maneuvered both hands down Roxie or Doxie's pants. I watched her pink tongue disappear in his ear like a woodpecker's beak in a tree trunk and wondered if he was, so to speak, going to poke her right there. Lost in that and other fascinating ruminations, we all were, I didn't notice for eight bars that the song now searing the airwaves was our own, "Waiting for Love."

The realization broke over us like four tidal waves, two hurricanes and one bar mitzvah. Stunned, devout, we stood silently while the modern god Warhol Fame zapped us with his fifteen-minute blessing. Then Tony Two began to bounce up and down like a basketball. Suddenly we were screaming and cheering, playing·phantom guitars and ghostly keyboards. I hugged Jenny. We sang. Anne and Danny kissed. Rock, Bird and Shelly danced. On one bed, sitting near each other, Tony Two and Ethan ogled Jenny. Near them, Bobby grinned, just grinned. Then, as I watched, my eyes not believing it, Bobby, the great man, my hero, Bobby stood and smacked Rankin with a pillow. A free-for-all followed as Mr. Binder's radio played our song, people bouncing on one bed whacking each other silly, like kids at a sleep-over while on the other, Ike Thomas, a man of slight discretion but impressive concentration did, in fact, so to speak, begin to poke her.

Two weeks later, a Friday afternoon, Bird, Danny, Jenny, Anne and I were crisscrossing Whalley Avenue in New Haven, Connecticut, hustling from record counter to record counter hunting our album. Ponce de León, who'd searched for youth's waters in the Everglade swamps, was as close to home as we were. Wednesday, the album's official release day, had dawned and darkened without a single copy of *Love Is No Reason* lighting the sky anywhere near Albany, capital of the mighty Empire State and site of our Wednesday and Thursday gigs. The city also lacked illumination. Neither Bobby nor my parents had turned up a one. Not at The Record Hunter on Fifth Avenue. Not in the Village. Not at any of the suburban malls where Arnie was buddies with the owners of Sam Goody outlets. *Nada*, zilch, goose-eggs.

And Streit and Parker, nasty scumbags who'd never liked him, and the feeling, Bobby allowed, was mutual; toads, tone-deaf accountant frogs who'd cheered loudest at Hershkoff's dinner, then humped hardest to replace him the morning after he died—when we spoke to him Wednesday and again Thursday night, Bobby said Streit and Parker, who now split Hershkoff's job, weren't returning his calls.

"Their secretaries say it's nothing, a small delay. Distribution said the same. So maybe it's nothing. But maybe . . ." His voice had trailed off into The Big Banana, The Great Nightmare. "Hey," his voice had come back, airy, paranoid, "how's the road treating ya?"

The road, I thought, as the combined forces of truth and justice ducked into Cutler's, the road had been treating us fine. We'd drawn well, primarily because Apex had spent advance bucks to ease the way. Radio spots, ticket giveaways and club posters plastered to every telephone pole and tree more than four inches in diameter had produced crowds in Poughkeepsie, New Paltz, Kingston, Woodstock and Albany. Local interviews had been arranged. DJs had been contacted, stroked, maybe bullshitted, and the day we were in town, "Waiting for Love" got airplay.

Local rock critics, whose sterling prose we digested over 2 P.M. breakfasts in silver-sided diners run, we hoped, by Greeks, who were not only Danny's people but the world's best short-order cooks—the reviewers were kind, at times loving.

They focused on Jenny. And *beautiful, dazzling, sexy, great pipes, huzzah-huzzah, wonka, wonka,* nothing was too fine for the talented younger sister of Bobby Hall. But the Albany writer also noted, and I quote, "The high quality of the original material, without being derivative, brings to mind the groundbreaking early work of Fleetwood Mac."

The review in the *Poughkeepsie Journal,* brought to our New Paltz gig by the Poughkeepsie writer himself, a kind and thoughtful dude whose eyes looked in different directions, said in part that "Waterfall's technical excellence, highlighted by veteran Rock Isaacson's guitar solos and Danny Grabonus's intricate mastery of the bass electrified and delighted a packed house Saturday night at the Last Chance." He urged his readers to "Look for *Love Is No Reason* when it appears in record stores. A Can't Miss!"

Well, Lord, we were looking and missing. Inside Cutler's we mounted a well-organized search. Danny, Bird and Jenny swarmed the new-release bins. With Anne looking over my shoulder, I flipped through Cutler's rock albums by artist, *J,* I tried. Flip, flip, flip. I tried *H.* Hall and Oates, Hendrix, shit. Moving several files to my right, I checked *W* for Waterfall, and the shrink-wrapped albums slipped through my fingers like money badly spent. When I looked up, Anne, leggy and slender, already knew. Her large eyes were level with mine and dark hair fell past her cheeks to the puffed shoulders of a fawn-colored silk blouse, an Annie blouse.

"Not yet."

Eyes locked in mine, whispering, she asked, "What's wrong?"

I shrugged, and she said, "Danny told me albums are always out a week before their release date. Is that true?"

I nodded, wondered why she was asking in such a tense whisper. Okay, if we hadn't been with our present lovers, I would have asked Anne to bed months ago and she would have come. But that was old news. And still watching Annie's eyes, these thoughts leaping more rapidly to mind than I could sort them, I understood. The more serious problem, much worse than the heat we generated between each other's knees and navels, was that quick, verbal Annie couldn't discuss the band with Danny. The band meant Jenny, who we all assumed was off limits for her. Danny was sweet and quiet, a technical genius, but as Bird had pointed out, a serious crank. Discussing something he didn't want to; well, the category didn't exist.

"Look," I said finally, though it hadn't been very long, "radio stations have their comps, and the tour is costing Apex ten grand a week."

"So?"

"So why should anything be wrong?"

Annie didn't answer. Not because either of us believed what I'd just said, but because a) we were scared, and b) Bird was throwing a scene in front of the store.

"My man," he boomed at the bespectacled, bearded store manager who sat behind the elevated front desk and looked as if he were more accustomed to answering questions about new releases of *Don Giovanni* and Chopin's *Nocturnes,* than fielding hot grounders from a big-nosed, slightly berserk drummer.

"My man." Bird indicated his retinue. "*We* are Jenny Hall

and Waterfall. *She*"—he pointed—"is the beauteous, the mul-titalented Jenny Hall." Bird paused. "What's your name?"

"Robert Townley—" he hesitated, "the third."

"Townley," Bird said. "We are hot novae bursting into rock's super heavens."

Townley seemed to realize Bird wasn't dangerous and relaxed a little. "I've seen your posters."

"So where's our album? Do you realize how many sales you'll lose? The wild excitement with which young fans are going to burst in here tomorrow? And they're going to blame you, Number Three. Your future's in jeopardy."

Townley was suddenly all business. "What's the label?"

"Apex," said Jenny.

Townley opened drawers, flipped through binders. "It was due last week. It's not out?"

I looked at Anne, who looked back at me.

"No," said Bird.

"One minute."

He picked up a phone; the intercom buzzed in back. Townley said, "You're right, it's not in."

"For once," said Bird, "I wouldn't mind being wrong."

He picked up another phone, Townley did, cold efficiency now, his neat beard and glasses reflecting fluorescent light.

"I'm calling my distributor," he said, his voice urbane, very sophisticated, edged with the right amount of a stranger's concern. "I understand how upset you must be."

A short conversation followed, on Townley's end something like, "Uh-huh, uh-huh," then a couple "I see"'s. The second "I see" sounded like death and all of us—Anne and I had joined the others in front of the store—avoided each other's eyes. Townley hung up.

"My distributor says, and he got this from an Apex rep—who is not precisely a bedrock source, I know the man, he drinks; nevertheless—there's a problem. Your record will be available"—Townley hesitated, and his eyes narrowed behind his bifocals—"but not until late next week or the week after. I'm sorry."

"You're sorry," Bird said. "Oh, shit."

I took Jenny's hand in both of mine. She looked up as Danny said, "Thanks for your trouble," followed by Bird's relatively lifeless "Yeah, Three, you're number one with me."

What was in Jenny's eyes, as we stood in the shadow of no time passing, wasn't outrage or anger. That would come later for all of us. What I saw, what I imagine was painted on all our faces was shock, animal terror, fear of darkness.

We shuffled out of Cutler's into the bright afternoon, managed to cross Broadway without being run down. Dead-eyed, we trooped back to our motel and called Bobby. Bobby said hang loose, he'd buzz Apex, threaten lawsuits and/or letter bombs, our choice, and get back. Which was why, a half hour later when the phone rang in the band's extra room, we assumed it was Bobby. Instead, hand covering the receiver, Jenny whispered, "Streit, from Apex."

Leaning on the chest of drawers/desk combo, the back of her head reflected in the mirror, the rest of us sitting on beds facing her, Jenny listened. Then she said, "Of course, we're upset. We were told it would be out. And we've been telling—"

To keep calm, I tried remembering what Streit looked like. I was pretty sure he was my height, paunchy, fortyish, with dark hair. The night of Hershkoff's dinner, he'd worn a three-piece serge suit when he told me, as we stood shoulder to shoulder in front of urinals, how much Sol loved the album, and how happy he, Streit, was that they were doing it.

Or maybe that was Parker. I hadn't paid attention, none of us had, to anyone except Sol.

"I understand," Jenny said. "But shit, we're only out another five weeks."

Gobble erupted from the other end of the line. Jenny rolled her eyes.

The First Time I Saw Jenny Hall

"I understand." Her eyes had taken on the enraged, boil-over glare which meant something untoward was liable to happen. "But why the fuck didn't you tell us, you must have known a week—"

Streit obviously disapproved of Anglo-Saxonisms. Jenny shot back, "I know who I'm talking to, a fat, stupid—"

Not a moment too soon, Ethan grabbed the phone, cupping the mouthpiece as Jenny finished, screaming "bastard." And enraged, around the bend which is past the last house on the psyche's meanest street, she tried to pull Ethan's hand off the phone, screaming, "Bastard, you're a lying bastard, Streit, you hear me?"

Ethan hid the phone behind his back. Looking straight at me, he wailed, "For Chrissakes!"

Not knowing what else to do, my pulse at 190, then 250, I lifted Jenny, kicking and screaming, off the floor. With every-one else watching, I mean, riveted, I dragged her away from Ethan, catching an elbow in the ribs, as Ethan finessed the phone to his mouth, saying, "Mr. Streit, this is Ethan Marks."

To no one's surprise, the line was dead.

Ethan reached Streit an hour later, and calm men of busi-ness, they discussed the matter calmly. Ethan promised we'd play that night, assuring Streit that Bobby, who'd implied otherwise, had spoken out of love for his sister.

Streit, harrumphing and making it clear, Ethan said later, that he'd never had much use for prima donnas, Streit read Ethan the riot act. We were to understand that following Sol's death and the end of his thirty-year reign, Apex was reevaluat-ing priorities in the face of changing musical tastes. While he neither liked our music as well as Sol had nor thought it on target in terms of where the market was headed, nonetheless, he, Streit, would see to it that the first available copies of *Love Is No Reason* were drop-shipped to retailers in our tour cities.

He apologized for the unavoidable delay, but stressed, and asked Ethan to stress, which Ethan did stress over our evening meal, a stressful 7 P.M. delight in the private room of an Indian restaurant where the walls and ceiling were hung with pink and green Indian sheets, that Apex was under no contractual obligation to release the album during the tour. Rather, they'd agreed to release two sides and an album within twelve months, nothing more, nothing less.

Finally, Streit announced that egotism, pure and simple, was our problem. Tour availability of the album would not significantly affect sales, and while he encouraged self-respect in his artists, he hoped Jenny would calm down, see that she'd over-reacted and get back to him.

"Are you saying," Jenny asked in the candlelit room, which smelled distinctly of jasmine incense, "that that lying shit of an accountant expects me to apologize?"

Ethan smiled and dropped his right hand over Jenny's left. "I'm afraid so." He gazed into her pale blues as if playing a seduction scene, and I wanted to choke the bastard. "As your manager, I think you should."

Jenny chewed her lip. She turned toward me in the candle-light, seemingly unaware that she was sitting in front of every-one with Ethan fondling her knuckles.

"What do you think?"

I thought she should take her hand out from under Ethan's.

"I think Streit wants you to suck up to prove to himself how important he—"

Before I could finish, Jenny fired back, "Maybe I should blow him."

Bird said, "Depends if you're any good. Why don't you try this here carrot?"

"What pisses me off," Jenny continued, her hand no longer under Ethan's, but that was small consolation, "is you're mad at me. Like it's my fault the album isn't out and that pig lied.

'If Jenny hadn't told him off, things would be better.' That's what you're thinking, isn't it?"

Jenny looked around the table. Then her eyes came back to me.

"I can't tell you how mad that makes me. I haven't heard word one of fucking support."

I couldn't get my breath. Then I could. "For Chrissakes, Jenny."

I grabbed her wrist as she was standing up; she pulled away.

"Leave me alone. Just leave me alone."

Rock stood at the head of the table. Eyes wide beneath his bald dome, which almost reached the low, sheeted ceiling, he said, "Sit down, Jenny."

She sat.

"I'm not trying to be inspirational, but it's important to play well tonight. Not only because I dig the music, which is all that matters anyway, but for rat-turd practical reasons, too." Rock lifted his water glass, sipped it slowly. "I fear you're about to be royally fucked over."

"No shit," shouted Tony Two from the room's far right corner. I glared at him; he glared back.

"Not because the record isn't out, but why it isn't."

"You think they're killing it," said Danny.

I turned toward Danny, sitting next to Rock, Anne next to him. Her eyes met mine. Rock nodded.

"What about our contract?" Jenny asked.

"If they don't release the album, go sue them. You got fifty thousand and two years?"

No one spoke.

"What usually happens is you have to beg them to sell you the masters, then peddle them to another label."

"But why?" Bird said. "I mean—"

"Just suppose Streit and Parker are paranoid assholes. They're unsure of their own taste and want to consolidate their new power. And just suppose, it's reasonable, right, they resented working in an old man's shadow. That dinner, we didn't give them the time of day."

Rock rubbed the back of his neck with one large hand, lifted the water glass to his lips with the other.

"We were Sol's last big project," I said. "So fuck us over."

Our waiter, a thin, polite Indian who looked like a graduate student in the physical sciences, glided into the room and asked if there was anything we needed.

"An ounce of coke," Bird said.

"Sir?"

"Just the bill," said Ethan.

I tapped Jenny's shoulder. "How're you doing?"

"How do you think?"

"This is happening to all of us."

She didn't answer, but I hoped that had hit home. The waiter returned with the bill on a black plastic tray, discreetly set it in front of Ethan, who covered it with the band's credit card.

Rock stood up again. "If I'm right about Streit and Parker, our best shot is to play the hell out of these gigs and get good reviews. That way, if nothing happens with the album, they'll look bad."

There was a rumble of voices around the table, a blend and blur of opinions rising with the jasmine. I heard Danny ask, "What else can we do?"

Tony Two growled, "I'll kill the fucker. I'll put a bomb up his ass."

Then Jenny, no longer angry, but desperate, near tears, Jenny said, "You really think they won't release the album? It's not fair."

"Oh, sweetheart," said Rock, "where have you been?"

Dreaming, I thought, and glanced from worried face to worried face. Even Bird looked scared.

"But hey," Rock added gently. "You're right, it's not fair."

The First Time I Saw Jenny Hall

*   *   *

We were hot that night. Ditto the next night in Framingham, and at the two Boston gigs. In Cambridge and Portsmouth we continued to smoke, scorched-earth, rock-and-roll guerrillas. Depending on whether or not it was a travel day, the morning after a gig we'd get up between eleven and two, eat breakfast, smoke a little dope, blow some coke, whatever. If we'd traveled, we'd set up and finish sound check by seven, then eat and dress for the show.

In the afternoons we talked about our lives and musicians we'd known. Ethan had a kid sister, fifteen years old, who was a ballerina in Balanchine's company. Bird admitted to spending a year at Tufts before dropping out to be a full-time drummer. Rock told stories, when pressed, about the old days. Dylan and Baez, how hot they'd been for each other; how he, Rock, had once walked in on them. He explained Dylan had treated her badly at the end, not because he didn't love her, but because he loved his own ego more.

Tony Two told Jenny, who told me, how much he hated his father. That for years he'd lifted weights, dreaming of becoming tough enough to get even with him for beating up on Rosemarie. But he would never be tough enough, Jenny believed. Under the hood exterior Tony was a sweet boy who wanted to be loved. Her heart, she said, went out to him.

Great. That same conversation, over a very late breakfast, Jenny told me about the golden days in the Hall household. Bobby still lived at home, her mom was healthy, and every Sunday morning, the family sang together on the screened-in porch. Her mother played the piano, Bobby the guitar, and Jenny sat beside Mom on the piano bench, turning pages for her, dreaming, but never believing that someday her voice would be as good as Mom's. May Hall. Her name was May, Jenny told me, and she was beautiful. Mom was so very beautiful.

But I was too far gone; nothing touched me. Until we went

on I remained numb. Not nervous or wired, not even keyed. Numb. Then we'd hit the stage, the lights would come up and wham. We'd play our asses off. We began doing monster shows, everything we knew, two hour-and-a-half sets. Manic, lost in the music, in the here and now. Released for as long as we played from having to consider what was really happening to us.

The day after the Portsmouth gig, Jenny and I were sprawled across our bed in the Abraham Lincoln Holiday Inn in Washington, D.C. Dazed, spaced and generally sore-boned from nine hours in the van, we were sneaking a half hour's nap. It was six-fifteen, and we'd arranged to be at the club by seven for sound check.

The night before we'd partied too late, then got stuck in Boston's morning rush hour. Entering D.C. at five o'clock, we'd snarled in rush hour again. In between, we'd battled trucks on I-95. Our vans, Spock and the Enterprise, which Danny had shopped for, Danny who was generally against extravagance and specifically trying to save money for that farm, our vans were solid and serviceable, little more. Air conditioning, not a chance. Shocks and springs, *eh*. Bumping south on the Jersey pike, the windows open because it was 95 and sunny, I found myself in the back seat between Ethan and Jenny. Tony Two sat in front, and horror of horrors, Bird was driving.

Truck exhaust poured through the open windows. On either side of us eighteen-wheel semis belched smoke, roaring like poppa lions, like momma snakes, striking terror in my wussy, automotive-phobic soul, the silver-bodied trucks squeezing us as if they were bookends and we were the book, until I thought my head would pop and I wanted to scream.

I pressed Jenny's hand, which she squeezed until my knuckles cracked. We rolled on in our valley of van between mountains of snarling semis, last night's four hours of sleep pressing against my eyeballs, when suddenly—it seemed to happen all at once—Bird turned to say something, we swerved left, Tony grabbed the wheel, the truck's air brakes squealed, Bird's eyes widened, he faced front and I hugged Jenny, thinking, We're going to die.

Ha. The truck veered left, and with Tony's help Bird missed it. A few miles down the road, everyone's stomachs still churning, Bird pulled into a rest area and Tony took over.

Staring at the blank ceiling above us, my arm around Jenny, whose cheek and forehead rested on my shoulder, I felt like I used to after a day's ocean fishing. My eyes burned and a curtain of brown haze hung between me and the world. When I closed my eyes the curtain went up and everything moved. Not as if the boat were rocking, but as if I still rode in the damn van, asphalt running beneath us, exhaust burning my throat, the sun cooking my mind.

I opened my eyes, acknowledged I no longer thought the record would be released while we were on tour. I didn't think it would be released afterward, either. Not in its present form and not by Apex. No copies had reached New England tour cities, and follow-up conversations with Streit and Parker got so nasty the Apex switchboard wouldn't put calls through from anyone except Ethan, who, if nothing else, could be counted on for charm and discretion.

I didn't know what to think and tried not to. No record. No fucking record. But if I didn't think the record would be released, I had to believe it would be. Otherwise, I couldn't have kept playing as well as I had been, no one could. Or so I'd decided while I waited for that semi to kill me.

Lying in bed in the half-dark, the brown gauze of burnout covering us, I was afraid to think about the future. We had three and a half weeks of long-haul touring left. South as far as Atlanta, then west to Chicago before returning east for the big dates opening for Laser Light, Apex's answer to Kiss, at the Syracuse Coliseum before finishing up at the Bottom Line in the city.

And who knew, who really knew? Late last night, lying in
bed in a different town, a different motel, Jenny had said,
"What's going to happen to us, babe?"

"The fame and fortune kids, right?"

"I'll tell you one thing," Jenny answered, her chin on my
shoulder as it was now. "They're not going to fuck me over.
I won't let them."

"What are you going to do?"

"I'm just not."

And feeling chilled, the air conditioner set on super cool,
I'd hugged her against me. As I did again, and felt her move.
Saw her lashes flutter, her mouth forming a full moon, a moan
escaping, her body tensing, then relaxing against me.

"Where, what time is it?"

"Still early."

"Tell me."

"Six-thirty."

She nodded. Her eyes opened and we were back on the
track of our shared obsessions.

"What are we going to do?"

"What do you mean?"

"If things get worse."

"Let's not think about it."

"I want it so bad," she said, and her eyes were suddenly
intense, shining, aglow. "Is that corrupt, am I horrible?"

"No."

"I want it so bad."

I hugged her for all I was worth.

Chapter Ten

·

THAT NIGHT, for the first time, the club we played was half empty. And none of us had heard radio spots, "Waiting for Love," or seen club posters tacked to telephone poles when we walked around Georgetown after sound check.

"They're pulling the plug," Rock said to Ethan between sets. Eavesdropping, I thought, Oh, God.

"They can't welsh on club guarantees," Rock added more loudly because he'd realized I was listening, "but they're stopping advance work."

"And no push," Ethan said, his handsome face rising hard, tanned and angular from his open shirt, "no reviews."

"Streit and Parker," Rock said, "are covering their paranoid assholes."

Oh, God.

Around midnight, second set, Jenny stepped to the mike to introduce "Waiting for Love." During the tour her outfits had been getting wilder. This one, a one-piece turquoise jumpsuit tight at the ass, belted at the waist, unzipped far enough to show the top of her breasts and a little bit more, was a real doozy. Her hair, from where I sat in the right rear of the stage behind my Rhodes, glowed red in the lights. There were maybe fifty people in the club, which could have held two hundred.

"This next song, 'Waiting for Love,' is our hit single."

She paused. I could hear the audience laughing, buzzing, chinking ice.

"Would you believe, near-miss single? Maybe you've been digging it on the radio."

"No," someone shouted at a table of men up close, their faces blurred by the lights. "But I'm digging you."

Laughter from his fellow clowns. None from Jenny, who turned, signaled me to start the intro. I did, high cascading sixteenth notes best done on a sequencer, but my poor mortal fingers would do the trick. G over C, G over C, G over C, G over C. D over E, D over E, D over E, D over E. The others came in, swelling bass and drums, the screech of Rock's guitar as he hit the analog delay, Jenny doubling Rock's sustained chord as she stepped to the mike.

> *"Many men have tried.*
> *They didn't understand.*
> *Stare into my eyes."*

Jenny hesitated slightly, drew breath as the melody rose to the top of her range, sang, "Swear they were my man!"

A short break built to Jenny's high "Waiting," which Bird, Danny and I answered in still higher harmonies, "Wait-ting," both lines following the sixteenth-note motif of the intro.

> *"Still waiting for love,*
> *Aching, shaking."*

Jenny's voice was almost a sexual moan now, "Still waiting for love."

We slid back to the verse. The pigs at the front table shouted, "Waiting for you, too, baby. Waiting right here."

It happened all the time. They were putzes, but I hardly blamed them. A beautiful pixie blonde shook her tits, claiming she was waiting for love, in fact, aching for it, they were supposed to react. And they did, all the time. Animals shouted and bayed. Classier guys sent flowers with notes asking her to meet them.

Sex appeal, I thought, fingers hardly feeling the keys, my mind light-years away, wondering what was going to happen to us. An empty house, an empty fucking house. And me out there in it watching Jenny, always Jenny, Potts with the yahoos, who were shouting again. Putzes, I thought, but I could deal with them, as Jenny finished, "Any way the wind blows / still waiting for love."

I began the rippling sixteenths of the chorus, Jenny singing, "Waiting," me, Bird and Danny answering, "Wait-ting," but my mind was elsewhere, wondering, What the fuck are we doing here? But even in outer space, I knew something was wrong. The sex vibes were fouler than usual. Tony Two, I thought, must be having trouble. He was always rushing around backstage threatening to waste someone for looking at her wrong, for shouting dirt, though how to define wrong, given Jenny's outfits and body language, my line coming up again, "Wait-ting," wasn't easy.

But the kid seemed to know, his hood's sense of high honor getting a workout every time we played, his dark brows flushing red. As it must be now, I thought, watching Jenny move her pelvis closer to the stand, cupping the mike with both hands, singing,

> *"Shaking, aching,*
> *Still waiting for love."*

Right then, the tall, dark-haired head yahoo stood up shouting, "I'm aching right here, Jenny," and grabbed his pecker.

I missed what happened next because we were starting a break and I needed to concentrate. The next thing I knew, the yahoo was onstage. Jenny didn't know what to do. She was supposed to sing, but between her and the mike, there was a big, dark-haired drunk in a cowboy shirt grinning and pawing at her.

No one knew what to do. The band kept playing. Bird shouted to the wings, "A bouncer, get a bouncer," while in the middle of the music there was a horrible silence where

Jenny's voice should have been. Suddenly, moving so quickly his limbs blurred, someone I knew had to be Tony Two raced out from backstage. Purple and red spots making him look like an avenging devil, the band still playing, Jenny frozen, not drawing back, frozen, Tony launched himself into the yahoo's gut. The putz's eyes bulged. His mouth opened like a fish's sucking air, then they went down with a boom, Tony on top, fists whirling.

Madness, insanity. In a daze I ran forward to hustle Jenny offstage, but she'd come to life, had already escaped. Front and center Tony was making hamburger of the yahoo's face. Rock was trying to pull him off. Some fool punched Rock in the side of the head, and the placid man lifted the fucker and threw him offstage. Then all the asshole's friends stormed the stage to prove their manhood. From the corner of my eye I saw Bird tackle one who was trying to kick in his bass drum. A blond guy with a fat gut and Bud on his breath materialized in front of me. Oh, God, I thought. What I said was "This is crazy, come on," which is when he hit me in the mouth.

He tried to hit me again, and really out of self-defense I ducked, wrestled the dipshit to the floor, thinking, Someone better call the police, that fucking Tony, but first I'm gonna kill this idiot. And rolling in the dust and my own blood, I forgot how badly the tour was going and hit the turd more than he hit me, bouncing his head on the stage as if it were a bowling ball zipping down the alley of life.

Ten minutes later the cops showed and took the asshole contingent away. I wanted them to take Tony Two, but no such luck. Instead, back at the Holiday Inn, me, Rock and Bird nursing war wounds, the most serious being swollen fingers on Bird's right hand, I listened to the little thug brag.

"Hey," I said, taking the bag of ice off my lip. "You could have led him offstage."

Seated on the next bed, Tony turned. He didn't like me. Maybe I represented his father, and by defending Jenny he felt he was finally being a good son and standing up for Rose-marie. Fine, but leave me out of it. His left eye was swollen, but tough boy, he tried to squint at me anyway. The whole bit, taken with his muscular neck, broken tooth and see-through adolescent moustache, gave his face a kind of comic, froggy look.

"He was touching Jenny."

Jenny sat at the window end of the room near a small coffee table, talking softly and laughing with Danny. Anne had gone home. To Tony, Jenny with her red-blond hair and small freckled nose must have looked like a demigoddess, a woman from another dimension, which was how she looked to me at times, Brooklyn Italian and Brooklyn Jew, after all, being first cousins once removed.

Bird said, "Listen, Sparky—"

"Whaddya mean, Sparky?"

Bird grinned. He was sitting beside me, soaking his knuckles in a bucket of ice. "Sparky, like spark plug. Means you got a temper."

Tony made the frog face. "Sparky, I like it."

Bird removed his hand from the ice, dried it on a towel. "Next time, just get him offstage. No tickee, no hittee."

"The creep was grabbing Jenny."

"I don't care what he was doing," I said. "The next time you beat up on someone, it's your ass. This is just what Streit and Parker want."

For a second Tony glared at me with pure, straight-out hate in his eyes. Then, from across the room Jenny called, "Leave him alone, Tony's my hero," and the kid's anger went underground.

Jenny stood, came toward us and kissed Tony's cheek, repeating in falsetto, "My hero."

The little shit grinned at me, the left side of his face puffy and the same color as an eggplant.

"But Steve's right, no more fighting. Still"—she smiled at

me—"it's nice to know someone will defend your virtue."
She began to laugh.

An hour later, lying crosswise on the bed in Bird's room,
staring up at the ceiling and speaking to no one in particular,
Danny said, "What scares me is that after compromising the
ideals that got me out of the city in the first place—"

"What ideals, ya fucking Greek?"

Bird also lay back down on the bed. Seeking solace in the
same ceiling, I lay on the floor below them, just the three of
us in the room.

"I'd only play music I really liked. Like I wouldn't do bullshit for money."

"You and everyone else."

In his soft, almost sultry voice Danny said, "Okay."

"Then why did you?"

"Because I thought—" Danny paused. "You know why."

Lying on the floor, I thought, They've forgotten I'm here.

Bird said, "What about it? Besides, the music's turned out—"

"Will you cool it? What I'm trying to say is after compromising my ideals, and ideals change, I see that, I'm afraid I'm
gonna fall flat on my compromised Greek ass. What I really
mind isn't the compromise or the fall, but how it's happening.
The band and the music deserve better."

"Thanks," I said.

"What do you mean, thanks?" said Bird. "It's not just your
music, Needle-nose."

"Thanks, you don't understand thanks?"

"Potts, my man, Jenny's calling you. Why don't you crawl
home?"

I stood groggily. My eyes met Danny's, who said, "I should
go, too."

"Sure, abandon me. What do those hussies have I don't?"

Bird grinned, walked us to the door. "Potts," he said.

"Lighten up on Sparky. Either that, or we really should fire his ass."

"*Sparky.*" I laughed. "The problem's not Sparky."

Bird nodded, then Danny and I were alone in the hall. From behind closed doors I could hear televisions, soft laughter. In the few seconds we'd have together, I felt I should say something, but didn't know what. We crossed the corridor. Digging for our keys, I looked into Danny's eyes, at his black ponytail falling down his back like braided rope. With his high cheeks and straight hair, he almost looked Indian.

"You want to smoke a joint?"

Danny's forehead was smooth, but around his eyes, which were the color of bittersweet chocolate, there were fine lines. He nodded, put his key away, and we walked two doors down the hall to 122, the band room, for which I also had a key. There might be someone inside fucking, I thought, Rankin or Ike, who was proving prodigious in such matters, and I hesitated before turning on the light, listening for the sibilance of skin and sheet.

The room was empty and Danny followed me in, sat at the desk, rolled a joint from the Baggie of tops he carried in his shirt pocket. The joint he passed me was a work of art. In ten years of smoking, I had never rolled its equal. Round, smooth and tight, a master joint. Danny was a master joint-roller. Danny, in fact, had mastered everything he did. There weren't many categories, okay, but he was master of them all.

He patted his pockets, reached for the Holiday Inn matches in the desktop ashtray. He studied the cover, struck a match and held out the flame.

"Weird, huh?"

Inhaling, I nodded. So much was weird.

"The whole Holiday Inn trip," he added, reaching for the joint. "Jenny and I were in Mexico once, and visited these rich Mexican friends of hers. We sat around smoking while their servants fed us cheese, dinner, then coffee and dessert. And the whole time we're getting more and more fucked up. Being served while smoking pot, that bent my mind. There was this one Indian girl wearing a white uniform, maybe she was sixteen. The whole night she never smiled once. Just kept serving us while we laughed our asses off." Danny passed the joint. "That was weird, too."

"But not as weird as this?"

The wrinkles edging Danny's eyes seemed to multiply. "This," he said, "is dislocating."

After that we passed the joint back and forth in silence until I said, "Which this? Holiday Inns, how they're fucking us over, or me, not you, sleeping with Jenny?"

Danny pinched what was left of the joint between his thumb and second finger, raised the roach to his lips. "What do *you* think?" He passed the roach.

"What about Anne?"

I inhaled, briefly wondered, my imagination stoned, crazy, tingling, if we should exchange keys, what the women would think if we did.

"What about her?" He took the roach.

"Do you love her?"

"Do you love Jenny?"

"Isn't it obvious?"

Instead of answering, he sat motionless with the roach between his fingers. Then he said, "Enough to keep her together when this blows up? They're never going to release that album."

"Who says?"

"Think about it."

"I have. I agree."

We stared at each other, then Danny said, "I don't think you love her enough."

"I say I do." I looked into his eyes again, which were almost black and, I noticed for the first time, too close together. "I sure hope so. I'm being honest. I hope so."

"But you don't. And I'll tell you something else. I do. Or I did." He tried to toke the roach, but it was out. "I still do," he added, "but it doesn't make any difference."

"Because of me?"

He shook his head.

"Anne?"

He shook his head again. "Because of Jenny. When this crap is done, I'm going to make a life in the country, but Jenny can't. She's changed, and she's the one who's going to get hurt."

You poor bastard, I thought. "You're crazy."

Danny stood up. "Sure. But when the shit hits the fan, you're going to decide we're all adults, and cover your own ass."

I stood up next to him. "You know what? You're a shit to Annie."

"Leave her out of this."

"Fine."

I was upset, but I could see I wasn't nearly as upset as Danny.

"You know what else? You think you really love her. And you may be as faithful as Rin Tin Tin and Tonto. But when it comes to Jenny you don't know your asshole from a light socket."

I thought he was going to hit me. Then he grinned.

"Neither do you."

Rankin quit us in the morning. Our best guess was he called Apex, told them he wasn't going on and they said fine. Or maybe Streit contacted him and offered to buy out his contract. All anyone knew for sure was the morning after the fight, Rankin told Ethan he was jetting to L.A. That afternoon, Old Sourpuss was gone.

I didn't like Rankin, no one did, and normally I would have been glad to see him go. At the Syracuse Coliseum, one of Laser Light's techies could do our board. The rest of our gigs, the clubs were small enough and our lighting sufficiently simple that the house man or Sparky could do it. It might keep the kid out of trouble, too.

But coming when it did, Rankin's desertion hurt; and driving south out of D.C., Jenny and I, everyone, really, was pretty down. We stayed down, playing half-empty clubs in Richmond and Chapel Hill, gigs that had been set up to give us something to do en route to Atlanta.

Not only were we down, we weren't getting along. After talking, Danny and I understood each other better, but we liked each other a lot less. I never mentioned our talk to Jenny, I'm sure Danny didn't discuss it with Anne, but somehow, everyone knew. Sunday morning (actually it was twelve-thirty, but after a gig, before 2 P.M. was considered morning), I left Jenny sleeping—she'd been out late drinking with some of the others—and went down to our motel's coffee shop. At a corner booth, as far as possible from the windows on the opposite wall, Rock and Bird were finishing breakfast.

"Hey, hotshot," Bird said when I joined them, "where's the star?"

"Still sleeping." I grinned, opened the menu. "She was out till four and puking till five."

Rock looked up from his eggs and home fries, his mouth full. Under their awning of brown brow and bare skin, his eyes looked enormous and judgmental. I read the menu. Last night was a blur. For the first time since we started touring, God, it was almost a month, we'd stunk up the stage. The first set was the kind of disaster all bands endure at one time or another. All night I'd told myself it wasn't remarkable it had happened, but that it had taken so long.

"How's breakfast?"

"Corporate home fries," said Rock.

I eyed his food. A sodden wad of chopped and pressed potatoes lay beneath prison bars of ketchup.

"Order french," Bird said. "I had five thousand, three hundred fifteen through thirty. Yours will make five, three, four, five."

Bird was keeping track of fries the band ate. Early on he'd predicted we'd hit ten thousand. Now that it looked as if we were going to fall a few thousand short, he ate them every meal, accused us of eating them on the sly or avoiding them just to prove him wrong.

A redheaded girl in a white dress stopped in front of our booth, waving a glass coffeepot. I turned my cup over. She filled it and when I thanked her she flashed me a smile which proclaimed the world was bright and beautiful. She topped off Bird and Rock's cups, replaced the pot on a warmer, pert buttocks slapping the inside of her white, cross-ribbed dress. We were all watching so intently no one realized Anne had entered the coffee shop until she arrived in front of our booth, squeezed in next to Rock. The waitress returned, pad in hand.

"Do y'all want more time?"

"Give me all you got," Bird said.

"I was talking to the lady."

"Coffee and English muffin," said Anne.

"Eggs over easy. Bacon, french fries and whole-wheat toast."

"Good man," Bird said, as the waitress jotted down the order, retrieved the coffeepot and filled Annie's cup.

"Little girl," said Bird, "anyone ever tell you your hind parts would make a dead man sit up and smile?"

"Not like that." She grinned and walked off.

"Ah," Bird said loudly, "sweet bird of youth," and the girl, knowing she was being watched, shook her bottom at him. Bird sighed, then said, "Where's the Greek?"

Anne lit a Merit from the pack she always seemed to carry.

"In bed, hung over." She pinched the cigarette between her thumb and index finger. "When did the party break up?"

I sipped my coffee. "Different parties, different times."

Anne looked at me, kept quiet, her eyes ringed with mascara and purple shadow: Annie maintained standards, even in the A.M.

After a nervous silence, Rock sitting rocklike in the corner, Annie chainsmoking, Bird drumming his fingers, me drinking coffee, Bird said, "Assuming the drunks can mobilize, let's leave at three."

"If they can't," Rock said, "one van goes ahead. For once, I want to get in before midnight."

"You're showing your age," Bird said. "Rock Isaacson, legendary fuddy-duddy."

Rock grunted. A minute later he excused himself. I found myself staring at Anne's dark eyes, at her long face. My breath began to catch. I wanted her, that's all there was to it. I loved Jenny, loved her as much as I was capable of loving anyone, but I wanted Anne. Suddenly I was thrilled to be sitting across from her, thrilled by the way she inserted the cigarette between her lips and inhaled. Her eyes came up to meet mine. Then I remembered Bird.

"God," I said. "We sucked last night."

"Yes, little man"—above his sharp nose, Bird's blue eyes quizzed me—"we did." Then, as the waitress arrived with our breakfast, he added, "I think we need a band meeting, maybe on the drive."

The waitress set our food down, refilled coffee cups, then waited for Bird to flirt with her. Sorry, angel. Bird had other things on his mind, and ass bouncing, the girl walked off. Anne spread her English muffin with grape jelly. I cut into my eggs. The yolks oozed. Bird said, "We've got a couple weeks left, and even if the album doesn't come out, I'm making good money. Shit, Potts, we'll be playing for fifteen thousand people in Syracuse, that's almost the size of Ithaca." Bird snitched a fry from my plate, popped it into his mouth. "I want it to be immortal, ya dig?"

"Everyone does."

"We're letting Apex fuck with our minds, that's what happened last night."

I'd salted my eggs, but they needed more, and I hit them again. Anne bit into her English muffin.

"It's only human to be depressed. They *are* fucking us over."

"You can fuck me," Bird answered, grinning, "but you cannot fuck my mind. My mind wears a chastity belt. My mind is mine. If you let people fuck your mind, then you really have sold out. Hell, I can go back to doing what I was before."

That got to me. "I'm not sure I can. I know I don't want to."

"Before he passed out," Anne began in her best Brooklyn-British, "Danny said Bobby's going to meet us next week in Chicago. Maybe things are looking up."

"Or maybe," Bird said, drumming his fingers again, "he's giving up making something happen in the city."

"How did Danny know?"

"I assume," Anne said slowly, "Ethan or Jenny told him."

Soon afterward Bird stood, told us not to take any wooden nickels, and said he was going up to shower. I watched his long back and crest of hair leave the coffee shop, then Anne said, "Everyone assumes Danny and Jenny got drunk together."

I nodded.

"Why shouldn't they?" Anne asked. "Danny's worried about her, he's—"

I touched the tips of Annie's fingers, which were halfway across the table, with the tips of my own.

"Jenny can take care of herself."

I increased the pressure. Anne didn't answer. Then her fingers moved against mine. "Honestly," she said, her eyes moving over my face, neither of us daring to look down, "I wish he'd stop worrying about Jenny. God, do I."

"You and me both." I wove our fingers together, unable to stop myself, excitement sparking from my nails up my arms. "It would be better for everyone."

Anne didn't answer. I found myself wondering what it would be like to make love to her, what her breasts looked like, the shape of her thighs, and whether she'd be wild or quiet when she came. I stopped myself, thinking, This is crazy. What am I doing?

"There are a lot of people," Anne said, "men who want to do things for Jenny. She seems to inspire that."

We stared at each other. Her eyes were large and luminous, holding nothing back.

"On the other hand"—her fake accent was particularly charming right now—"I understand why they want to."

She disentangled our fingers; Tony Two and Ethan were approaching. A few minutes later I returned to our room. Jenny was still sleeping, cheek on her pillow, blond hair falling over her face. I stood beside the bed, listened to her steady breathing, then bent and kissed the border of her hair and forehead. Her eyelids trembled open.

"Hi."

"How are you, babe?"

"Hung over."

"How about some aspirin?"

She nodded. "Do you love me, Steve?"

"Very much."

She smiled. I kissed her cheek, which tasted slightly of bourbon and tobacco.

"Boy," she said, "was I stinko last night. So was Danny."

"I know. Anne told me at breakfast."

Our eyes met. Jenny's were pale, mine feverish and dark. There was trouble in that look. What? I didn't want to know. Then she said, "Get me the aspirin, and I'll love you forever, huh?"

What an offer.

Chapter Eleven

•

ATLANTA WAS STEAMY. One night, late, coked up, Jenny, Bird and I, a few of the others, wandered through the Peachtree Plaza Center, stared up at the stacked balconies as if we were gladiators facing the crowd. Plant tendrils hung down linking tier to tier, and the effect was beautiful, slightly surreal, at once warm and menacing. But hell, at that time, the shape we were in, a soft-boiled egg seemed dangerous.

Another night someone told us about a jazz club where the players were good, black and progressive. It was a small cave-like room, and the walls were painted charcoal, the decor self-consciously modeled after a 50's beat café. Musicians changed, played for little or no money, and the jam continued till dawn. At one point Bird and Danny joined them; and listening, despite being at the same table with Jenny and Anne, I dissolved into the sound, the rainbow of subtle rhythm, melody and counterpoint, the bullshit business side of our lives simply not there. The music went on and on, long lovely riffs, players trading solos. And me at the same table as Anne and Jenny, released from worry, the music going on and on, something timeless about it after all.

Other than that, of the next few days I remember the driving and the phone calls, the lack of real conversations about what to do. Endless unribboning miles running north and west, hours in the van, heat rising from the black asphalt, the perfume of summer mixing with dust, exhaust and our own sweat. I remember the back of Tony Two's thick neck, Tony who was always in whichever van Jenny and I rode because he was always near Jenny, a goo-goo-eyed baby hood; Tony at the wheel in a sleeveless T-shirt and wraparound shades, a cassette of "Born To Run" blasting from the van's four speakers. Tony, who barely spoke to me, grunted when I asked him something, but who, when Jenny smiled at him, would grin as if he'd just held up a liquor store and got away clean.

From the Atlanta motel room I called my parents. My mother answered, then Arnie picked up the downstairs extension.

"I still can't find the album."

"They're not releasing it."

"Are you sure?"

"Sure enough."

There was a pause and through the line, I could feel their distress.

"What about your contract?" Arnie asked.

"When the tour's over," I began, and realized I didn't want to discuss it with them. I'd thought I had. When I called I'd wanted them to comfort me, but it was no good.

"Well?"

"Afterward we're going to sit down with our lawyers."

Arnie began to shout. "You should have used my lawyers. No, you knew better."

"For Chrissakes, Dad."

"What about her brother?" Mom asked. "Can't he help?"

"I told you. There was a power struggle and we're on the wrong side. Besides, our music, timeless as it is—"

Irony sounds grotesque on long-distance calls. My mother said, "It *is* wonderful."

"Our music's not considered hip by the new powers-that-be, which is the semiofficial excuse they're in no hurry to release it. The real reason is the new bosses hated Bobby for years and this is their revenge."

Normally, I wouldn't have allowed the conversation to reach such a dead end. It wasn't kind.

"How's Ziggie?" I asked.

A pause, then Mom said, "You tell him."

"For shit," said Arnie, his voice rising. "He kept stumbling, banging his goddamn stubborn head, so we made him a bedroom downstairs."

"When?"

Another pause. Then, speaking matter-of-factly, which was supposed to help but only made me feel worse, my mother said, "A few weeks ago. We didn't want to spoil—"

"He still won't have the operation?"

Arnie exploded, which I now knew—I hadn't understood as a kid—was a scam to make himself feel better.

"That fucking fortune-teller. I'm going to have Ziggie declared incompetent."

"No, Dad."

"That's what I've been telling him."

"I know," said Arnie. "I know."

Suddenly, the distance between us dissolved, and sitting on my rented bed in Atlanta, I felt close enough to hug my parents in their large green house with the kids gone and the old man going blind; Arnie with his ridiculous temper and curly hair, Mom the calm pool in Arnie's wild stream. She was saying something.

"He keeps making me promise we'll take him to your concert in New York. As if we wouldn't."

"Can I talk to him?"

"He's asleep," said Arnie.

"But he'd like to hear from you and Jenny," my mother said. "It's amazing, I think he's in love with her."

Him and everyone else.

"We'll call from Chicago."

"Drive safely and get some sleep. I know you don't sleep enough."

"Sure, Dad. How's business?"

"Business," said my business-minded father, "is business. You take care."

We hung up.

Bobby flew out in time to be in the audience for our first show in Bonaparte's, a club in Chicago's New Town area. We were doing "Love Is No Reason" for a mediocre house, Jenny singing, "Where did our love go wrong / was it ever right?" when I looked up and saw Bobby making his way toward Annie's table. He looked great; the excess weight was finally gone. And listening to Jenny—whose voice, even when tired, was so special, a living thing I knew and loved—while seeing Bobby in the glow of club light, the famous smile, dark eyes, chest hair peeking through workshirt buttons, I forgot what I was doing and blew the chord change. Bird caught my eye and whispered, "Schmuck." I mouthed back, *Bobby.*

Bird didn't understand. When we finished I said it aloud, "Bobby." Then everyone knew. Suddenly, for the first time since Washington we were hitting all the marks and, as they had in Portsmouth, Poughkeepsie and Boston, girls got up and danced with each other in front of the stage.

We finished "Fall in Love Again," started Danny's "Wrong Number Lovers." My fingers owned the intro, flew into the verse. Jenny stepped to her mike, hips thrust forward, pouting like Jagger.

> *"Rozzie had a new phone,*
> *She was getting calls*
> *For some other girl.*
> *There was this guy named Mike."*

The music was fun again, and I realized that for two weeks we'd been scared shitless, scared green. Now, because Bobby's here . . . and doesn't the man look great!

We shifted to a minor key for the chorus. I leaned into my mike, joining the rest of the band's voices:

> *"Wrong number lovers,*
> *Met on the phone.*
> *Wrong number lovers,*
> *Couldn't wait to be alone.*
> *Wrong number lovers,*
> *Wrong number lovers."*

Rock stepped forward, poised on his toes, knees slightly bent under his belly, those great shining orbs reflecting pure spirit, the soul's true mirror. He began his solo, and though his eyes glowed with peace, wild rock screamed from his guitar, long runs that sounded as if they'd been torn from a dream. Painful, pristine, building until he had nowhere to take it, but Rock always found somewhere, building again until he let it fall back to begin once more.

The girls in front of the stage bounced and danced, twirled each other, vying for Rock's attention. One girl, tall and willowy, a peroxide blonde with long arms, wore a red top with a ruffled collar and holes, deliberately made, the size of silver dollars in all the right places. She bounced and screamed and bounced to attract Rock, Rock whose eyes were wide but saw nothing. She was so stoned, she didn't seem to see much either; when she bounced her breasts popped free. Sometimes she'd notice, sometimes not, and she'd bounce, one copper-colored nipple winking until one of her friends shoved the wayward tit back inside her blouse.

She bounced, screamed, made eyes. We played, hanging back under Rock's solo, then Jenny was singing again. One of her breasts popped free. Or maybe she urged it out, and a beautiful full breast it was, putting the bouncer's tit to shame. Or maybe I imagined the whole thing, Jenny's singing and sex were completely tangled in my mind. But I don't think so. The audience screamed. Bobby was shouting, too. And in the way of suicidal lemmings and feeding frenzies, "Wrong Number Lovers," which normally took four minutes, went on for fifteen and could have gone twice that. At the end Rock and Jenny bowed, holding hands in a room suddenly close, dark and intimate as a lover's tongue. Then Jenny let go of Rock's hand, and unselfconsciously wiping perspiration from her face, she said, "We have a special guest tonight."

She paused. As I sat behind my keyboards, a large white follow spot pinning her, all I could see was Jenny's back and hair, light spreading around her.

"My brother, Bobby Hall!"

Ooohs, ahs, maybe a few "Who's he?" 's, then the spotlight raised Bobby. He stood, bowed, and still standing, faced us. Smiling, the extra weight gone, it could have been 1968 again. I mean, the man was beautiful, and I was so moved, something stirred so deep inside me, it was as if they were cheering for me.

He made his way to the stage, jumped up and kissed Jenny. The audience howled and whistled. The bouncing girl in red chiffon began screaming "Bobby, Bobby, Bobby." And while I sat wondering what would happen next, the room's excitement level soared like the temperature inside a sauna after you dash water on the rocks.

Bobby turned. "Steve, play 'To the Country,' wouldja? In D."

I nodded. Bobby and Jenny whispered, then Bobby lifted Danny's vocal mike from its stand, and I started the intro to the song Bobby and I had written together; the song that was about Jenny leaving the country, but more generally, about Bobby's and everyone's lost Eden: the politics of hope and shared dreams.

Jenny began the melody, Bobby a third, sometimes a fifth below her. Then they traded and Bobby took it. And their performance was so beautiful, the moment so precious I wanted to cry. Okay, I did cry. So did Bird. Jenny, too, as soon as the song was over. Somehow, Bobby singing with us and looking well again, Bobby singing with us made up for a lot.

I don't know how to describe what I felt, watching Bobby and Jenny sing in the same reddish spot, Bobby's voice okay at least in the lower end, except to compare it to the emotion an audience feels at the end of a well-made movie. After long struggles the heroes or lovers stand together, not triumphant, but ready for the future. They've suffered, but have kept faith, and we see them smile, touch, perhaps even sing. That small gesture gives the audience hope for their own lives, and when the credits come on, there's not a dry eye in the house.

That's how it was for me in Chicago.

Rolling from bar to bar to bar, all anyone could talk about was how spectacular Jenny and Bobby had sounded together; how Bobby's arrival had made the show. Later, we stayed up in the band's extra room until three-thirty, smoking, rapping, snorting some of the good coke Bobby had brought with him, everyone except Rock, Bird and Ike, who were off with the bouncing girl and two of her friends.

"My voice started healing a few weeks back. The top's gone, but I sounded okay, right?"

"Okay?"

Struggling to seem cool and elegant, Ethan Marks was ready to pop. He was sitting next to Bobby on one of the room's two double beds, beaming at him; Jenny, on the other side of Bobby, was also beaming. I sat opposite them on the other bed beside Danny and Anne, Tony Two somewhere in the background standing guard, and I suddenly understood what all this beaming was about. Ethan was a luxury item, committed to the right clothes, the right smile, the right ideas about the world. For anyone of a romantic, radical sensibility, Bobby, the way he'd looked and sounded tonight, the way he'd looked and sounded in the 60's, was as right as you could be, and being his best friend confirmed Ethan's idea of himself. Through the 60's, it meant that he, too, was saved; that his life was justified; and tonight, with Bobby back onstage, Ethan Marks had also been resurrected.

Watching Jenny and Bobby beam at each other while Ethan searched for a superlative, I understood that Bobby's rightness, the way the Kennedys had at one time seemed *right*, was beyond talent or even personality. For a few minutes listening to Jenny and Bobby sing, I felt, as I've heard people say about seeing a young Nureyev and Fonteyn dance, that it was like watching the supernatural onstage. Something—

"Okay?" Ethan repeated. "Merely perfection. And those dildos at Apex—"

Jenny said, "We're not discussing them tonight."

"Apex who?" asked Danny.

"Streit my ass," I said.

"I can probably do a couple, three tunes a night without straining."

"You know?" Jenny began, her voice and the look in her eyes dreamy and far-off. "The last time we sang together, I think it was at Mom's piano."

Bobby hugged her, kissed Jenny's cheek, and watching them, I was happy. Bobby arriving and singing was the first good news in two weeks. But it wasn't undiluted joy I felt as I watched Bobby, Ethan and Jenny on the other bed. And glancing past Danny, who sat between us, I could see that Anne, who was smiling, didn't only look pleased, either.

Bobby said, "Of course, it's up to the band." He grinned. "I wouldn't want to cash in on family connections."

Suddenly, everyone was looking at me.

"I don't know about anyone else, but I couldn't be happier."

"Same here," said Danny. I turned, and over his shoulder Anne caught my eye. As I stared at her, just for a second, something inside me trembled. Then Danny finished, "It'd be an honor."

That's how it happened: Bobby, Jenny Hall and Waterfall. The next two nights at Bonaparte's, Bobby sang three songs each set. His numbers were good, they were fine, but not like the first night. His voice tired easily, and by the second set he was raspy and hoarse, not as bad as at the silver-suit fiasco, but off enough that a couple times it hurt to listen. One more thing that wasn't quite working out, a little more chaos and pain I couldn't help with; the absolute rightness of Jenny and Bobby's performance that first night eroded. Not much, just a little, but enough that I noticed and grieved for it.

Jenny must have noticed, too, but we didn't discuss it. I didn't see her much after Bobby joined us. We slept in the same bed, but that week in the Midwest—Chicago, Milwaukee, Madison, then Cleveland on the drive east—the afternoon and evening hours which, during the early weeks of the tour, we'd reserved for private time and making love (we were generally too tired at three or four in the morning), she began to spend that free time with Bobby, Ethan and, increasingly, with Danny.

They were planning, ostensibly, what was going to happen next. Nothing was going to happen next, not for Jenny Hall and Waterfall. Then for whom? Our second night in Chicago, Jenny returned to our room after eight, which left her just enough time to dress before driving to Bonaparte's.

"Where have you been?" I asked, as she unzipped her pants and in one movement slid them to the floor while walking to the bathroom.

"At the *Chicago Tribune.*"

She reached to her waist, pulled her purple Indian print blouse cross-handed over her head, then tossed the blouse in typical Jenny fashion inside out onto the bed.

"Their rock critic caught last night's show and wanted to write about the singing Halls. You know, he was late, we were late, then there were drinks."

Jenny hooked a thumb on either side of her panty waist-band, guided the panties right-handed to the floor, stepped out of them, left the pink panties on the carpet. I caught a peek of blond hair, then she turned and, trim buttocks flashing, strode to the bathroom.

"You couldn't call?" She turned. "I waited on dinner."

"Ethan didn't?"

I shook my head.

"That fucker." She smiled one of her pure, luminous Jenny smiles. "I'm sorry, he was supposed to."

She hesitated, naked and beautiful at the bathroom door, then wrinkled her nose. "Give me a second to piss, then talk to me in the shower."

After the toilet flushed I joined her. The curtain was half drawn. The shower was already running, and under it, back to the nozzle, water striking in the middle of her back, then skiing her flat ass, Jenny was reaching up with both hands washing her hair. Because of the motion and position of her hands, her breasts rode higher than usual, and the nipples, like her face—to keep soap out of her eyes—pointed upward. I sat on the closed toilet and watched her. It was an amazing performance.

"Bobby's news from New York," she said, eyes closed against the shampoo, "is we're completely fucked. Streit claims it's just a matter of time. Because it's only a month late" —lather rose like meringue from her scalp—"which happens all the time for legit reasons, no other label can talk to us without looking as if they're tampering."

She stepped backward under the spray. Lather streamed out of her hair, down her shoulders, ass and thighs. Jenny's was the most beautiful body I'd ever seen naked, a statue in a fountain, and while there was a way in which she didn't care, another part of her used that beauty against me; which, I knew, was why she'd invited me into the bathroom.

"So we're stuck," she shouted over the spray. "But it is just time. Other people *are* interested."

"Who?"

"What?"

I stood, put my mouth near the curtain. *"Who?"*

She opened her eyes. "Bobby didn't say."

Jenny reached for the small bar of motel soap, began lathering her armpits, her breasts, her thighs, then smiled.

"Looks like fun," I said.

"Too bad you're dressed."

"There's not enough time, Jenny."

"I know."

She rinsed, turned off the shower and I handed her a towel. Still inside the tub, drying, she asked, "Could we raise eighty thousand? Bobby says one solution is to buy back the masters and sell them to another label."

I didn't answer. *We* meant my family. Then I said, "I don't know. By the way, Ziggie said hello."

Jenny looked up, her eyes wide. "Oh, shit, we were supposed to call him."

I nodded.

"Now I really am sorry." Our eyes met. "How is he?"

"Almost blind. My mother says when he thinks no one's watching, he walks from room to room holding on to the wall."

"I'm sorry. I really should have gotten back."

I didn't disagree. Jenny said, "Why don't we make love, Steve? A quickie, huh?"

"There isn't time."

"So we'll be late."

I followed Jenny out of the bathroom. On the bed that wasn't covered with her clothes, she helped me out of mine. Jenny took me in her mouth until I was hard, then guided me inside her, and we made love quickly, effortlessly, like masters. We were late, but only a little, and no one cared.

After the show I begged off going drinking. Instead, when Jenny, Ethan, Bobby, Bird, Danny, Rock, Ike and Tony Two drove off in the band's vans to a South Side club owned by Ike's brother, I took a cab to the motel. Earlier, huddled in one corner of our crowded dressing room, I'd told Jenny I was tired and depressed about Ziggie.

"Should I come home with you?"

"You'll have a better time with Bobby."

"I'll have a better time if we all go."

"Believe me, not tonight."

Jenny kissed me, then walked off gaily and, I thought, somewhat relieved, to talk to Ethan. Back at our motel, a Holiday Inn, I lay on my bed and thought. I was pretty sure Bobby and Ethan were putting together a post-tour plan for Jenny which didn't include me. It wasn't anything they'd said, but the way at lunch today and in between sets tonight that conversation died when I entered the room. There was the new intensity of Tony Two's sneer, Tony who seemed to be pulling guard duty for Ethan, warning him when I approached. They had some sort of sister-and-brother act in mind, or a solo gig for Jenny. Maybe Bobby knew of a name band looking for a singer. Something, some way around the contract with Apex.

Maybe, I thought, lying in bed hands behind my neck, I was imagining the whole thing. Too wacked out to think. One thing, though, I was sure of. Two doors away down the green-carpeted hall, Anne was alone. Once or twice a week, she skipped our show to stay home and draw. She had tonight, the first time since our brunch in Chapel Hill. Returning in the cab, I'd considered going straight to her room, to *their* room, decided instead to head for *ours* and think.

Think. I walked to the bathroom, washed my face. With my silk shirt still tucked in my jeans, I unbuttoned it, slipped out of the arms. The shirt hung down my legs but didn't fall. I washed my armpits, dried them, and chest bare looked at myself in the mirror above the sink. Dark hair and Potzgovitz eyes. Ziggie's, which were dying. *This is wrong,* I thought. *Everything is wrong.*

I walked down the hall, knocked softly. No answer, and I knocked again.

"Who is it?"

"Anne," I whispered. "Steve."

Anne opened the door wearing a pale green nightgown which didn't quite reach her knees.

"Aren't you going to invite me in?"

"Should I?"

"They went to hear jazz on the South Side."

Annie stepped back. Before the door was closed, I took her in my arms. Her lips against mine, finally, were full and soft. Her tongue moved like water against the edge of a lake. Through the silk of my shirt and the satin of her negligee, I could feel her nipples bumping erect. Kissing me, Annie locked the door. Leading her toward the bed, still kissing, ecstatic, I slipped the thin straps from her shoulders and her nightgown slid to the floor with a hiss. Her pubic hair, shiny and almost black, was the first dark sexual hair other than my own that I'd seen in nearly a year. I kissed Annie's mouth again, moved my lips down her neck to her breast, and she drew back.

"Steve."

"I know, I know."

I pulled her slender body to me. I wanted her, I thought, more than I'd ever wanted anyone, or why would I be doing this? I saw Danny kissing Jenny, kissed Anne again, and whatever doubts she felt had vanished. She kissed me, moaned, fell backward on the bed, pulling me on top. I moved my hand to her crotch, felt hers at mine, and I don't remember much else except that the whole time we made love I kissed her. Not thinking about anything or anyone, not listening for footsteps or keys in the lock, we made love, while I kissed the girl's bright eyes.

A half hour later, tempting fate, we were at it again. Afterward, we arranged to eat breakfast. I dressed, thinking, Schmuck, don't leave anything, socks or underwear. I kissed Annie, then crept down the hall, thinking, What am I doing?

I showered to get rid of the smell of sex, then climbed into bed, too excited and worried to sleep. Yes, it had happened. Yes. And remembering, guilty as hell, I got a hard-on. Five minutes later, at most ten, I heard voices. The door opened.

"Steve," Jenny whispered.

I didn't answer.

"Steve."

"Unnnh," I murmured.

"I love you," I thought I heard her say as the door closed. Or maybe I wanted to say it myself. When she returned two hours later, I was awake and furious she'd been out so late without me. She slipped into bed, guiltily, I thought, trying not to wake me. She smelled of whiskey, cigarettes and sex. She smells of sex. I lay there maybe fifteen seconds, so distanced from both of us I wanted to die. Then, with an acting job that should have won me an Oscar, I woke up. I kissed her breast. One eye slitted, I looked up and Jenny smiled. Her hand found my penis, which was already hard.

"What kind of dreams have you been having?" she whispered.

Oh, God. My mind and body in different galaxies, parts of my heart in both, I ended what had been the most extraordinary and upsetting night of my life as I'd begun it, making love to Jenny.

Chapter Twelve

•

W HEN I ARRIVED AT TEN, Anne was already in the coffee shop. I slid into the booth and placed my hand on her bare knee.

"How'd you sleep?" she asked.

"Badly." I looked into Annie's dark eyes. "I was too excited."

The waitress arrived, filled my coffee cup, took an order for eggs. She departed, and I traced esses and whys in the hollow behind Annie's knee.

"Don't."

"I couldn't resist."

I grinned. It was important, I thought, to act natural. Remain cool. Above all, don't be morbid or guilty. Of course, I had no idea how to act.

Annie said, "It was good you left when you did. Danny got home ten minutes later."

"Did he stay?"

"I don't know. I dropped right off." Annie smiled sideways at me. "Isn't that shocking?"

I stirred nondairy creamer into my coffee. "Jenny came home, then went out again."

Fingers fumbling at the matchbook, Annie lit a cigarette. Pinching it between her thumb and second finger, she inhaled, then stared into the vast distances of the coffee shop, her left hand crossed in front of her, cupping her right elbow. Smoke rose from her nose and mouth, from the cigarette balanced between her long fingers. She turned. "Be honest, Steve. Are you using me to get back at her?"

"I could ask that about Danny."

She didn't answer. I realized I'd hit closer to home than she had, which made me feel in control, something I rarely felt with Jenny.

"I've wanted you since we met. And you know what did it? The way you laughed at Bird when he spelled farty."

"I've wanted you, too."

We touched fingertips.

"I don't feel guilty," she added. "I thought I would."

"You're lucky."

"Are you sorry?"

I smiled at Anne over my coffee cup. "No, I'm ecstatic." I glanced around the coffee shop. "I'm also terrified someone's going to see us and know. I feel like it's written all over us."

The waitress brought my food. Annie, who'd already eaten her English muffin, watched me salt and pepper eggs and home fries.

"What do you think will happen if they find out?"

"Whatever shit hasn't already hit the fan—" I filled my mouth, chewed and grinned. "We'd probably break up."

"You mean the band?"

When I nodded she said, "Do you want to stop?"

"No, and neither do you."

"I guess that makes us pretty corrupt." She stubbed out her cigarette, tapped another from the pack. "I never thought of myself as corrupt before."

"Me either, but I can't think of anyone I'd rather be corrupt with."

We laughed. All things considered I felt pretty good. I finished my breakfast. Annie lit another cigarette.

"Tell me, do you love Danny?"

"That's the funny part." She inhaled; then, in her stylized, precious way blew a smoke ring, which floated, expanding slowly toward the ceiling. "I love him and want his children. What about you and Jenny?"

I confessed what was then the truth.

"I'm not sure."

I've never been much of a liar, but the next few days I got good at it. Chicago, Milwaukee, Madison, Cleveland, Annie and I screwed our way across the Midwest. Generally, we found time in the afternoons, though there was one morning quickie when the others were eating breakfast. Twice, we slipped away when everyone else was in the band room partying after gigs, once to their room, once to ours, and proceeded to fuck like fiends, hypnotized by the sex, seduced by it, unable to think of anything else, which was awfully convenient.

The night Annie and I used our bed we were in Cleveland, city of lights, city of wonder, if you can believe Randy Newman, which you can't. Afterward, I returned to the band's party room, which, since he'd joined us in Chicago, had become Bobby's. No one suspected. How could they? Potts sleeping with Danny's Anne? Madness. Fresh from her arms, from Annie's long legs circling my waist, her head tossing on Jenny's pillow, Annie whispering, "Yes, Steve, yes, yes," then biting my shoulder to keep from screaming, I didn't believe it was happening. Kissing Jenny, telling her I wasn't sleepy after all, laughing with Rock, asking Ethan about the Syracuse Coliseum, where we'd open for Laser Light in two nights, fifteen thousand people, it wasn't happening, it couldn't be; not me, not Anne.

No one suspected, but Bird knew. Bird always knew. That night in Cleveland he took me aside after I'd finished talking to Ethan about Bobby's plan to raise money for the Sandinista revolutionaries in Nicaragua. I said I'd think about it, and head swirling with revolution, with dreams of the 60's, Bobby

The First Time I Saw Jenny Hall

in Chicago, I sat with Bird at a small round table in the corner, as far from the others as we could be in that motel room. We snorted a few lines. Then, grinning at me, blue eyes shining with the drug, Bird asked, "How's it hanging, brother?"

"Just fine." I sniffed. "Hey, I thought you were going to make it with that redhead."

"Nah." Bird leaned across the table till his nose almost bumped mine. "I don't approve of casual sex."

I laughed, he laughed, then Bird said, "So how's Annie?"

Bird grinned. After a second, I answered, "Asleep, I guess."

"Are we brothers, or what?"

I nodded.

"As your brother, I want to say you're letting me down."

I turned, watched Ethan whisper to Jenny, saw her throw her head back and laugh. Bird said, "I know the shit that's been going down is hardest for you and Jenny. You're bent out of shape, I can see it."

"And you?"

"Different dreams, man." Bird smiled, touched my hand with his. "But don't confuse desire and despair, you hear what I'm saying?"

I looked down at the table, at my hands on it. I felt like a hole, like a tunnel with no light at the end. I peered at Jenny across the room surrounded by her court: Ethan, Danny, Tony Two standing guard behind them.

"Tell me," I whispered. "What are Ethan and Bobby planning for her after the tour?"

"What are you talking about?"

"They're always whispering. And those interviews Jenny and Bobby do, four in five days. Now this Nicaragua shit. Danny must know what they're planning. I thought maybe—"

"You're kidding, right?"

I shook my head.

"You're wacko, you know that?"

"I don't think so."

Bird didn't answer, and I sat at our little table listening to the sounds of the party. Bird said, "You really think they're planning to screw you? You think Jenny would do that?"

I felt like crying. It was late, my mind was confused, burned out on craziness and coke, and from three feet away I knew my fingers smelled like Annie's crotch.

"I guess not, huh?"

"Ask her," Bird said softly. "One thing about Jenny, she'll tell you if you ask."

I stood up. "I'm going to sleep now."

Bird winked. "Coke always tire you out?"

"Maybe I'll think awhile first."

"Think about despair and desire."

I nodded.

Bird stood, looped an arm over my shoulder. "Hey, Big-nose, you okay?"

I shrugged and Bird said, "I know what you mean."

We left for Syracuse at noon the next day, which was Thursday. We'd discussed taking the Southern Tier Parkway, which would have allowed us to swing north through T-burg, but decided, finally, to drive straight. The tour was in shambles, but Friday and Saturday nights, fifteen thousand people, including most of Jenny, Bird and Danny's Ithaca friends would hear us. An extra day to get comfortable with the larger venue and Laser Light's monster sound system, for meeting their light man—it obviously made sense.

There were other reasons. Bobby and Ethan thought that Apex execs might be in town with Laser Light, who were one of the label's top-selling acts. Not Streit or Parker, but two of Bobby's friends who'd been passed over when the accountant frogs replaced Sol. Bob Crawford was a producer whose work I knew. Vico, no first name, just Vico, was a marketing whiz who'd broken in writing record reviews. Maybe, the reasoning went, there *was* some way around the frogs. If nothing else, Vico knew the latest dirt and could evaluate our chances of seeing the album released, or of getting out of the contract.

I didn't believe it. My theory, supported by Rock and Bird, was that we were screwed. That we'd be at Apex until the contract ran out with no action, at which point, if we raised enough money and kissed enough ass, Apex might sell us or a new label the masters. If the band was still together, which was unlikely, or if Jenny and I still were, which, riding beside her in the van from Cleveland, I didn't want to think about, we'd do some kind of deal and hope would sally forth. Once more I'd be Potts the Innocent, Jenny's charm against despair and corruption, and we'd fly into the future, the wind blowing her hair straight back like the streamers on a little girl's bicycle.

Somewhere on that drive east Jenny, who'd been asleep with her head on my lap, legs curled, her feet just touching Bird, Jenny began to moan softly. Her legs twitched as if she were running.

"No," she murmured. "No, please," and I shook her till her eyes opened.

"You were having a bad dream."

"I was?"

She blinked, recognized me and smiled, I thought, quite sadly. She crooked the second finger of her right hand, reached up with the left guiding my mouth to hers. We kissed, then, sitting up, she whispered, "What's wrong?"

Our eyes met, terror and guilt in mine. Some magic charm.

"We're not sharing much anymore."

I glanced past Jenny to Bird, who was sleeping. Since our talk last night, I hadn't been alone with Annie, but I'd decided to break off. So there was no need to tell Jenny, not with Bobby, Ethan and Tony Two in front.

"It's easier to be madly in love when everything's going well," I said.

"No shit."

"Since Chicago," I dropped my voice to the softest whisper possible, "I hardly see you and when I do your mind's somewhere else."

Liar, I thought. *You worm.*

"We don't even go to the same bed. I mean, at the same time."

"I know, Steve. I'm afraid nothing's going to work out. I'm scared."

She hugged me, and ashamed, I buried my face in Jenny's hair, told her not to worry, that everything would be okay.

That evening, Jenny, Bobby, Danny and I stood before 15,540 empty seats on a bare black stage. Rows of red, blue and green rose three tiers above us like mountains surrounding a narrow valley. The effect was eerie, awesome, and the vast enclosed quiet weighed on me until I was afraid I'd never move again.

Jenny said, "This is it."

She stood six feet away, Bobby and Danny another ten beyond her.

"What?"

"Those seats."

I gazed into the void.

Jenny crossed to my side. "Last fall, when we were writing in your apartment. Did you ever think—?"

I nodded.

Jenny said, "I was very happy then."

"So was I."

Danny said something to Bobby about monitors. I turned to listen and Jenny began to sing.

> *"Time stretches out*
> *Like an unbroken road . . ."*

I joined her:

The First Time I Saw Jenny Hall

"Steals from my hand
Like the mountains erode,
Then they're gone."

Our voices faded in the distance, and the huge space was
quiet except for Danny clapping once, then following Bobby offstage. Jenny said, "After the tour's over, have you
thought—?"

"No, have you?"

"Bobby's organizing that Nicaragua benefit." She hesitated. "And some other things."

"Like?"

Jenny took my hand. "I still think Waterfall can work. I
want *us* to headline here next time."

"Sweet dreams, babe. Waterfall's dead."

Her eyes widened. She squeezed my hand. "What's happened to you?"

"You mean Potts the whizbang? The magic charm?"

"Who'll keep bad things from happening to me."

She smiled and something broke inside me.

"Listen, do Bobby's plans for you include me?"

"*My* plans include you." She paused, added in a low voice,
"If you want them to."

"What does that mean?"

"What does it sound like?"

"It's not my fault Apex killed the fucking record."

"I'm talking about us."

"You're talking about your career, Jenny, there's a difference."

"What's got into you?"

"I'm just saying, if you think I'm holding you back, do what
you want."

"I can't believe you said that."

Jenny let go of my hand and faced me, knuckles on her hips.

I shouted, "Why not? You think because Danny follows you around like a fucking puppy, I can't say no?"

"No, I thought—" Rage swelled her eyes. "Oh, fuck off." She walked away. *Jenny,* I wanted to shout, *Jenny.* Instead I looked out at the rows of seats until the others had gone. Then, low and miserable, I walked backstage to the runway which led past the dressing rooms with stars on the doors where Laser Light and maybe Bobby would dress tomorrow, but not me. I pissed in a ladies' room, let myself out a side door and started back to the motel, which was only a few blocks away and where, no doubt, a party was in full swing—Bird's friends from Ithaca.

I watched the sunrise, but didn't see Jenny. When the phone rang at ten, my wake-up call to meet Annie, she still wasn't home. Replacing the receiver, my eyes and feet throbbing, I looked down realizing I'd fallen asleep fully dressed with my shoes on. I unlaced them, massaged my soles to get blood flowing. Then, rubbing my eyes and pushing hair off my face, I thought, Oh, my, and don't this lonely room look wide.

"It's beautiful outside," Anne said when I reached the coffee shop. "Let's walk and eat afterward."

We walked. Last night, when I left the party at two, Jenny, Ethan and Bobby hadn't been seen in hours. I thought Danny might know where she was, but he'd been giving me hard looks and I didn't dare ask. At the door, Rock told me the Apex people were crosstown at the Regency, and that's where they probably were. Oh, I'd said, thanks, then returned to my room.

Annie and I walked. The sun shone sweetly. Blue sky hung bravely above us. A breeze blew from the west. Annie wore a faded cotton jumper and swung her arms happily.

"Tell me."

We were strolling down a commercial street of old brick

buildings. People passed us, hurrying about their business.
"Tell you what?"
"Anything." Annie grinned. "Lie to me."
"I walked in on Danny and Jenny last night."
A policeman turned the corner, strutted past us.
"You're kidding."
"I'm kidding. Jenny didn't come home."
"I'm sorry."
So much for conversation. We walked until we left the downtown and reached a small corner park. A patch of grass, a few old oaks, wooden bench, a stone table for checkers. Sitting on the bench, Annie said, "Danny told me you and Jenny had argued."
"I bet he did."
Annie found a pack of Merits in her purse. I lit one for each of us off the same Holiday Inn match. My life had become a Holiday Inn with dirty sheets. Exhaling, the sun in her eyes, Annie said, "Considering we've been fucking like bunnies"— she laughed—"I don't know why, but I feel like your big sister, I do. I wish you'd knock Jenny up and marry her or something."
"That would be tidy."
A pigeon landed at our feet and pecked dust, hoping to be fed.
"What makes me mad is Danny knows she doesn't want him, but it doesn't make any difference. I could just scream."
I remembered screaming with Jenny above her pond and the memory nearly did me in. I dropped my cigarette, buried my head on Annie's shoulder.
"I'm sorry, Steve. I am."
The sun still shone. Birds sang. Annie hugged me against her. The pigeon at our feet flew off. When I felt better, I said, "So what are you sorry about, pretty girl?"
"I'm sorry we don't love each other." She smiled. "We're so reasonable."

I kissed her. Her tongue circled my teeth, my lips, and I felt a familiar excitement shimmer through me.

"Reasonable, that's why we're making out in a park." I stood. "We'd better get back."

A block or two from the motel, a platonic arm's length away, Annie turned, asked suddenly, "Why do you want to be famous?"

"Do I?"

"It's all over you."

"Why does anyone?"

"I don't. Nor does Danny, you know he doesn't."

"Is this a serious question?"

She nodded. Sunlight reflecting from her broad forehead caught in her smile, narrowed her eyes.

"Growing up I was the best student, best athlete, the only son, an all-around whizbang. I believed there was a real connection between talent and success. So I never considered going into Potts and Pans, it wasn't special enough."

The motel was on the next block. I stopped walking, leaned against a building and took Annie's hand. A few walkers passed while I looked into her long face framed by sky.

"I thought if you were good enough at something you'd get famous and somehow your life would matter."

"You still believe that."

"Dumb, huh?"

"You're a sweet boy, Steve. Misguided, but sweet."

I smiled. "Why don't you go in? I'll meet you in the coffee shop."

"I think I'll see if Danny's up, do you mind?"

"Not if you kiss me."

She did. Watching her cover the half block to the motel, I wondered if anyone had seen us. Then I knew no one had. I was invisible. Besides, I didn't care.

I ate in a small Greek diner, bought a Syracuse paper, and returned to the park where Annie and I had sat. Two old men were playing chess and I watched. Then, looking out for dog and pigeon shit, I lay on the grass to read my paper. It was an ordinary summer Friday, not much news. Another murder in Buffalo, a rape, a forest fire burning out of control in California, and suddenly I was exhausted. I must have fallen asleep because when I woke up the paper had blown away, the sun was no longer overhead, and the blue sky had aged to gray and white.

I began walking to the motel, read a window clock and started to run, passing men in business suits, women shopping, kids on street corners, everyone eyeing my long hair as I dashed past, shirt open, sweating in the hot afternoon, running until I reached the motel.

Jenny's things were gone. I marched to Bobby's room and knocked. Voices, footsteps, then the door opened just wide enough for Tony Two to peer out. He grinned, showed his broken tooth.

"We don't want any."

He closed the door. I began beating on it.

"Go away, ya creep."

I beat the crap out of the door. Uppercuts, combinations. Other doors opened. I decided if Tony reappeared I was going to lay him out. That was it, deck him and walk. The door opened.

"Let's go," said Bobby.

I hadn't locked my door, hadn't even closed it. I followed Bobby in, poured myself three inches of bourbon, drank it off.

"If it makes you feel any better"—butt against the desktop, Bobby leaned forward, grinning—"she's in the same shape you are."

I poured another drink, quickly downed it. "Then why can't I see her?"

The question must have sounded as puerile to him as it did to me.

"Sound check's in two hours, just be—"

"You know she won't talk to me."

Bobby took the bottle, swigged it, handed it back. "Look, Potts, is there anything you want to tell me?"

"I want to talk to Jenny."

"Not now, this can be a real big night."

"For who?"

"There's a lot of Apex brass here. Ask yourself why."

"I've been asking myself where she slept last night."

"Remember what I said about talent?"

"What?"

"I'm beginning to think your greatest talent is impersonating an asshole."

"You're one to talk."

"I *am* one to talk." He grinned, slapped me on the shoulder. "Pull up your socks, huh?"

I nodded and he walked out.

Sound check was a disaster. Laser Light were Kiss imitators. Four hard rockers from Des Moines without much talent but possessed of an incredible sound system, good theatrical sense and a stage show built on special effects. Their current hit single, "Born To Be Nasty," featured smoke bombs, fireworks and a finale in which the lead singer rose above the stage on invisible wires. It took forever to set up, and by six-thirty, when we were supposed to be finished, we hadn't even started. By seven, I'd told Tony Two I was going to fire his ass off the tour. He told me just try it. By eight-oh-five, show time was nine, we were done. The only words I'd had from Jenny were yes, no and yes, all in answer to direct technical questions. Walking offstage toward our dressing room— I'd volunteered to return to our motel with Bird for our stage outfits—I drew up beside her.

"Turquoise jumpsuit and black heels."

"I want to talk."

"So talk."

The First Time I Saw Jenny Hall

We were standing in the runway leading from backstage to the dressing rooms. People were passing all around us: Ethan, Tony, Danny, some of Laser Light's crew.

"Alone."

She shook her head. "You'll just upset me."

"I promise I won't."

"I bet you do."

I took a deep breath. "Why don't we talk after the show?"

"I'm busy."

"You were pretty busy last night, too."

"Leave me alone, Steve, okay?"

For a second I was tempted to smack her. That passed, and I said, "I'm sorry about yesterday."

"You should be."

She turned and walked away.

When Bird and I reached my room, the red message light on my phone was blinking. "Better see who forgot what," Bird said. "I'll get dressed."

He slammed out the door; I dialed the front desk.

"Here it is," said the operator. " 'Call home. If no answer, 212-790-7000, room 1114. Mom.' "

No answer at my parents' and I tried the other number.

"Saint Vincent's."

"Eleven-fourteen."

"Busy, will you hold?"

I held. Bird returned wearing tight jeans and a black T-shirt with a silver flash *Jenny Hall and Waterfall* logo. One look at me and he asked, "What's wrong?"

"I'm not sure."

"In that case, my man, let's go. It's eight-thirty, very important date—"

The call went through. Arnie answered the second ring.

"Dad."

"Steve?"

"What's wrong?"

"Did your mother call? Goddamnit—"

I could hear Arnie bellow, my mother's protest, then Arnie's voice came back. "Ziggie broke his hip. He's on the critical list."

"What?"

"He's a stupid old man," Arnie shouted, and I could see him, his ridiculous curly hair, balding head, his large face blood red. "He fell going upstairs, he—"

"Let me talk to Mom."

While they exchanged, I told Bird. My mother came on.

"I thought you'd want to know."

"What's critical about a broken hip?"

Static filled the line, sweat and craziness. My mother said, "He also broke ribs. He's having trouble breathing, they—"

"Is he dying?"

"No, he—"

I heard Arnie bellow, a Jewish elephant, then he must have grabbed the phone because suddenly, very loud and clear, he was shouting, "Isn't tonight the big concert?"

"Yeah."

"Goddamnit, it's eight-forty. Call in the morning."

"Dad—"

He hung up.

We snagged in traffic entering the Coliseum lot. Then we had to fight our way through crowds of identically made-up Laser Light fans at the stage door—yellow-lightning-zig-zagged foreheads, black-starred cheeks—and didn't reach our dressing room with everyone's clothes until five to nine.

"Nice of you to drop in," said Rock, who was in the doorway, looking out for us. Then everyone was shouting, "How the fuck? What? Where?"

Jenny was especially furious; no surprise to me. Wearing only panties and a top, eyes sparking, she grabbed her jumpsuit and heels, stormed off. In the farthest corner of the dressing room, back to the rest of us, she pulled her blouse over her head. Flash. The side of her breast, the small mole on her right shoulder. She stepped into the jumpsuit.

"You're welcome," I called. Someone squeezed the back of my left arm. I whirled, pulled free. *Ethan.*

"Haven't you upset her enough?"

"Don't touch me, you prick."

Bird stepped between us, led Ethan away. I'd made him promise not to say anything about Ziggie until after the show but he must have; I watched Ethan nod a few times and look back at me with his snake's approximation of sympathy.

Bobby burst through the door. "Five minutes."

Jenny screamed, "These are the wrong fucking shoes!"

Something shattered, a mirror, perfume bottle, I didn't look. The next thing I remember was leaving our dressing room. People I didn't know smiled and nodded, touched my shoulders, told me to break a leg. Someone said "Now." I followed Bird and Danny down the runway to the black stage in the quiet and half-dark that precedes a concert and makes me feel as if I'm on the ocean just before the sun has risen when it's neither day nor night, dark nor light and anything can happen.

I climbed behind the keyboards. My pulse thundered, but my heart wasn't there. It was with Jenny and Ziggie the night we became, at least briefly, a family. With Jenny above her pond and the wind was howling, sobbing. The moon rose, spotlighted Jenny, a guitar at her waist. An amplified voice said, ". . . recording artists Jenny Hall and Waterfall," and we began to play.

We were flat the first two tunes, overanxious, and the huge house, keyed for Laser Light, didn't know what to make of us. Then we started "Waiting for Love," and so much energy poured off the stage, it was as if our souls had exploded and begun soaring through our instruments. First Jenny. Singing, moving, her voice a dazzling, once-in-a-decade thrill. Rock stepped forward, belly out, up on his toes and took a lead. I could hear Danny, perfect-time Danny. Then Bird was on a solo, sticks high, flashing in the lights, and we were beyond goodness or talent, we were right. And playing, singing backup vocals, seeking my own bit of rightness, I remembered what Bird had said about being immortal tonight, and I thought, Yes, good buddy. You got it.

Jenny sang the last two lines, "Though my heart's been broken / my door's still open," we did the chorus, and wave after wave of sound rolled out of the audience, like nothing I'd ever felt or heard as a performer. Fifteen thousand people standing and screaming for us. I thought I'd died and gone to heaven.

After that we could do no wrong. Standing ovations for every tune. Bobby came out, sang "To the Country." Then, signaling for quiet, he stepped to the mike.

"We'd like to dedicate this song to freedom-fighters around the world. To the freedom we have to fight for in our lives and in our hearts. To the freedom I'd despaired of and have found again. To freedom everywhere, but especially to the Sandinista cause in Nicaragua."

He paused, and though most of them didn't know what he was talking about, the crowd roared.

"We're doing a benefit for the Sandinistas next month in New York. I hope you can all make it."

He stepped back, and as agreed, we played Bobby's "White Guns." When we came to the famous ending

> *It's freedom, don't you see,*
> *Not I, but the wind that blows through me.*
>
> *When our time has come*
> *They'll remember what we've done,*
> *Not you, not me, not us,*
> *We'll be turned to dust.*

The First Time I Saw Jenny Hall

It's freedom, don't you see,
Not I, but the wind that blows through me.
Freedom, don't you see,
The wind that blows through me

all fifteen thousand people felt that wind. I certainly did. It lightened my heart.

We finished on Danny's "Lazarus," did "Fall in Love Again" as an encore, then raced backstage smiling, laughing, hugging each other. Twenty-five people crowded into our dressing room meant to hold ten. Champagne corks peppered the ceiling. Bird hugged me. I kissed Annie. Bobby introduced me to Vico and Crawford, who wore open shirts and Sol Hershkoff blue blazers. Crawford was tanned, his hair touched his collar, and he sported a gold chain. Vico was an odd little guy whose face disappeared behind thick glasses. They shook my hand, Crawford told me he loved the tunes, then they pushed past, moving toward Jenny, who was at the far end of the room in front of the makeup table. I watched Tony Two and Ethan hug, then kiss her. I drank my champagne, talked to Rock, looked up to see the lead singer of Laser Light already in stage makeup, yellow lightning on his forehead, an ugly black star circling his left eye and cheek, move across the room toward Jenny, everyone letting him pass. She said something; he laughed. Then, looking around the room for me, or maybe I imagined she was looking for me, Jenny began to flirt with him. The flirting I didn't imagine. The packed room filled with sex vibes like a swamp with muddy water. A second or two later, the Laser Light cretin, I've blocked his name, bent and kissed Jenny on the mouth. When I turned away they were still at it.

Jenny sang a couple of tunes with Laser Light. Afterward, there was a party in Laser Light's suite of star dressing rooms I don't remember much of because of the memory-diluting effects of champagne, coke and thai stick consumed in large quantities. It's possible I told Laser Light's lead singer I was going to break his fingers if he kissed Jenny again. It's also possible he hit me in the head, but I doubt it.

Certain fundamentals I'm sure of. Jenny and Mr. Laser Light stopped playing Post Office. Bird did more coke and champagne than anyone in the room. I ran a close second, Jenny third, and by twelve-thirty she was feeling loose enough to plant a moist one on my ear, and whisper, "Hi, Pecker, how's your Potts?"

"Present and accounted for."

And who knows what might have happened if Bobby, who'd spent most of the evening huddled with Ethan, Vico and Crawford, hadn't called her away.

Just before one, word spread the party was moving to Vico's and Crawford's rooms at the Regency. Sitting alone on one of the dressing room couches, smoking a joint, I watched Jenny, her arm around Danny's waist, say something to Anne, to Danny, then laughing, to Anne again. A minute or two later, Annie sat beside me.

"If Danny goes to that party, take me home. I'm exhausted."

Annie didn't look tired. Miserable yes, tired no.

"Annie," I mumbled. "To the ends of the earth."

Jenny left in one van with Bobby, Ethan, Danny, Crawford and Vico, her entire fools' court. Bird, Rock and Tony Two set off in the other van with four or five women who'd made their way backstage, Tony Two driving. A few minutes later, they were followed by Laser Light's silver eagle party bus, a yellow lightning bolt on the side panel, the half horde of groupies the boys from Des Moines hadn't invited on the bus shrieking and running after it across the parking lot, arms and legs waving in the lights.

"Please," they screamed. "Please."

Annie and I returned to the motel arm in arm, Annie supporting me. I was stinko, snookered, and everything blurred, shimmering at a great distance. We were halfway home before I realized it was raining.

"Hey, Annie." I winked. "You're a pretty girl."

"I could kill her."

"Wha—?"

"Danny was coming with me until she talked him out of it."

I began to feel unpleasantly sober and fumbled in my pockets for a joint. Annie said, "If she wanted him. But she doesn't. I could kill her."

I pulled Annie against me.

"She doesn't notice."

"Don't make excuses for her. Not you."

We walked on in the misting rain. Then Annie slid her arm around my waist.

"It's not your fault."

"Partially."

"Bird told me about your grandfather."

In the shadow of the streetlights, our eyes were the same color.

"Ziggie's tough," I said. "Let's try to be."

She nodded.

Annie suggested her room. We showered, made love, then I guess we passed out. The next thing I knew someone was shaking me. When I was awake enough to see, I realized it was Danny.

"Get up," he was chanting. "Get up, fucker."

A half second, maybe less, then I remembered the more important facts. I was naked, the naked body beside me was Annie, I was in Danny's bed. Whoops, I remember thinking as I swung my legs off the bed. *Whoops.*

Danny hit me in the mouth. I fell backward on Annie, who moaned. I stood again. Danny hit me in the nose. This time I crashed to the floor and began bleeding into the carpet. By then Annie was awake and screaming at Danny. He hesitated, turned, and I tackled him. We rolled around for a while, bouncing off the bed and wall. We knocked over the lamp and coffee table and somehow I landed on top, sat on his chest, pinning his arms with my naked knees.

"Stop," Anne shouted. She was standing above us. "Stop it!"

I looked down at Danny's olive skin, enraged black eyes, his cheeks and chest dotted with blood from my nose, and knew he wasn't going to stop anything. But I felt too guilty to hold him down and do what was necessary: knock him senseless with a lamp base. I let him up and jumped back. He rushed me. Annie threw herself between us and held on, crying, "Danny, please!"

We held it maybe ten seconds, three bodies in a row, two of us naked, me leaking blood, Annie between us crying while Danny glared at me wild-eyed over her shoulder. Suddenly, he tossed her onto the bed. She bounced and fell to the floor, screaming. Assuming this was round two, I put up my dukes.

Danny shouted, "To hell with you both. I'm going home."

He strode across the room, banged out the door.

"Steve," Annie said. "Are you okay?"

I sat on the bed, watched blood drizzle onto my thighs. Even my dick was red. "What are you crazy? He broke my nose."

"He did?"

She sounded thrilled; I didn't hold it against her. She probably figured my cracked schnozz was a marriage proposal. I looked around. There was blood everywhere. Blankets and sheets lay snarled in heaps; tables and lamps embraced on the floor. I sat back, allowed myself the luxury of a long groan.

"What are we going to do?"

"I'm going to my room and put ice on my nose."

I peered up at her. Annie looked terrible. Swollen eyes, tangled hair. My blood rouged her left tit.

"And you," I said, "are going to get dressed and find Danny."

"You wouldn't mind?"

She was already throwing on clothes.

"Mind?" I coughed. Blood spurted onto my lip. "If Danny misses tomorrow night, certain people—"

Annie disappeared in the bathroom, emerged a minute later and started toward the door.

"You're okay?"

"I'll be fine. Name your first son after me."

She blew me a kiss.

I plugged my nose with t.p., rearranged the furniture. Dressed in a sheet, carrying my clothes, I returned to my room, stopping on the way to fill a cardboard ice bucket. I wrapped the ice in a towel, pressed it against my nose and lip, called the front desk. It was four-fifteen. I lay on the bed and moaned. Moaning helped. Then I began to feel the ice through the towel, and the cold helped even more than moaning. After ten minutes the curl of toilet paper protruding from my nose stopped staining red. I lay on the bed, waiting.

The phone rang, Anne in the lobby. Danny was gone. I told her not to worry. The fucking pacifist loved her enough to break my nose, he'd be back.

"He's hitching."

"How do you know?"

"I ran into Bird, he—"

My door began to rattle.

"Someone's here," I said.

"If you need me, I'll be in the lobby. Maybe he'll—"

The pounding at the door grew louder. "Fine." I hung up, wrapped myself in the bloody sheet, climbed off the bed.

"Who is it?"

"It's your fucking conscience."

I threw the lock; Bird staggered in, followed me to the center of the room.

"What's this toga shit?"

"Danny walked in on us."

"Annie said. You were fucking?"

"We were asleep."

Bird struggled to focus. "What happened to your—?"

"Danny was mad."

"The Greek hit you?"

I nodded.

"Fucking-A. What did you do?"

"I bled all over him."

"Tough guy, huh?" Bird emitted his high ringing laugh, then sat on the bed. "You know what?"

I shook my head. Bird's eyes went hard, and he said, "You're a user, Potts, a scumbag. You and Jenny deserve each other, you hear what I'm saying?"

"I'm sorry."

"You sure are."

My nose began bleeding again. I touched it with the sheet, which came away red. Bird struggled to his feet.

"I know which way Danny's hitching. I'm going to bring him back for Annie."

"You're too wasted to drive."

"Bullshit."

"Wait till morning, we'll go together."

Bird shook his head. "Won't come now 'cause you're waiting for Jenny."

I nodded.

"That's your problem," he said, and started past.

I grabbed his arm. My sheet began to slip.

"Let go, Potts."

We stared at each other. Bird's eyes were sky blue. His pupils were enormous.

"Please." I let go of his wrist, pulled up my sheet. "If you can't drive, pull over."

He grinned. "If I were you, I'd change my sheet before Jenny got back. Different color, maybe."

"You promise?"

"This is the Bird, remember?"

"I'm sorry, I really am."

He nodded. And if I hadn't been bleeding and holding up that fucking sheet, I would have hugged him. Then he was gone.

When a key turned in the lock maybe forty-five minutes later, I was sitting up in bed, exhausted but wide awake on nerves and body speed. I'd fixed my nose plug so it didn't protrude past my nostril. I'd taken Bird's advice and put on a workshirt, jeans, and a silk scarf around my neck.

Jenny still wore the tight turquoise jumpsuit. She stepped out of her shoes and waited at the foot of the bed. She was tired, her makeup smudged, but she was still the remarkable Jenny Hall. Large light eyes, high freckled cheeks, a tangle and fall of blond hair. I'd stayed awake planning what I was going to say, but nothing came.

"You're still up."

I nodded.

"How's your nose?"

"Bigger than ever."

She smiled. "I can see that."

"Who told you?"

"I've been talking to Annie. She was in the lobby."

My mouth went completely dry. "What do you think?"

"We've been acting very badly. You maybe worse than me, but it's close."

"You haven't been—"

"Finding Annie asleep in the lobby waiting for him"—Jenny sat on the edge of the bed—"it was all there. I could see what a bitch I've been to Danny. And it wasn't you or the record. It's been going on for years."

We looked at each other. Jenny said, "I told her I'd do what I could. That I knew she was right for him and I wanted them to stay together. Even if it meant forcing Danny out of the band."

"I'm glad," I said. "I like Annie."

"How long have you liked her?"

"About a week."

We grinned.

"Promise me," I said, "if you've liked anyone, don't tell me about it."

"What about us, Steve? I've been pretty mad at you."

I uncrossed my arms, placed my hand on the bed near hers.

"I'm more fucked up than I've ever been. The record not working out, it's like I was crumbling inside. I couldn't tell what was true anymore." My fingers finished their pilgrimage across the sheet and touched Jenny's. "But I do love you."

"I know."

"Maybe—"

"There's a chance," Jenny said, "Streit and Parker are going to be canned."

"Says who?"

"Crawford. If they are, Crawford and Vico will be promoted and release our album."

"Are you sure?"

"I've been there all night."

"Tell me later. Kiss me?"

"No." Jenny stood up. "How's Ziggie?"

"Who told you?"

"Ethan, then Annie. Call home."

"It's five-thirty."

"I don't care."

I reached for the phone and dialed. I was about to hang up when Arnie answered.

"Huh?"

"Dad."

"Huh?"

"How's Ziggie? It's Steve."

"Who?"

"Steve, how's Ziggie?"

"Fine. Who is this?"

I hung up, told Jenny, and this time she kissed me on her own.

"Careful, or I'll bleed all over you."

"I'll be careful." She kissed me gently on the lips. "This time we'll be so careful."

We lay on the bed holding each other. I was slowly sliding into sleep when someone began pounding the door.

"Steve," Annie shouted. "Steve!"

I ran toward the noise, dazed, tucking my shirt in my pants. Jenny followed me. I opened the door and Annie leapt into my arms.

"A wreck." Her face streamed tears. "Bird."

"And Danny?" asked Jenny.

"Just Bird. I was downstairs, the police came."

She began to sob and scream. I hugged her against me. "How bad?" I said. "Tell me how bad."

"They said he's dead." She began to shake. "How could Bird be dead?"

"Who said?" Jenny asked.

I met her eyes and all I could think was, I let him go. I waited for you and let him go.

"The police," Annie cried. "How could Bird be dead?"

· PART FOUR ·

Love Is No Reason

Chapter Thirteen

•

T HE REST IS NIGHTMARE and rock history. Streit and Parker were canned, and in September, after getting permission from me, Danny and Bird's estate, Apex released a remixed version of the album, called simply *Jenny Hall*. The album and single, "Love Is No Reason," climbed the *Billboard* and *Cash Box* charts, reaching four and two, respectively. In November, *Rolling Stone* put Jenny's face on the cover above "Jenny Hall—Too Good to Be True?" Christmas week, in Ziggie's darkened bedroom, I caught a video of her new touring band on "Don Kirschner's Rock Concert." I recognized no one else, but there was Jenny, six inches high, my heart's once and future star inside an electronic box.

"Not bad," said Ziggie. "Eh?"

Bird was buried in Boston on a day remarkable for the blueness of the sky, which everyone said matched his eyes. Of his laughter, however, there was no equivalent. The service was traditional and Catholic. Black words, solemn clothes; Bird would have hated it all. Sweating in the July heat, I kept expecting him to walk up and grin, a cocaine high sparking his eyes, his nose wagging at the bulldog sun and white-haired priest. Buzz off, big buddy, he would have told the sun, the father and Holy Ghost. Buzz off.

Bird's parents turned out to be university professors, his mother at Harvard, Mr. Murphy at MIT. Only Danny had known. The South Boston background, the Irish working-class accent—all nonsense, self-creation, Bird's fantasy. The Murphys were far too civilized to hold a wake, but that night, staying in one last Holiday Inn together, Bobby, Rock, Ethan, Jenny and myself; some of Bird's friends from Ithaca; Dickie, who'd flown in from the city; everyone, in fact, except Anne and Danny, who left after the funeral—in Bird's memory we snorted all the cocaine we could lay hands on and gave him the send-off we told ourselves Bird would have wanted. Laughing, dancing, telling dirty jokes till dawn.

"What's the difference between dead and hard?"

"It stays dead forever."

Jenny was asleep when I entered the bathroom a few hours after the party broke up. Lying in bed too stoned and miserable to sleep, I'd been wishing I were in the van with him. Not to have saved him—I was nobody's magic charm—but so I could have died, too. And crazy from the coke, loving no one, crazy with everything that had gone wrong, I smashed the bathroom mirror to see my face shatter. I fingered a spear of glass, wondering what it would feel like, wondering which wrist to do first, but knew in the cold recesses of my heart that I was posing. God knows how long I would have made myself stay there if Jenny hadn't heard the mirror and burst in, she thought, to save me from myself.

We drove to New York, dropped our things at her apartment, and headed downtown to visit Ziggie. He was a mess. He could barely see, there was a pin in his hip, and his left lung had collapsed. That afternoon was his first out of an oxygen tent.

"Mister and Missus Rock Star," he whispered, his voice so thin and brittle I couldn't believe it was Ziggie.

"Don't talk," Jenny said.

"The Bottom Line, I—"

"There'll be other times." I pressed his dry palm. "You get better."

"I wanted. . . . Tell Bird—"

"I'm going to sing for your birthday," Jenny whispered fiercely. "Do you understand me?"

Ziggie nodded and closed his eyes.

I couldn't sleep the next few weeks without getting wrecked. I couldn't talk to Jenny, either. Then word came Streit and Parker were gone. That night in bed, I told Jenny I was moving out.

"I don't understand."

We lay on our sides, my arm on her hip, the city's summer music screaming up through the open window.

"I'm not surprised, but I don't understand."

"All I think about." There was no easy way. "I feel like we did it. If we hadn't been so worried about ourselves, about our careers, our—"

"Steve."

"If I'd gone with him, if I hadn't waited for you."

Jenny began to cry. "Hold me," she said.

I hugged her, and we cried in each other's arms.

Two days later, Jenny flew to California to visit her father. I moved back to the hovel on East Seventh, boxed the clothes and books Bird had left behind, gave them to the Salvation Army, and began seeing a shrink. I visited Ziggie every afternoon. I called Bobby, told him I wasn't going to make the Sandinista concert, but good luck anyway.

"How're you doing, Potts?"

"Don't ask."

"That's what Jenny said."

I couldn't think of a snappy comeback. Bobby said, "She's still in California."

"Uh-huh."

"Is there anything I can do?"

"Maybe later."

"Call me, huh?"

The album was released, soared through the charts, and

suddenly Jenny Hall and an unknown writer named Steve Potts were the hottest names in New York. My phone began ringing off the hook. I went to parties, fucked women I didn't know. Producers called, asking for songs. I changed to an unlisted number, and when my lease was up in October, I moved to a new apartment with a river view.

A week later Jenny called and asked if I wanted to tour December 15 to March 1.

"Are you crazy? I can barely tie my shoes."

"You're still mad at me."

My heart began to beat so fast, my head began to pound so badly I thought I was going to pass out. I leaned against the frost-free refrigerator in my new frost-free kitchen, and began saying anything that popped into my mouth.

"Ziggie's coming home from the hospital next week. I want to be there to take care of him."

"He told me."

"They've scheduled the cataract operation for January, before his birthday. Can you imagine that? He says the fortune-teller must have seen the lung and hip, that medical science wasn't so good in Poland."

"He told me. Steve—"

"What?"

"I thought maybe I could come over."

Back against the refrigerator, I took deep breaths. "When I think about you," I said, "all I want to do is cry."

"We can cry together."

"We tried that."

"Please, Steve."

"You got what you wanted."

"I wanted us to be happy."

"You wanted to make it. You thought we couldn't have both."

She didn't answer, and I could imagine Jenny in a hotel suite or new apartment, lying in bed, puffing a cigarette, blowing smoke to the ceiling, watching it until it disappeared.

"You said we could be successful and still be nice to dogs and small children. I believed you."

"I was wrong."

"You were right, Steve. I was wrong to expect you to do it for me. We should have done it together. Then—" She hesitated; her voice was getting softer, losing itself in tears, and I pressed the receiver to my ear. "Then when things started going bad, you wouldn't have given up and slept with Annie. I'm sorry, I wasn't going to cry."

I listened to the scratch of telecommunications, to Jenny's tears, and thought my heart was going to break, yet again.

"When I think about you." I stopped. "Look, Bird's dead."

"Punishing us isn't going to change that."

"Neither is going on tour."

"Listen to me, Steve. You're no saint. And even saints sin. But you're no devil either."

"Bird's fucking dead, and you're talking to me about sinning."

"And you're alive." She paused. I could hear her breathing, then she screamed, "For Chrissakes, Steve, why can't you grow up?"

"I'm trying."

I spent the rest of the fall in my apartment, thinking, diddling at the piano, and on the advice of the shrink, whom I stopped seeing after two months—he never said a word, I couldn't bear it—I began writing down this tale of yuks, stupidity and sorrow.

New Year's Day, around eight in the evening, my doorbell rang. I was wearing a bathrobe and needed a shave. New Year's Eve I'd been to a party and gone home with an English model whose name was either Margaret or Maggie. I'd left her sleeping, her makeup still intact.

The First Time I Saw Jenny Hall

The bell rang again.

"Coming," I called, belting my robe. "Coming."

I opened the door. Bobby handed me a bottle inside a brown bag. He wore a parka, his face was red from the cold and he looked healthy.

"It's Wild Turkey." He grinned. "Hair of the bird."

When he realized what he'd said, he stopped grinning. I closed the door and he followed me to the couch.

"Nice place." He pushed newspapers to the floor, making room for both of us to sit down. "How've you been?"

I slipped the pint of Wild Turkey out of its sack, broke the seal and drank.

"When you're down, you loathe everyone. How have you been?"

He made that funny move with his left eye, which I took to mean he remembered saying the same thing to me.

"Busy, benefits and press. Ethan and I are going to Nicaragua next month."

"Sounds dangerous."

Bobby grinned. He liked to be thought of as dangerous. "How's Ethan?"

Bobby swigged the bourbon, wiped his mouth and handed me the bottle. "The same. You don't like him, he doesn't like you. I didn't come to talk about Ethan."

I sipped the Wild Turkey. "Why did you come? You got something for me to sign?"

"You want the truth?"

"Sure."

"Jenny asked me, but I was planning to anyway."

I didn't answer and he said, "Why don't you ask how *she* is, schmuck?"

"How is she?"

"Playing full houses. San Francisco last night, tomorrow it's L.A."

"I'm glad she's happy."

"I didn't say she was happy."

Bobby took the bottle back, tipped it up once, then a second time. "I didn't know you had all this suffering in you, Potts. Always thought you were a party boy."

He squinted at me and I said, "You didn't know jackshit about me. I used to care."

Bobby lit a cigarette, offered me one. "I want to tell you something. The last week of that tour, I was pretty sure you were fucking Annie. I saw you eating breakfast together in Chicago. Didn't feel right."

"What about it?"

"I never told anyone. I even convinced myself it wasn't happening." He puffed his cigarette. "I wish now I hadn't. Bird might be here."

He sipped the bourbon, passed me the bottle, which was already half empty. My knees were sticking out of the robe and I covered them.

"I didn't want it to be true. Working with the band, fighting for you in New York, though things were going badly, made me feel alive again. As if there were causes worth living for."

He looked at me. Then, as if reading my thoughts, he said, "You may not think so. But the Sandinistas, the poor in this country, the blacks in South Africa, they know real suffering. In our business, it's easy to become confused, to get lost in bullshit."

I peered down at my feet, puffed the cigarette. I looked up. Bobby said, "I didn't call you on it because I wanted to believe there was something right in the world, you understand?"

He took the bourbon from me, drank, passed it back and wiped his mouth with the back of his hand.

"And as long as I'm being honest, I was afraid to confront you. If I was right, I knew the tour might blow up, and for business reasons I wanted it to keep going. I didn't expect you to get caught in the fucking saddle, dumbo."

I stubbed out my cigarette. "Tell me, were you and Ethan arranging a deal for Jenny that didn't include me?"

Bobby grinned. "You know something, all this suffering has been good for you."

I almost threw the bottle at him. "Don't patronize me."

He grinned wider.

"You're always so fucking sure of yourself. Even when you were depressed, you were sure of it."

"Give the people what they want." We looked at each other. "You know, you were a lot easier to get along with when I was your hero."

"That's because I couldn't tell my ass from a hole in the ground, but thought I could."

"Now you can't, but at least you're self-aware, huh?"

After a minute, I said, "What about that deal for Jenny?"

"You want the truth?"

I nodded.

"Yeah, we had something set up."

"Had Jenny agreed?"

"The truth?"

I nodded again.

"No, even after your fight in Syracuse, she said no."

"Was she fucking Ethan?"

Bobby's eye made that funny move, the cosmic squint. "You have a low mind, Potts."

"Was she?"

"I don't think so. What does it matter?"

"It doesn't, but I'd still like to know."

"Can't help you there."

I stood, walked to the kitchen and returned with a joint, which we smoked. Afterward, he put his coat on, and still in my robe, I walked him to the door.

"I'm glad you stopped by. I appreciate it."

"Sure, but I want you to do something for me. Look Jenny up when she gets back to town. It's confusing for her, all these changes. She's lonely."

"I'm not sure I can do that."

"What are you afraid of, Potts?" Our eyes met one last time. "You're already a sinner."

"Don't get killed in Nicaragua."

He nodded.

Ziggie was operated on on January 15. Dr. Kolesnick said the procedure was a success, but Ziggie still can't see much. I offered to move back with my parents to take care of him, but Ziggie wouldn't let me. Said he wanted to stand on his own and I should, too.

Last week he beat the curse, turned eighty-three on Tuesday, and tonight, keeping an old promise, I'm taking him to see Jenny at the Palladium. Why is why, at eight-thirty on a cold Friday night, we're driving across the Brooklyn Bridge. D.C.'s tires whine as we cross the ancient middle span of the bridge and I turn toward him. Below his dark glasses, the old man's lips are moving.

"You want to fill me in?"

"I was thinking, eh? Now that I'm eighty-three and plan to live forever, I need a job."

"Any ideas?"

Ziggie laughs. "I saw an ad for male strippers. You want to try out together?"

The Palladium is packed. A friend who works in the box office got me the seats and swore he wouldn't tell Jenny or any of her entourage. I also made Ziggie promise, but after Bobby's visit, I'm not taking any chances. I'm not sure exactly what I'm afraid of, but I'm not sure of much anymore. In the old days, when I was certain of things, Potts the Innocent, I was sure I'd never betray hearts that loved me. That knowledge, that the world is corrupt, that we do evil to each other, that the problems in their father's life produced Vietnam, was Bobby and Jenny's birthright. Me, as Dylan sings, I'm learning it these days.

Anyway, I've timed our arrival so that Heat Wave, the opening act, is in the middle of its set. Our seats are in the tenth row and we walk down the center aisle under the cover of darkness, me holding Ziggie's arm, Ziggie tapping the ground with the cane he now uses. We settle into our seats. Kids are getting high all around us, and after a few minutes Ziggie says, "They're smoking marijuana?"

I nod. Heat Wave's lead guitarist is jumping up and down, carrying on as if he thinks he's Townsend or Keith Richard. Unfortunately, as a lead guitarist he's a good plumber. Ah, I think, the human ego.

Ziggie taps my arm. "Do you have any?"

"Any what?"

"Pot, what are you, a *schtumie*?"

Ziggie and I smoke a joint. He doesn't feel anything and we smoke another. He still doesn't feel anything, but I'm totally wrecked. The pot is $200-an-ounce sensimilla. I give Ziggie the last of the three joints I've brought. Halfway through he bumps my shoulder.

"My neck's stiff."

"So?"

"I don't know. But my neck's stiff."

"Is that all?"

He giggles. "It's enough."

Ten minutes later Ziggie asks me to take him to the bathroom. We walk up the aisle and I hold onto his arm, terrified he's going to break his hip again. I glance at him and see the old man is twirling his cane in a Charlie Chaplin imitation.

"Ziggie!"

"Wait till I tell Potts and Pans."

When we get back to our seats, Heat Wave has departed.

Jenny is due on anytime, and up in the balcony her fans have started to chant, "Jenny, Jenny, Jenny."

"It's none of my business," Ziggie says.

"Jenny?"

"So who else?"

"It's none of your business."

After a minute I decide maybe it is. "When Bird died I couldn't look at her without thinking it was our fault."

"You still feel that?"

"I don't know, I haven't seen her."

"Why does it have to be anyone's fault?"

"Because it was."

"Suppose it was."

Ziggie pauses. A cheer goes up from the crowd. In the half-dark, I can see Jenny's band coming out onstage.

"Suppose it was," he repeats. "Bird was your friend. You loved him, and you're still alive."

"I don't know," I say. "I don't know."

The band begins to play what I recognize as a slick, worked-up intro to "Waiting for Love." Suddenly, she dashes out. A spotlight pierces the gray, picks her up, and a booming voice announces, "The amazing Jenny Hall!"

Jenny wears a white satin blouse and thin tight pants. Her hair is shorter than when I last saw her; she's changed guitars. She starts singing, and the words, which I wrote with Danny, mean nothing, but her voice burns its way inside me.

> *"Stare into my eyes,*
> *Swear they were my man!"*

Midway through the song, Jenny and her lead guitarist, a tall, dark-haired pretty boy, trade solos center stage, their thighs and guitar necks almost touching. At one point the guy's crotch presses up against her thigh, then ass, and the crowd goes crazy. Me it launches into Space City, which is where I stay, wondering if I ever knew her. Wondering what

I'm doing here, and if I'm going to get through the show without losing my mind.

The song ends. Fans cheer, stomp and whistle. Someone up close throws a rose onto the stage. Jenny smiles, picks it up and bows. Ziggie touches my shoulder.

"Huzzah, huzzah," he says.

"Huzzah, huzzah, yourself."

Jenny does another song, then another. I remain in a state of nonbeing, doing my best to simply not be there. For a half hour, I don't even breathe. Then the piano player begins the introduction to "Love Is No Reason." The audience recognizes the hit single and roars its approval. Someone in the balcony screams, "Jenny, I love you." Then everyone quiets down, Jenny's alone in the spotlight, and she doesn't look like a performer to me now. As she begins to sing she looks like Jenny, my Jenny.

> *"Long before I left you,*
> *Long after the end,*
> *I'd hear the same questions*
> *Time and again.*
>
> *"Through broken, lonely, fearful nights,*
> *Watching the morning sky grow light,*
> *Where did our love go wrong?*
> *Was it ever right?"*

And suddenly, I'm afraid I'm going to cry. I remember writing the song running through the Village, so proud, dumb and unaware, writing the song about Danny. Now the words sear my heart and I know who they're about, as Jenny's voice leans into the chorus, the way walking up her hill we'd leaned into the wind.

> *"Love,*
> *Love is no reason, you say,*
> *Love,*
> *Love is no reason, to stay,*

> *Love,*
> *Love is no reason, this way*
> *Running our lives in circles*
> *Day after day."*

Then she's singing the verses again and I'm sitting there but not hearing it. I'm there but I'm not, and suddenly I think about Annie. I know, somehow I'm sure, she's pregnant, and I promise myself to call her. Then I'm remembering Bird. I see him grinning at me. Nose brother, he calls me. A user. Then I can't help it, I am crying. I'm crying and sobbing. My shoulders shake, and I don't even hear the rest of the fucking song.

The applause dies. Jenny steps to the mike. Her voice a little tight, she says, "We have a very special guest tonight."

I sit up, surprised Bobby is back in the country already. Jenny says, "The man who wrote all these great songs, Steve Potts."

"Ziggie," I hiss. "I'm going to kill you."

"Get up."

I don't move. I can't move; my face is soggy with tears. Ziggie crunches my big toe with his cane. I jump out of my seat, the spotlight hits me and everyone cheers.

"Take a bow, putz."

I bow to the house, turn toward the stage. Jenny's smiling; I don't know what to do. She steps forward, away from her mike and out of the lights.

"Steve," she says. "Come up here."

I don't move. Hands, people I don't know push me toward the stage. Then they don't have to. I clamber up the side steps. The spotlight finds me, Jenny hugs me, and a roar goes up.

"Glad to see me?"

I remember a happier time and say, "Does the Pope piss purple?"

"Depends what he's been drinking. What do you want to sing?"

"How about 'Fall in Love Again'?"

Jenny grins. She's a little thinner, her makeup covers dark circles, but she's the same Jenny.

"You're a romantic, Steve. That's one of the things I always loved about you."

"I've been trying not to be."

We look at each other, then a techie hands me a mike. The piano player begins the intro, my intro. I come in on cue, our voices sound good together, and I hit all the notes. We bow holding hands, and bowing, Jenny whispers, "Wait for me backstage."

"I've got to get Ziggie."

"Someone's getting him."

We stop bowing. She squeezes my hand, releases it, and I turn to walk off.

"Be sure to wait."

She blows me a kiss, then bends for her guitar, thighs straining against her tight pants.

Offstage, strangers pound me on the back, tell me I was great. Tony Two walks by, looking a little older. I nod at him, but he ignores me. I stand in the wings, as close as possible to the stage without the audience being able to see me, look out and watch Jenny. Her band finishes the introduction, the stage lights come up, washing her in a hot purple glow, and she begins to sing:

> *"Dust rising from the road,*
> *Blue horizon where it showed."*

Watching her, I think, There's nothing for me here. I ought to leave. And yet. And I have to wait for Ziggie. Then I'm not thinking about anything or anyone, not even about Bird. I'm looking out from the wings at Jenny, her face in profile, the purple lights on her hair. The music swells, the chorus begins, and she's singing my song.